Nab Yoga

Jeffrey R. Crimmel

Copyright © 2016 Jeffrey R Crimmel

All rights reserved.

ISBN: 1537724282
ISBN-13: 978-1537724287

DEDICATION

Nab Yoga, in the Brain Bleed series, is dedicated to my fellow yoga classmates and teachers at the Yoga Breeze studio in Cave Creek, AZ and all the other studios where I find myself bending, twisting and sticking my legs up the wall. During my two years with the Arizona classes I learned different stretching techniques that enabled me to improve my back alignment and stop visiting the chiropractor. I decided to write the third book in the murder mystery series as a way of thanking them and to encourage this type of exercise for everyone.

Just be careful when you go to your car in the parking lot.

The Paris yoga studio in the book belongs to my sister-in-law and I used it so we would have something to talk about at the next family reunion if we ever have one.

ACKNOWLEDGMENTS

I would like to thank my writers group in Peoria, AZ for adding their insights and corrections to this and the first two books in the Brain Bleed series. We don't agree on every issues I covered but we survived.

Also my wife, Suzanne, who gives me her insights into the material and lets me know if I go too far off the reservation. She is an avid reader and knows about styles and writing techniques.

My cover designer, Rita Toews, has helped me with three covers so far and is a dream to work with.

Books by Author

Living Beneath the Radar

Learning to Love the Peso

Centavo, A Dog From Mexico

The 60's, If You Remember it You Didn't Live It.

Brain Bleed

Ian's Revenge

Types of Yoga

Anusara Anusara is often described as Iyengar (a purist form of yoga) with a sense of humor.
Ashtanga Six established and strenuous <u>pose</u> sequences — the primary series, second series, third series, and so on — practiced sequentially as progress is made.
Bikram Bikram features yoga poses in a sauna-like room. The heat is cranked up to nearly 105 degrees and 40 percent humidity in official Bikram classes.
Hatha By definition, hatha is a physical yoga practice, which is pretty much all yoga you'll find in this hemisphere.
Iyengar Iyengar yoga is all about precise alignment and deliberate sequencing.

Kripalu Kripalu is a three-part practice that teaches you to get to know, accept, and learn from your body.

Kundalini The practice of kundalini yoga features constantly moving, invigorating poses. The fluidity of the practice is intended to release the kundalini (serpent) energy in your body.
Restorative Less work, more relaxation.
Sivananda
An unhurried yoga practice that typically focuses on the same 12 basic asanas or variations thereof every time, bookended by sun salutations and savasana (corpse pose)
Vinyasa / Power
An active and athletic style of yoga adapted from the traditional ashtanga system in the late 1980s to appeal to aerobic-crazed Westerners.
Yin
A quiet, meditative yoga practice.

Chapter 1

Two men waited in their van outside the home of Robert and Julia Forrester snapping photos of Alan Hogan and his girlfriend, Cathy, as they got into their car and drove away. The Forrester's wedding party ended an hour before and this couple was the last to leave. Neither of the men knew anything about Robert Forrester, the former Robert Woods.

Alan's company, Geek Mingle, went public a month earlier in New York. When a company is traded on the NYSE, the founders usually do well financially in a short amount of time, and Alan was no exception.

"And you're sure that's him?" Dawg, the bigger of the two men asked.

"Yes, I'm sure," Barry answered. "His picture's been in People Magazine, and the local rag for a month. He and his girlfriend are newsworthy, except he never goes anywhere. The article I read about him said he doesn't like to attend social gatherings and parties where the rich and famous hangout. This gathering seems to be an exception. It must be a close friend who had a party."

A patrol car came down the street and the two men ducked down and remained hidden. Dawg sat up first and gave the all clear.

"That could be a good thing for us," Barry said. If

he's a homebody, and we now know where he lives, this job could be a piece of cake."

"How do you mean?" Dawg asked.

"I'm sure he has a tight security system. A person who goes to work and stays home a lot has a routine they follow. If we follow him as well the woman and map out their routine, we may be able to find a vulnerable time of day to grab one of them. We can't hurry this, Dawg. Let's get out of here and plan what to do next."

The two men drove down Tumbleweed Road that took them back to the main route towards Albuquerque. Barry, the brains of the two men, had a two-page rap sheet. Extortion and bank fraud made the list of his most repeated offenses. He served ten months in a low-security prison in Arizona five years ago. His small size kept him from committing violent crimes. An ugly scar on his neck earned in a high school fight, told him he needed to stay away from any physical altercations and hire someone to do the dirty work.

Dawg, Barry's partner, was the muscle in their newly formed alliance. He met Barry six months before in a bar and did a few small jobs with him, breaking into warehouses and selling whatever they could get their hands on. His high school football days ended ten years before and he was lost in the world of 'what to do'. A life of crime paid the bills for now. He went to his school reunion last year but had nothing to show his fellow classmates as far as any physical possessions. Several of his close football teammates married school cheerleaders and now worked for their father-in-law's family business.

At six foot four, Dawg stood out in a crowd. His boyish looks could not disguise his inability to attract women. As soon as he opened his mouth and attempted to engage them in conversation, the game was over. 'Me Dawg, you Jane,' did not cut it with the modern woman in a bar crowd.

The two men drove past the address where Alan and his girlfriend lived. They'd followed Alan and Cathy to the Forrester house several hours before, after staking out their home. Metal gates and a surround security system made the property secure. The actual house, small in comparison to what other billionaires lived in, still portrayed to those passing by that the occupants lived well.

"Look at the security, Dawg." CCTV signs were posted on the gate telling anyone that the house is well protected. "We may not be able to get past that. Whatever we do, the grab needs to happen outside the gates."

"You're right, Barry. We'll need to document any routine Mr. Hogan or his girlfriend takes during the week. This isn't like breaking into a warehouse. The sentence is a lot higher for kidnapping but this gig could be our last job. A couple of million for either one of them would be a lot of money for us."

"Yeah, but pocket change to them," Barry said.

Dawg glanced at his partner with a puzzled expression. "How do you mean?"

"When you're a billionaire, you have a thousand, million dollars. Take away two million and you still have 998 million left." Barry knew how to count.

"Well put," Dawg said. "Kind of like seeing a billionaire differently."

"No shit. Let's get back to the apartment. We've got some planning to do."

Chapter 2

Robert Forrester and his wife of one hour, Julia, walked around the pool area picking up glasses and taking them into the kitchen for their cook, Carla. A few of Carla's relatives, who attended the wedding, were also helping in the final clean up.

As soon as the last dishes made their way into the dishwasher, Carla packed up her family and left. The house returned to the newly weds. Quiet once again settled over the pool area where Julie and Robert sat, contemplating the activities of the day.

"What do you want to do now, Mrs. Forrester? Everything is cleaned up." Robert knew what he wanted to do.

"Well, Mr. Forrester, now that you've returned from the dead, what is the first thing that you feel like doing?"

"Does sex with a Zombie sound exciting or should we relax and watch a movie?" Robert pretended to be dead for several months until he made his appearance three hours before. His fake death played a huge part in taking down a group of madmen bent on controlling the world through drinking water, but that's another story.

"We could do both. Let's choose two films, set up a candle light dinner between shows and consummate this marriage after the second movie." Julia was excited about being married to Robert but needed to set the stage for their romantic encounters.

"Can we wait that long?" Robert asked. He didn't need a movie to get him in the mood.

"Sweetheart. We've been together for eighteen months. We can watch both movies first. Anyway, I have a surprise for you, but I need some time to get ready. You pick the first movie and I'll start the popcorn."

When it came to surprises, Julia could excite Robert in ways he never knew. "I'm game. We haven't seen that space movie yet with Sandra Bullock. It's on Netflix."

"Fine with me, Mr. Forrester. Popcorn in five."

Robert and Julia operated an investigation business together. Robert used to have the last name of Woods, but circumstances caused him to change his name. Only his closest friends knew Robert Woods and Robert Forrester was the same person. His last step towards completing his identity change would happen in two weeks. A facial procedure and hair color makeover were necessary to remain dead in the eyes of the Albuquerque police and anyone else in his past. The couple would run their investigating business with new names and different physical features.

"Popcorn's ready. How about the flick?"

"Almost. Before we start this, did Peggy finish downloading that information on the Bryan case?"

Peggy was Robert's computer assistant who replaced Alan after he started his Geek Mingle site a year and a half ago. Alan and Cathy were the Forrester's closest friends.

"We just got married today, Robert. There'll be no business talk until tomorrow, and that's final."

The rules of engagement had changed.

Chapter 3

Marcos Crane stood at the entrance of the ferryboat, waiting to board the cruise boat that would take him on a journey through the Stockholm waterways. He'd lived in Sweden for several years, and he was finally going to see the city from the canals surrounding the city.

All of a sudden a couple pushed their way through the short line in order to get ahead of the queue. The woman was determined to get the last two remaining seats in the outdoor deck area in order to work on her tan during the tour. She was a Scandinavian TV actress traveling with Olaf, her 300-pound Olympic shot-put boyfriend who, at six foot five, acted as an enforcer for her bad behavior. Marcos was just about to step onto the ferry when he felt a massive leg pin him against the side of the boarding ramp, making room for Helga, the actress.

"Stay still for a minute and you'll be fine," Olaf said to Marcos in Swedish. Helga was showing the ticket conductor her ID and going on about how she was a star and needed to board the boat at once in order to secure the two remaining seats on the sun deck.

Olaf had no idea who he had picked on to throw his weight around. Marcos assessed the situation, reached into his right coat pocket, removed the Taser C2 and placed it in the groin area of the Swedish giant. Fifty thousand volts of electricity brought the man to his knees on the wooden ramp. Marcos grabbed the man by his collar and jerked him off the boat into the water between the dock and the side of the boat. Olaf hit his head on the way down and blood was seen spurting from his forehead as he floated in the water, face up.

By now, Helga could see her boyfriend was no longer available to back her demands to board the boat. She turned toward the ramp and the stranger who attacked Olaf, screaming in Swedish, "Don't you know who I am?"

Marcos understood Swedish fairly well but answered her in English. "Don't you know who I am?" and gave her an electric shock to the neck, crumbling her to her knees in a heap. Marcos knew he would not get to enjoy a cruise today. He turned around in the line and walked to the exit gate as several people in the queue applauded him. He got into his car, which was parked in the lot and drove away.

The authorities arrived twenty minutes later and were taking statements from the eyewitnesses as well as retrieving the body of Olaf from the water. He was alive, but would not be training with his teammates for at least a month due to the concussion he received from his fall into the water. Helga would also miss a few weeks of work due to the shock to her system. None of the witnesses supported the TV actress and her outrageous claim that she and her boyfriend were attacked. Marcos

Crane was gone and the policeman leading the investigation decided not to put a lot of effort in finding him.

*****

Marcos was now five miles from the ferry that would take him to Denmark. He decided he needed to leave Sweden for a while and lay low. He didn't want to be questioned by the police, and in his line of work staying out of trouble was most important. He'd call his girlfriend tomorrow and send some money to cover the apartment rent. He'd use the excuse he had to go to Paris for business.

"One ticket," Marcos told the ticket master as he drove onto the ferry. He spoke in English even though he could get by in Swedish.

"Yes, sir. One way or round trip?" the conductor asked in perfect English.

"One way. I'll be back, but not for a while."

Marcos had plenty of money to keep his apartment in Stockholm where he and his girlfriend lived. She'd keep an eye on the place while the situation with the couple on the ferry cooled down. He did have business to attend to in France and he decided to make his way back to Paris and take care of it.

Chapter 4

Barry and Dawg spent the next five days observing the routine of Alan Hogan and his girlfriend. Mr. Hogan went every day to his business in the industrial section of Albuquerque, while the girlfriend seemed to remain home. She only went out to her gym, yoga classes, or did errands for the house.

"It seems to me that the woman might be easier to grab instead of Alan Hogan," Barry said to Dawg. "He never stops anywhere else other than work, and she's all over the map."

Dawg added his gathered information to the conversation. "She even does the grocery shopping and that's something I never expected from a billionaire's partner. She's probably still getting used to being rich, and may not trust anyone else buying her food."

"You might be right," Dawg said. "If we grab her, I'm sure Mr. Hogan will get the money to us quickly. I know I'd pay right away if I had a girlfriend who looked like her. Let's follow her for another week, and see if her yoga classes are always at the same time. What's the name of that place again? Yoga Ease?"

"Yeah, I think so," Barry said. He looked at his notes. "Also few men who do yoga at that place, so if we grab her there we'd have an easier time."

"Good point," Dawg said. "I did see two men walk into the studio on Tuesday carrying long swords. They might have a special class on that day so let's avoid Tuesday for sure. Since I'm the muscle, I think I can handle a few women in tights if they try to save her but men with weapons might be a little much."

"Don't get too cocky, Dawg. Some of those ladies look pretty fit. You get four or five of them all over you, and you could have your hands full. I saw one woman who was at least six feet tall. I know I wouldn't try and take her on."

"Let's make the grab quickly, and don't give them a chance to tackle me," Dawg said.

"We'll also have to get her out of Albuquerque to set up the money swap," Barry said. "The police will be all over this, and Albuquerque is not big enough to hide in."

"Where do you suggest?" Dawg asked. He hadn't traveled far from Albuquerque his whole life and did not feel safe going far away. He was a home-boy through and through.

"My mother used to take me to a small mountain community in Colorado when I was a kid," Barry said. "The cabins were isolated and had no phones. It's one of those places for people who really want to get away. We could hold the woman there until we get our money."

"Why don't you set up the place in Colorado and I'll make sure she follows her yoga schedule," Dawg said. "She goes about three times a week. One of those classes is around two in the afternoon when office people are at work so there's not much foot traffic. That might be the best time to grab her."

"Good thinking, Dawg. I'll leave tomorrow and return in three days. You monitor the woman and find out more if you can. The article in People's Magazine said her name is Cathy. Her last name is probably in the article as well. I just don't remember it."

*****

For the next three days, Dawg arrived at the Yoga Ease studio around the time Cathy took her classes. He waited in the parking lot and watched her go into her class and marked down when she left. She was consistent with her attendance. Few people attended Wednesday's session so he decided this was the best time to nab her.

Dawg owned an old set of license plates salvaged from a car at the local junkyard and decided to put them on the van the night before making the kidnapping. A bed mattress covered the back of the windowless vehicle, and all the maintenance was up to date. Dawg felt confident nothing would break down on the drive to Colorado.

Barry returned to Albuquerque on Friday with good

news. He'd found a cabin that was away from all the others and could reserve it with a phone call. It was always the last one people rented and almost guaranteed to be available when they needed it. The manager left the renters alone so no one would be checking up on them while they were staying there.

"What did you find out about the woman, Dawg? Does she regularly go to that two o'clock class on Wednesday?"

"Not only that, there's no one around after it lets out. She also visits Starbucks, a couple doors down from the studio after every session. By the time she returns with a drink, the parking lot is empty. This is going to be a lot easier than I thought."

"Have you gone into the studio to check for security cameras? Also, we don't want any men around if possible. The less muscle to interfere with this the better."

"I went inside last Monday before she showed up. I asked about yoga and what was involved and the owner gave me a tour. Her name was Chris. She had one of those hyphenated last names and I can't pronounce it. I think it was foreign. Most of those women are really hot, Barry. Anyway, I saw no cameras but I did see some unusual stuff in the big yoga room."

"Yeah, and what's that?"

"There was a huge gong with Chinese writing on it, long cushions, a box of belts, and some straps hanging off the wall. I asked what the wall belts were for and the owner told me they were for hanging upside-down. All this time I thought yoga people just bend in funny ways in order to get limber. What's up with the hanging upside-down crap? Are they in training to become the next 'Bat Woman'?"

"Dawg, I have no idea," Barry laughed. "Just be careful because some of these women look pretty buff."

"I'm not worried about that right now," Dawg said. "We know what car she drives so all we need to do is park next to it, and grab her before she gets in."

"I'll get the chloroform to knock her out," Barry said. "Let's do this next Wednesday. We need to strike right away. In a couple of weeks, we could be rich men, Dawg. What do you think about that?"

"Fine with me. By the time my fifteen-year school reunion rolls around I plan on driving up with one of those Mercedes cars with the top down and wearing some fancy duds. That should impress my old teammates, and give me some respect."

What a dim wit thought Barry. This asshole wants to impress his high school classmates, and he's almost thirty years old.

"What are you going to do with your share, Barry?" Dawg asked.

"I'm heading to the tropics to drink rum and coke with hot babes. I'm never coming back to this city again."

Both men had their personal agenda, but in reality, they were not too far apart.

*****

"I'm going to the office, Cathy. What's your day look like?" Alan asked.

"Food shopping and yoga at two. Pretty much the same schedule I always have on Wednesday. Do you want to go out to eat? We haven't done that in a while and Carmen's not here tonight. I really don't feel like cooking and we need a change of routine."

Alan thought for a moment and then answered. "Okay, I'll be back around four and find a restaurant we haven't been to. How does that sound?"

"Surprise me," Cathy answered. "Just drive us there and don't tell me the name. You know what foods I like so it's all in your hands, Mr. Hogan."

Cathy and Alan were approaching the year mark when they started living together. Alan had the Geek Mingle website going when Cathy showed up in his life and she added the spark and personality needed to interest investors. Cathy was good at talking to people and attracted some big money towards their startup cost.

Now that they had gone public, investors from all over the world kept the finances pouring into the business and many of those working for Alan and Cathy were now millionaires due to their stock options that came with their pay. Five more countries had just come on-line and the total in the world numbered nine.

"I have a meeting with my department heads and should be done by three."

The couple kissed good-bye and headed in different directions. Cathy decided to food shop first because she usually felt calm after yoga and didn't want to go to a noisy grocery store afterward.

*****

A white van was waiting at the far end of the yoga studio parking lot to not draw attention. Dawg and Barry were ready to take action when the time came.

At 1:45 the VW hybrid pulled up and Cathy got out with her yoga mat under her arm. Colorful yoga pants and a tight fitting top emphasized how well yoga kept her body in shape. She was a real distraction for single men when she shopped for groceries, and more than once she had to let these creeps know she was not available. She loved Alan.

After Cathy went inside the studio, Barry drove the van up to the spot next to the driver's side of the VW. The sliding door opened just where she would be standing when she got into her car. The trap was set.

"Here is your mask, Dawg. Put it on before you grab her. Add the chloroform to the rag just as she gets here so it's potent and doesn't evaporate."

"Mexican wrestling mask?" Dawg asked. "Where did you get these?"

"In a Mexican second hand store in Albuquerque. Put it on before you get out to nab her."

"What time is it?"

Barry looked at his watch. "Three-twenty p.m. She should be coming out soon." A few women walked by holding yoga mats. "Wow, look at the ass on that one, Dawg. Some of these women are built like a brick shit house."

"Wait, there she goes now," Dawg said. "She heading towards Starbucks and should be back in ten. Are we ready?"

Dawg put on his wrestling mask and had the cloth in his hand. He poured the chloroform onto the rag. His other hand was on the door handle as he waited for Barry's command.

"I can see her coming, Dawg. Get ready."

Cathy was still sipping her coffee as she held out her key and beeped the door to unlock.

"Now!" Barry said.

Dawg opened the sliding door and stepped out. Cathy turned to face the masked man and instantly knew she was in trouble. She quickly removed the lid from her hot coffee and threw the contents at the mask face. Dawg's eyes and mouth received the hot liquid full blast. Cathy followed the move with a swift kick to the groin just as Dawg grabbed her shoulder and gave her a pull. He was in extreme pain and blinded at the same time. He swung his other arm around where he thought Cathy's head would be and hit pay dirt. The cloth slammed into her face just as she let out a scream.

The material muffled most of the verbal cry for help, but the yell still alerted the owner who was also returning to her yoga studio carrying a coffee. She saw a woman in the arms of a masked man, but she was twenty-five yards away. She took off running towards the two struggling bodies but by the time she reached the van it drove away. The New Mexico plate number was etched in the mind of the owner as she ran back to the studio and called 911, passing the information on to the authorities.

Within five minutes, Barry was close to the freeway on ramp and heading towards Colorado on the 25. The turn off to the 550 was just ahead with Durango as their destination.

"Is she out?" Barry asked.

"Yes," screamed Dawg.

"I think that woman back in the parking lot saw our license plates. We need to pull over and replace the fake ones," Barry yelled back.

Dawg bent over in pain. The kick was a direct hit. "I'm hurt, Barry. This bitch nailed me. I'm still seeing stars."

By now, both men had removed the Lucha libre masks and Dawg sat in the back with a cloth over his eyes. The hot coffee had temporarily blinded him and it was a toss up as to what part of his body hurt more, his eyes or his balls.

"Is she still out," Barry asked again.

"I think so but I can hardly see. We better pull over soon and replace the plates. I have a magnet advertisement to put on the side of the van. We'll get pulled over if the cops block the roads so we better do the switch now."

"There's a rest stop coming up, Dawg. I'll pull into the back behind the bathrooms. You put up the signs and I'll remove the plates. Do this as fast as you can. We have to get out of this state pronto."

Dawg was moving slowly. He had duct-taped Cathy's feet and hands so she couldn't move and applied a strip over her mouth. He grabbed the electrician business signs for a fake company located in Albuquerque and attached them to both sides of the van. Barry removed the front and rear plates revealing the originals attached to the van. They were back on the road within ten minutes without being seen.

"Man, I'm in pain," Dawg repeated. "Who knew she had defensive skills."

"She's making us earn our money. Maybe we should add on another half a million each for pain and suffering," Barry added.

"You're not in pain, Barry. I am. How long is the drive to the cabin? Also, do you have any aspirin?"

Barry reached into the glove box and removed a bottle of Tylenol. "Here, take two of these and see me in the morning."

"Funny, Barry. This has been the most difficult job we've ever attempted. This better work out because I'm going to need some recovery time for sure."

"Quit crying. You must have been kicked in the balls while playing football in high school, right?"

"I wore a cup. That was a direct hit and it had lots of force. Maybe I'll add another half million to my take."

"Get over yourself, Dawg. If we walk away with a million each, I'll be content getting that. We should be there in a couple of hours so just lay back and relax. Check on the woman and see if she's breathing. Don't want to damage the goods, now do we?"

Chapter 5

Alan arrived home around four p.m. and was surprised Cathy was not back from yoga. He parked his car in the garage and plugged it in. He had enough power for a few more days, but he liked to keep it fully charged. At four-thirty he made a call to Cathy's cell phone to see what was holding her up. The call went directly to voicemail.

Now that is odd, thought Alan. She always picks up.

Just then a call came through.

"Hello, is this Alan Hogan?"

"Yes, it is. Who is this?"

"I'm Detective Louis from the Albuquerque Police Department. I met you last year at the funeral of Robert Woods. Do you remember?"

"Yes, Detective Louis, I do remember. You played a big part in solving the case. I remember sending a fruit basket to your office. I talked to a woman officer and asked her for gift advice and she suggested the fruit basket."

"Was that officer named Parsons?"

"Yes, I believe it was."

"She did that as a gesture to our boss who is trying to add more fiber to his diet. We're off the topic, so anyway here is why I called. Does your wife practice yoga?"

"We're not married, but yes she does. Is she all right?"

"We received a 911 call from the owner of Yoga Ease. She witnessed a woman being grabbed in the parking lot near the studio, but she was too far away to make out any faces. The kidnappers wore masks. It happened next to a VW Passat. The license plates are registered to a Cathy Chambers and the address is the same as yours. We do not have all the facts and we're sending a car to the yoga studio right now. Have you spoken to Miss Chambers in the last hour?"

"What? Are you kidding? She's been taken? How is this possible?" Alan felt weak in his knees and had to sit down.

"All we know for sure is that the incident took place next to the car that she owns. We're following up on all leads. Do you know where Miss Chambers is?"

"No, and I tried to call her a few minutes ago. It went directly to voice mail. She was supposed to be home by four and it's now five."

"Mr. Hogan, can you come down to the station and talk to us. There may have been a kidnapping and we'll need more information from you before we start working on this case. All we have now is a license number of a white van and a man wearing a funny mask. The yoga owner couldn't see the face of the woman being taken and the van was gone before she could reach it."

"How long ago did this happen, detective?" Alan asked. "Cathy had a two o'clock yoga class and was coming home after the session was over."

"The time the incident took place was between three-thirty and three-forty-five according to the owner of the studio. This could possibly be Miss Chambers. Are you able to make the drive downtown and give us some more information? We have an APB out on the van so hopefully, we can get a name of the owner within the hour."

"Yes, I'll be right down. I have one call to make and should be there in thirty minutes." Alan was still trembling and felt sick but he had the presence of mind to make a call to the one man who could really help him. He punched in speed dial to his neighbor, Robert.

"Robert, it's me, Alan. I think Cathy's in trouble."

For then next ten minutes, Alan repeated the information he had received from Detective Louis. His voice was trembling as he spoke and he was on the verge of breaking down with every word.

Robert listened carefully and took a few notes. When Alan finished, he gave him directions for what to do next.

"Alan, you're probably in shock so I'll guide you

through this as best I can. Get down to the police station and give Detective Louis everything he'll need to help find Cathy. Bring a recent photo of her and maybe a piece of clothing that has not been washed recently. If they use dogs to try and find her, then an item that has her scent will help. I'll start putting the pieces together, but we may need the police's help with this because they've put out an APB on the van. More than likely you're going to get a ransom call or letter because this has to be for financial gain. Cathy hasn't been in Albuquerque long enough to make enemies, and she's not the type of person who would rub someone the wrong way."

"Robert, you're right. It has to be for money. We've been all over the news, in national magazines and the local paper after going public with Geek Mingle." Alan started to feel more grounded. "If it's money the kidnappers are after, I'd have no trouble giving them what they wanted. One more thing I completely forgot. Cathy and I have GPS chips implanted behind our right elbows. We got them six months ago."

"I've heard of those. I know they first started putting them into pets so owners could find them if they got lost. You're the first person I know who had it done. What's the range of the tracking?"

"Fifty miles," Alan said. "We could track Cathy from her cell phone if she turned it on, but I tried that. It's off and probably in some trash can somewhere. I'm sure the person who took her knew about dumping the phone."

"Maybe, Alan. Call the company who monitors the chip and have them start a search. Let the police know as well and let them take it from there. It's not going to do us any good if we find the location because we don't have the muscle to back us up. This is a police job. If the kidnappers took her somewhere nearby then we might have a chance to find her right away. Hang in there, Alan, we're going to get her back."

"Thanks, Robert. If anyone can find her it's you," Alan said. He was devastated and right now Robert was his only hope.

"Call me when you're finished with the police," Robert added. "They might get this case solved right away. After all, they did have a lot to do with solving the Ian case."

"Yeah, but with you leading them the whole way." Alan knew how good Robert was with investigations firsthand.

"I have no problem with that. Let them get the credit and do all the paperwork. It shows our taxpayer's money is going to the right place."

"You're the best, Robert. I have complete faith in you. I'll come over when I get back from the police station."

"I'll be waiting."

Robert knew he had his hands full. Alan was his closest friend and helped him solve many tough cases with his computer skills. He knew Alan was in a bad headspace right now and ransom cases sometimes went bad. If Alan was ready to pay and get Cathy back, they had to make the exchange themselves. The police sometimes are more concerned about capturing the bad guys than protecting the victim. There was little he could do at the moment until Alan returned from town.

"Was that Alan?" Julia asked. "It sounded like he's in trouble."

Robert repeated the whole story to Julia as she sat on the couch. She and Cathy were roommates in New York before they met their partners. They remained close and now lived down the street from each other.

"What are we going to do, Robert?"

"We're going to wait for Alan to come back from town with information from the police. He'll give them the GPS tracker company phone number to find Cathy, and they'll probably circle the state until they pick up a signal. Either that or a ransom message will arrive. Helping Alan get Cathy back is our only goal. He has enough money to make this happen."

"When we get Cathy back we need to catch these

assholes. No way do I want them to get away." Julia had a deep sense of justice ever since she was a cop in New York. Making sure Cathy was safe was her main concern.

Chapter 6

Marcos Crane was now in Paris after driving most of the day from Denmark. He called his girlfriend, Monica, in Stockholm, explaining the situation. He told her he was suddenly called away on business even though she did not know what Marcos did. All she knew was that his boss lived in Paris and Marcos helped escort wealthy people. She'd lived with him for two years and he treated her fairly and with respect, which was her main concern.

Marcos called the man he worked for in Paris.

"Poppy, what do we have lined up this time?" he asked. Marcos was English and did not speak French.

Poppy set up the clients and took care of all the transportation problems in their business. Marcos was well compensated for his service. With his Taser C2, he made sure any takedowns went smoothly, and no one got hurt. The victim had to be in good shape at the end of their ordeal.

"We have a client staying in the Paris Hilton La Defense," Poppy said. "Her name is Claudette Monroe and she's the daughter of Mark Monroe, who's involved with the nuclear power industry in France. His daughter could bring us five million Euros easily. She lives the spoiled, rich girl lifestyle and travels all the time. Only the best hotels and private nightclubs are on her itinerary, and she always has a bodyguard with her. I believe she plans to be in Paris for the month because Miss Monroe is making an appearance on behalf of her father at a few conventions. She works for him in some capacity, showing up at a few high-end social functions. It's her way of thanking her father for supporting her jet-set lifestyle."

"When do you want this job done?" Marcos asked. He wanted to get back to Sweden soon. "I can be around for a few weeks so the sooner the better for me, Poppy."

"I think we can pull this off right away. We have Miss Monroe's routine schedule tracked and my team thinks one of the nightclubs she visits is the best place to grab her. We can use the safe house you used on the last job. You still have a key, right?"

Marcos reached into his pocket and pulled out a ring of keys. "Yes, I still do."

"Good. You might want to use Paula again on this job because we're going after a woman. She can deal with Miss Monroe. You could have your hands full with the bodyguard."

"I'm fine with Paula. She's good at what she does and doesn't talk a lot. I can't stand talkative women," Marcos said.

Poppy paused a moment and then continued. "I'll let Paula know she's hired and send her the Monroe woman's schedule. Why don't you meet Paula tomorrow at that café across from Notre Dame? You know, the one with the blue umbrellas. Say about two p.m. After you set up your plan, let me know. I'll get you a car that can't be traced and have someone at the safe house keeping an eye on our hostage."

"You'll do the negotiations with the father as well, correct?" Marcos asked.

"Naturally. This'll be just like the last grab. As long as we hit the high-end targets and don't get greedy, the Paris police will never catch us. I still have someone on the inside working for us."

"Everything sounds like a go, Poppy. Tell Paula I'll see her tomorrow."

*****

The next day Marcos and Paula met at the café and laid out their plan of attack. The high-end private nightclub called La Rue became the location where the grab would take place. Miss Monroe went there every Thursday night when she was in Paris, just to dance and drink. She always had a few regular friends that showed up as well and they had a table reserved for them in the back of the club.

"We need to go together as a couple and isolate Miss Monroe in the woman's bathroom," Paula said. "There's an alley exit out the back where our car will wait for us. Three minutes tops and the job's done."

"The most difficult part of this grab is getting the stun gun into the club," Marcos said. "Taping it to the inside of your leg should do the trick because they never check women's bodies entering the building. Only their handbags."

"No problem, Marcos. If we're going to do the job this Thursday then you better give me the stun gun now and I'll be ready when you pick me up."

"Be careful. Don't squeeze your legs together or the gun might activate and you could get the shock of your life in a sensitive area. That much electricity could affect your reproductive organs forever."

"I'll be fine," she answered. "I'll point it down so the jolt only hits the ground. Anyway, once we get in and are seated, I'm giving it right back to you. This is your toy. I'll isolate the girl while you take out Bruno."

"You mean her bodyguard?" Marcos asked.

"Yes, and be sure you have the gun on maximum power. I saw him when I tracked Miss Monroe. He must weigh 300 pounds, and it's all muscle."

"And you know this because?" Marcos asked with a grin.

"I have my sources," she said with a return smile. "Anyway, he's big, so don't take any chances."

"Our driver will pick you up around nine," Marcos said. "I'll be at the entrance waiting. We'll go in together and sit near her table. I'll reserve ours today."

"Anyway, It's good to see you again, Marcos. You still live in Sweden?" Paula was trying to make some connection with her partner of few words. This was her third job with him and she knew little about the man.

"Yes. I want to get this done and head back. It's still a little cool there, but when summer comes, the long days make for fantastic weather. I really love the people."

"I'm glad for you, Marcos. You seem to have found your home. I can't say much for the French so I spend more time in Italy in between jobs. The south of Italy is warming up now and that's where I'm heading after this grab."

Marcos had stopped listening to Paula. "I'll see you Thursday. Here's the stun gun but be careful. Ciao."

Chapter 7

Cathy opened her eyes and tried to move her arms and legs. Tape bound them together as well as a strip over her mouth. The bed she was lying on had a blanket covering her lower body. A pillow was under her head. She thought whoever took her spent a lot of time keeping her comfortable, so maybe she was taken for ransom.

The van crossed into Colorado twenty minutes before and was not far from Durango. The isolated cabin was a short drive from town. Barry's plan was to secure the woman in the cabin before Dawg went back into town for supplies. Neither man knew how long they would have to wait before the ransom was paid.

"How much longer to the cabin, Barry? She's starting to wake up and I need to take a piss."

"I'll pull over at the next rest stop. Make it quick. I don't want anyone coming near the van."

The rest stop was the next exit and Dawg made the short walk to the men's bathroom. He was in pain and every step he took demonstrated that fact.

Cathy had no idea where they were, and her arms were beginning to cramp. She rolled over to her side to allow the circulation to return to her fingers and tried once more to move her feet. No luck. The tape held them tightly together. She still wore the yoga attire from the class she took earlier that day. By now, she was sure someone was looking for her. Remaining calm was important for survival. She got a good kick in earlier with the big masked man but he grabbed her before she could back away and make a run for it.

Barry looked over at his two million dollar prize and could see she was starting to move around. "This won't take much longer, Miss Chambers. We have no intention of hurting you, so relax. All your boyfriend needs to do is pay the ransom, and you're free to go."

Cathy couldn't answer, but felt relief nothing would happen to her. They had to know Alan was loaded, she thought. The dinner Alan planned for her was ruined. Pain racked her body and she needed to pee. These assholes are going to pay.

Dawg returned to the van and they were back on the road. Twenty minutes later they drove through Durango and to the cabin outside of town. The transfer of Cathy into their unit took place quickly with the side door of the van pulled right up to the front door. Barry told the owner he and his partner didn't want to be disturbed. As far as the owner was concerned, he didn't want to bother two men in their cabin retreat anyway. What they did was their business.

Dawg carried Cathy into the cabin and put her into a chair with her hands and feet still bound. He was not going to give her another shot at his manhood.

"Miss Chambers," Barry said. "Here's the deal. We're in an isolated cabin away from anyone. I'm going to remove the tape from your mouth so we can feed you and allow you to use the bathroom. If you try to scream, kick either of us or attempt to get away we will tape you up again. You'll have to relieve yourself in your yoga pants and that will not be a pretty sight. Is that clear?"

Cathy nodded her head. She knew she had to play along with the two men and do what they said. They'd traveled farther than fifty miles and she was out of range from the GPS monitor picking up the chip in her arm. Either Alan would pay the ransom to free her, or somehow she'd run for it when she could.

Dawg approached Cathy from behind and removed the tape from her mouth. He still ached from the kick she gave him in the parking lot.

"I have to use the bathroom really bad," Cathy said. She was calm in her demand and knew getting hysterical would do no good.

"Dawg will cut the tape from your feet. The bathroom is through that door. I'll release your hands as well. Any attempt to run and we put you right back in the chair, tape and all."

"I get it. I promise not to try anything." Cathy kept looking at Dawg who now stood by the only door out of the cabin. Trying to escape was futile.

After a bathroom visit, Cathy returned to the main room. It was basic living. A couch, two chairs, and a coffee table made up the living room.

A sandwich and glass of apple juice completed her lunch. Dawg went into town for more supplies after Cathy was fed. Barry was not big enough to handle Cathy by himself, so she was handcuffed to the bedpost.

"What do you plan to do with me?" Cathy asked. She was less afraid now and knew she'd be free in time.

"The ransom demand call happens tonight after we make sure we're not followed," Barry said. "You'll provide us with your boyfriend's cell phone number so we can make this happen. The sooner the demand is met, the sooner you'll be free. Are we clear?"

"Crystal," Cathy answered. She guessed these kidnappers were amateurs and were trying to pull this job off with no knowledge that she had a GPS chip in her arm. They probably had never done something like this before and were lucky to get this far. "Give me a paper and pen and I'll write the number down. I want this over as soon as possible."

Barry was pleased Miss Chambers went along with the plan without any throwback. He wanted this to be over as well. He felt he was over his head but this could be his last job if everything worked out. Dawg grew up Albuquerque and Barry knew it would only be a matter of time before the 'big guy' landed in jail if he returned home. His plan was to fly out of Denver and never look back.

Dawg left the cabin after Cathy gave Barry the phone number. He needed a beer right away to calm his nerves. Probably several.

*****

A call from an unlisted number appeared on Alan's phone around ten p.m. Alan had a trace put onto his phone and knew he had to keep the person on the line for a least three minutes to be able to locate the caller.

"Mr. Alan Hogan, please."

"Yes, this is Alan Hogan."

"We have Cathy Chambers and she is safe. Let's make this quick. We want two million dollars deposited into this account tomorrow morning before ten a.m. Write it down. Wells Fargo account number 3874983-2. After the amount is transferred, I'll let you talk to Miss Chambers and give you her location. She can be home by dinner tomorrow night. Are we clear?"

"Yes, but I......"

'No, Mr. Hogan, there is nothing to discuss. That's it." Barry hung up. He had seen enough cop shows to know that if he stayed on the line any longer he could be traced.

He used a burner phone but still took no chances. He had to make sure the money transfer happened before he'd proceed any further.

Alan was cut off before he could ask to talk to Cathy. He wrote the account number down. The transfer meant it could be completed right away. He was relieved the kidnapper only wanted two million.

"Robert, they called." Alan trusted his friend would know what to do.

"The people who took Cathy?"

"Yes. They were on the phone for ninety seconds so no trace was possible. I have officer Parsons here at my house with a machine that can trace calls but there was not enough time."

"What do they want you to do?" Robert was sure it was money they wanted but he had no idea how much.

"I have to wire two million to a Wells Fargo account tomorrow morning. After they get the money they'll let me talk to Cathy, and then give me her location."

"Has anything turned up as far as that GPS chip in Cathy's arm?"

"No, not yet. The police are making wide circles around the state hoping to pick up a signal. Last I heard, they are making a loop about 100 miles outside

Albuquerque. They said they're going to continue this all night and should get a fix on a location soon unless the kidnappers hopped a train and are a thousand miles away."

"What time is the money transfer?"

"Tomorrow morning before ten."

"You know how to trace accounts, Alan. We could follow the money electronically and get him at the other end after we secure Cathy."

"I'm all shook up about this. I can pay the two million and be done with it. She has to get home safely. We've already started making wedding plans."

"It's up to you, Alan. What if the police pick up a signal before tomorrow? Do they have the okay to go in after her?"

"What do you think I should do, Robert? I'm not thinking clearly right now, and we don't know how dangerous these kidnappers are."

Robert thought for a moment. He knew Cathy was the number one person in Alan's life. He had to make sure she got home safely. "Are the police going to call you if they get a signal?"

"Officer Parsons is in the other room and has contact with the company monitoring the signal. I can ask her and call you back."

"Do that. We may not want them going in with blazing guns. Maybe we should hold back and get Cathy first and then go after them electronically."

"I'll pass the information to the police station through Parsons," Alan said. "She's really nice and understands how I feel about Cathy."

"Good, Alan. We'll' get her back. After she's safe, I may go after these assholes myself. They could have just as easily targeted Julia and I'd be in your place. I need to stop them from ever doing something like this again. They messed with the wrong family for sure."

"Thanks, Robert. I knew I could count on you."

Alan hung up and went back into the living room where Officer Parsons had the phone tracing equipment set up.

"Officer Parsons, I have a decision and I need the police to cooperate with this. I know you're trying to follow up on the GPS signal but my worry is these men might have guns. I would like you to call Detective Louis and let him know I plan on paying the ransom. Even if they find the location of Cathy from the signal, I want her out of harm's way before the police move in."

"I completely understand your concern, Mr. Hogan. Here's what I suggest we do if we find their location."

"Go ahead. I'm listening," Alan said.

"If she's in another state, we have to let the local police handle the case. We can surround the area where she is and wait. After the ransom is paid, and the men leave, the police should follow them. If they take Cathy with them, we stay undercover until she's released. Then we take them down but not until we know she's safe."

"That should work, but be sure the police aren't seen. She has to be in police custody before you move in on the kidnappers." Alan liked the plan and it made sure Cathy's safety was the objective.

"I'll let Louis know because he'll do what I suggest."

"How do you know he will?" Alan asked.

"We've been dating for a few months now and I know how he works. It's all in the presentation. I'll make him feel like the idea was his and then it'll be a slam dunk."

"Is that how women work?" Alan asked. "You've given me ten years of knowledge in one sentence. Cathy does that with me all the time. When we get her back, I may get to interact on a level playing field."

"Don't kid yourself," June answered as she rolled her eyes. "Women have several more tricks up their sleeves. Men just think they have the upper hand. Just look at all the great presidents and see who their wives were at the time. Eleanor and Martha should be on that list. I even like Michelle, but this country is still dealing with racism and it's been a tough administration because of it."

"Cathy's the backbone of our company and deals with tough problems. I do better with the employees because they're geeks like myself. I'll pay anything to get her back."

"I'll call Louis right now and get this plan into motion. If we have to go out of state, we'll alert the local police and have them follow the kidnappers. We're going to get her back, Mr. Hogan."

*****

"How did she sleep, Dawg? Did you get up in the night to get her anything?" Barry asked as he stood by the cabin door.

It was now day two of the kidnapping.

"I don't believe she's thinking about escape," Dawg answered. He was in the kitchen making coffee. "She knows her boyfriend can pay the ransom and we're not using any guns. She seems to be waiting out the time until she's free."

Barry was pleased the night went by without incident. Cathy remained handcuffed to the metal bed frame and Dawg slept on a mattress in front of the door, blocking any chance of escape. Barry slept in the loft by himself. He woke up several times and pointed a flashlight towards the bed downstairs to make sure their financial investment was safe.

Before the grab, Barry set up an account in the Cayman Islands. The money from Wells Fargo would transfer automatically as soon as the funds cleared. Another transfer into a second subsidiary bank on the island covered their transaction tracks. The banking laws were different in the Caymans. Any knowledge of where the money went after reaching the first Cayman account disappeared without a trace.

"Dawg, come outside for a minute. I want to explain to you how the money transfer is going down." Barry didn't want Cathy to hear what he was saying.

"You mean we're not going to get it in a suitcase?" Dawg asked. He wanted to touch the cash and didn't know much about transfers and banking practices.

"Hell no," Barry said. "This is the 21st century. Close the door so she can't hear us." The door closed. "Money is transferred by wire. We don't want to have any contact with Mr. Hogan, or anyone for that matter."

"So how are they going to pay us?" Dawg asked, a little perturbed. He envisioned himself arriving back in Albuquerque driving a new sports car with the trunk full of hundred dollar bills.

Barry spent the next ten minutes explaining to Dawg

about the wire transfers from Wells Fargo to the Cayman Island account and then on to another account.

"Everything is done within an hour of the money first going into the Fargo account."

"How do I get my share?" Dawg asked, sweat appearing on his forehead.

"First, we need to get away. When the money is transferred, we drive to Denver and fly anywhere we want to go. I'll set up a separate account in the Caymans for you but I suggest you only take what you need. I'll call and give the location of the girl to Mr. Hogan. Then we're done."

"What about the van and our apartments back in Albuquerque?" Dawg asked.

"I walked away from mine and put everything I own into storage. I may try to get it some day but probably not," answered Barry. "They'll sell the contents after a year."

"Here's my situation, Barry. I have all my old friends back there. I can't walk away," Dawg said as sweat beads continued to collect on his face. This was not how Dawg thought the money transfer would go.

"You're on your own after we get paid, Dawg. I'm out of here. I may disappear in Europe for a while before heading to some Caribbean island. After Denver, we may never see each other again."

"Really? I thought we were a team?" Dawg said.

"We were until now, but this is it. You can live on a million bucks for the rest of your life. A billionaire can't but I can. I suggest you get out of Albuquerque because your face is going to be on the news soon. That woman in there will give a sketch of what we look like to the Albuquerque police, and if you go back, it's just a matter of time before they find you. I'm leaving for good."

"What if we take her out?" Dawg was really scared now.

"Dawg, I don't kill people. Even if we get caught, our money would be waiting for us in the Cayman account. Kidnapping someone without a gun, and no violence might put us in jail for five years with good behavior. A million can earn a lot of interest in that amount of time and we would get free board and room during those years behind bars."

"I don't want to go to jail," Dawg yelled.

"Neither do I, so don't get caught. I really hope you don't go back to Albuquerque. I'll be long gone if you do get nabbed, so don't expect me to come back for you. You're on your own."

Dawg started to feel depressed. He had no idea where to go, and only knew his way around New Mexico.

"Where do you suggest I go, Barry? I'm starting to freak out."

"Let's get this done, set up a Cayman account in your name and decide things when we get to Denver. We'll keep an eye on the news and see if the police come up with any leads."

The two men went back inside just as Cathy sat up in bed. She was ready for this day to end and head home.

*****

"We have a location boss." Louis was awake since five a.m. when he got the call from the Colorado police. Two officers remained in the woods parked outside the cabin with orders to hold their positions until further notice.

"Where did they end up?" Martin asked.

"Some little cabin retreat outside Durango," Louis said. "Can you believe it? They went all the way to the next state to hide from us. The chip in the victim's arm gave us the location."

"What time is the money transfer?"

"Sometime around ten," Louis said. "After that, we can grab them if they're still in the cabin."

"Has anybody contacted Mr. Hogan to tell him we have a location?"

"Yes, about an hour ago. Mr. Hogan and Parsons are heading to the location as we speak. I gave her permission to accompany him. Mr. Hogan wants to be there when she's freed."

"What about the money transfer? How does he pull that off while driving in a car?"

"He has a secretary who's making the transfer at nine forty-five."

"Has anyone had eyes on the kidnappers yet?" Martin asked.

"Two of them went outside the front door for a few minutes. The local police believe they're still in the cabin."

"Any more phone calls from the kidnappers?" Martin wanted to know everything he could.

"Mr. Hogan has his phone with him. He doesn't expect another call until after the transfer. That's when he'll get the location of Miss Chambers."

Martin waited a few seconds before saying anything. He looked at his watch and finally said, "Twenty minutes to go. Who gets credit for their capture when it happens? Us or the Colorado team?"

"We pull this off then both states get credit. We gave the information to the police in Durango and they're taking the risks if any gunplay is involved. I'm happy sharing the credit," Louis said.

Martin nodded and said, "You're right, Louis. If this plays out the way we expect, have Parsons take pictures of the cabin where they held the woman and the couple embracing when she's freed. We can use them in the local paper and write the story ourselves."

"Will do boss," Louis answered. "I'll give her a call right now."

Louis had June on speed dial and pushed the button. "June, hi, it's me. Where are you two now?"

"We're just pulling into Durango. This guy is driving like a bat out of hell." She looked over at Alan and could see he still had his earphones on and couldn't hear a word she was saying. "I could've given him three speeding tickets since we left Albuquerque, but I know he wants to be there before ten when the money exchange happens."

"It should happen any minute now. Martin wants you to take lots of pictures after Cathy is safe. Also, take pictures of the cabin where they kept her and the two hugging when she is freed. Martin is still on his 'glory run' and he can't get enough publicity. How are you doing? I miss you."

"This is part of what we do. I miss you too. We hope to wrap this up and be back in Albuquerque by dinner."

"Just be careful. No one knows if they have any weapons and Hogan is willing to let them get away with the money just to be sure his girlfriend is safe."

"Durango turn off just appeared and the GPS locator says we'll be there in fifteen minutes."

"Just stay out of sight until Alan gets a call. Even if anyone leaves the cabin, wait. Still, don't know how many people are in the cabin with the woman. Martin would never let us hear the end of this if we blow it."

"That guy needs to eat more fruit, Louis. I think he's backing up and the shit is depositing in his head. You know the expression, 'shit for brains.' In Martin's case he may be getting close," June said with a laugh.

"You're too funny, June. Hey, since you are in Durango, pick up a variety of their home crafted beers. They have a lot of them from that state and anything dark is what we both like."

"Great idea, Louis. You cook tonight. I'll be a little tired after this trip. I may be doing the driving when the two lovebirds get together and start making out in the backseat. Can I give them a ticket if things get too steamy?"

"Just let them be. I'm thinking of giving you another stakeout assignment so I can show up and we can try the back seat some time as well."

"No more stakeouts, Louis. You promised. Anyway, we do much better in the bedroom with more area to play around."

"Can Hogan hear us?"

"No, he has earphones on. He's listening to music to calm his nerves while waiting for the phone call from the kidnappers. He can't hear a word I'm saying."

"Okay, so call me when you can and we'll make plans later. Love you"

"Oh stop, Louis. You just want my body," she teased.

"Yes, I do, but you know I love you, so get used to it."

"I love you too, Louis. Talk later."

Officer Parsons looked at the GPS again and pointed for Alan to take a right on Pine Drive. The cabin was located about five minutes up the road from the turnoff.

Chapter 8

The car arrived for Paula at nine and took her to La Rue. She had the stun gun tied to her inner thigh. The dress she wore was not tight so she could move without revealing the fact she was packing a weapon on her body.

Marcos sat at the table he booked near Miss Monroe's reserved location. He decided not to wait outside for his partner. When Paula arrived, she found Marcos and gave him a kiss on the cheek.

"I'm going to reach up my dress and get the Taser, so cover for me," she said.

"By doing what?" Marcos asked.

"Just put your arm around me while I untie it. It's awkward and starting to hurt."

Marcos did what he was asked. Paula removed the gun and quickly withdrew her hand, placing the device between Marcos' legs. He quickly slipped it into his coat pocket, returned his arm to the table, and took a sip from his beer.

"See, that wasn't too difficult, Marcos. You're all set. Now we just wait for our target to arrive. I thought you were going to stand outside to make sure the Monroe woman was coming."

"I got thirsty and needed a drink. She's coming,"

Marcos said.

After twenty minutes passed, some people arrived and sat at the Monroe table. This was a Jet-set crowd. Expensive suits and designer dress with plenty of cleavage exemplifying the dress code for these people. They were loud, obnoxious, and didn't care what people thought of them because they had money to do anything they wanted. Marcos despised this type of person and looked forward to putting one of them in their place.

"Keep an eye on the big guy, Marcos," Paula said. "He's the one you have to be careful of. He follows the Monroe woman everywhere, even to the bathroom. That's where we have to grab her and duck out the back door."

"Are you ready with the syringe?" Marcos asked. "You'll have to inject her and get her out the bathroom door on your own. I'm sure the Taser can knock out Bruno, or whatever his name is."

"I hope so, Marcos. There's a lot of beef on his bones so be careful."

Marcos and Paula sat for the next hour watching the table with Miss Monroe and the other three couples drinking and occasionally finding their way to the dance floor. The club was typical retro with loud music and high levels of noise. Marcos hated these types of clubs but counted on the high volume level to help him and

Paula contain their target and make their escape.

Around ten-thirty Miss Monroe stood up and walked towards the bathrooms, followed by her three hundred pounds of protection. Paula made her move and headed to the *salle de bain* as well. Marcos followed two minutes later and came around the corner to the restrooms hallway. The huge bodyguard stood outside the women's entrance and looked up towards Marcos as he came around the corner. Marcos' hand was already on the Taser in his left coat pocket, away from the bodyguard. As soon as he walked by, he swung around, placing the weapon to the man's neck and pulling the trigger.

The bodyguard shook but did not fall. His eyes glazed over, but instinct kicked in and he reached towards his attacker and grabbed his coat. Marcos felt the power in this man's grasp and knew another blast was needed right away. As Marcos was pulled towards the mountain of muscle, a second blast at the chest was all he had time for. Two blasts and the guard went down bringing Marcos with him.

By now Paula had isolated Miss Monroe as she entered a stall and injected her in the neck before she could lock the door. The drug took effect instantly. Paula grabbed her before she fell and dragged the body into the hallway, telling the two women in front of the mirrors not to worry. "My friend had too much to drink," she said.

The two women, more concerned about their looks,

returned to their lipstick and chatting.

Marcos pried the fingers of the bodyguard off his coat and stood up when Paula opened the door to the Ladies room.

"Grab her feet. The car is waiting just out that door," she said.

Marcos grabbed the woman's legs and backed towards the exit with a *Sortie* sign written in red neon. The back door of the car was already open and the target was inside within fifteen seconds. Marcos jumped into the front seat with the driver and Paula rode in the back seat, guarding the target.

The driver had been waiting in the alley for an hour and placed street cones to block any traffic wanting to park in the back of the nightclub. He drove over the cones in his escape from the Le Rue nightclub, took a hard right, and proceeded down the street, traveling at the traffic speed advertised. Getting pulled over for speeding was not an option.

"Did you have any problems?" Paula asked. "It sounded like you were having a struggle with the big guy before I came out."

"You're right." Marcos was still breathing hard. "His size enabled him to withstand the first shock. I had it dialed all the way up, but he still was able to grab and pull me down. It took two jolts to knock him out. That guy was a beast. What about the woman? Any trouble with her?"

"Not at all. Whatever Poppy uses to knock people out, it sure works fast. The two bitches doing their face couldn't care less about me pulling someone out of the ladies room. They were too busy comparing lipstick shades and only gave me a glance."

"We should be at the safe-house in twenty minutes," Marcos said. "After we get this woman into the apartment I'll call Poppy and let him know how everything went. He'll make the necessary ransom calls and then we can get out of town."

Twenty minutes later the car pulled up to the apartment, located in a small, dark street. Few people walked by the building at night but Marco and Paula took no chances. They braced the woman up in a standing position and walked her into the downstairs apartment with her feet dragging behind. It appeared as though they were helping a drunken friend get home.

The apartment on Rue du Bourg was used before to hold captives. The access to a main street, on both ends of the Rue, provided a getaway if necessary. It was rented under a false name with no trace back to anyone in the kidnapping ring.

Marcos called Poppy. "We're settled in and have the

target. The driver is taking Paula home and I'll remain here until the caretaker arrives."

"I just got off the phone with my contact in the police department. What happened with the bodyguard? He was found dead in front of the bathrooms. His heart stopped, according to the report. I thought you said that toy of yours didn't kill anyone."

Marcos waited a few seconds before answering. "Damn it, that was not intentional. The guy was so big the first shock didn't take him down. He grabbed me, and I had to give him another blast to the chest. I still ended up on the floor and had to pry his fingers from my clothes. I had no idea he might need a second blast or that his heart would give out."

"This changes a few things. This is the first time someone died on one of our grabs. Now it's a murder case and not a simple kidnapping. We'll get the money but the police will be coming after us for murder. As soon as the caretaker arrives to watch Miss Monroe, you and Paula need to leave Paris. If I were you, I'd leave tonight before any facial sketches can be made."

"You're right, Poppy. Let Paula know what happened. I only have to pick up a few things back at my hotel. Call me in a few weeks after things calm down."

"I'd ask you where you're going but right now I'd rather not know." Poppy shook with anger. "I plan on getting the letter off to the father tomorrow, and get this deal over with as soon as possible. I'll wire money to your account after we're paid."

"Sorry about the bodyguard, but it had to be done," Marcos said.

"Lay low and stay away from Paris for a while. I'll let you know if your face comes up in any ID photos. If it does, then another trip to the plastic surgeon may be in order."

"I've only had to do that once before," Marcos answered, "and now my mother wouldn't recognize me."

"I thought you said she was dead?" Poppy asked.

"Well, yes, she is, so that would ensure she wouldn't recognize me."

Chapter 9

"Park over there, Alan," Officer June said. "We don't want anyone in the cabin to see our car. The GPS location shows me Cathy is in that one. This is the only road out so let's stay hidden."

"All right," Alan said. "The money's transferred and I should be getting a call from these people. Look, here comes a white van. Stay down. We don't want them to see us in the car."

The van, fitting the description of the kidnapper's vehicle, passed Alan's car. June got a quick peek into the cab, just as it passed. There were two men in the front.

Parsons called on her radio and gave instructions to the Durango police, waiting in an unmarked car near the main road entrance.

"There's a white van heading your way. Follow them, but stay hidden. We still don't know if our victim is in the cabin, or in the van. I'll know in a while. There's a team watching the place. I'll stay here until we get a call from the kidnappers telling us where she is."

"Affirmative," the Durango police officer said. "We'll keep them in our sight and make sure they don't get away."

*****

Dawg and Barry headed towards Denver. After twenty minutes, Barry received the statement, on his cell phone, that the funds had been transferred from the Wells Fargo account to the Cayman account. Cathy remained cuffed to the cabin bed, but she knew what they looked like. They'd catch a flight as soon as possible and disappear before a sketch made it to the internet.

Canada was their first stop. In Barry's mind, everything played out perfectly. Miles later, just outside of Denver, one last maneuver became necessary.

"Dawg, quick, pull over to that carwash and prepare to move quickly. We have to change vehicles."

The sign for Quick Wash appeared in the distance.

"You want to wash the van before we get to the airport?" Dawg asked.

"Just do as I tell you. I think we're being followed," Barry answered.

"Are you sure?"

"Ninety percent sure. Do you see that black sedan about four cars behind us? It's been the same distance since we left Durango and that was hours ago. We need to make a move here and get a new ride."

The van pulled into the carwash and got in line. It was the style of carwash where four cars at a time went through the system, passing through the three cleaning cycles one after another with the driver inside.

The Durango police, following the van, pulled into the parking lot and waited. Their orders were to keep the suspects in sight.

The two officers saw the van enter the carwash chamber. The process took about ten minutes. Finally, the cleaned white van emerged, passed through the dryer, and rolled towards the parking lot. Instead of stopping, the van kept on rolling and eventually crashed into the retaining wall separating the parking lot from the main street.

"Something's wrong," the officer in the passenger seat said. "I don't see a driver in the van."

Both policemen left their car and walked over to the van. The owner of the carwash walked out of his office and approached the van.

"What the hell just happened," yelled the owner. He reached the van and opened the door. "There's no one inside."

The officers, standing right behind the owner, were just as stumped as he was.

"Don't tell me we lost them?" the lead officer asked. "How'd they do that?"

*****

The blue Honda Accord, that was second in line in the car wash minutes before, was on the I70 heading towards Denver. The woman driving the Accord was petrified when two men jumped into the back seat of her car in the middle of the washing cycle. Both men were soapy wet.

"Just drive out of the carwash, take the exit to the right and you won't get hurt," Barry told her. "We just want a ride into town, and from there you can be on your way."

The woman didn't say anything to the two men and did exactly what they asked. The larger man had his hand on her shoulder in case she tried to jump out of the car.

The occupants of the Honda didn't speak until the first exit into Denver appeared. Barry told her to take the off ramp.

"Pull over to the curb by that bus stop and let us out. Here's a hundred for your trouble." Barry handed the woman two, fifty-dollar bills.

The frightened woman took the money, her hands shaking. Barry and Dawg got out and the woman hit the gas as she pulled away. They were in luck. An airport express bus was just pulling up and they quickly got in. By the time the woman made a call to the police, Barry and Dawg were on the way to the airport.

"Man, that was close," Dawg said.

"Yeah, too close. I can now call Alan Hogan and let him know where his girlfriend is. There's no way they know where we are."

Barry made the call to Alan, who'd been waiting in the car for three hours outside the cabin. He knew Cathy was still inside because of the tracking chip in her arm, but he didn't know if there was another kidnapper with her.

"Move in. That was the call," Alan said with relief.

The other two officers, waiting outside the cabin, were already in the room cutting the cuffs off Cathy. By the time Alan and Parsons walked in she was free from the bed. June had her cell phone camera and started videoing the meeting between Alan and Cathy. She also took footage of the cabin interior and the conditions Cathy had to endure while being held hostage.

Kisses and hugs insured the ordeal was over. The last hours were the worst for Alan because he sent the money but the return call never came until much later.

"I knew you'd come, Alan. How come it took so long?" Cathy looked stressed.

"I had to wait for a phone call to get your location. We were parked outside the cabin but didn't know if there was anyone inside with you. I wasn't taking any chances."

"So the chip in my arm worked," Cathy said. "You tracked me, but had to wait for a phone call? Let's get out of here. Maybe we can get home by dinner. I need a bath and about three beers to unwind."

Officer Parsons was almost ready. She was on the phone with Louis and gave him an account of Cathy and the news she was safe. She'd do the paperwork in the morning and promised to pick up the assortment of beers in Durango before heading back to Albuquerque.

"It's 200 miles to Albuquerque, but I'm going to mount the portable police light I brought with me, and make it back in two hours."

"Drive safely, June. I'm glad the woman is safe. It looks like the suspects got away just outside Denver. That's the worst part of this case so far."

"What? How'd that happen?"

"I'll tell you when you get home. It's interesting, but I don't want to spend time telling you because I would rather have you here."

"You're sweet, Louis. I'll hear the story after a bath and a beer."

Cathy, Alan and Officer Parsons got in the car and drove into Durango. Alan paid for a room at a nice hotel and waited for Cathy to take a shower and wash her hair. Meanwhile, June picked up a case of dark beer but Alan paid for it.

"This is a small token for supporting me through this ordeal," Alan said. "It's the least I can do."

June drove at 110 mph with the red light flashing on the hood of the car, while Cathy slept on Alan's lap in the back seat. She was exhausted and the ordeal left her completely spent.

Chapter 10

"We're safe." Alan was able to place a call to Robert after Cathy fell asleep on his lap. He spent the next ten minutes going over the events leading up to the release of Cathy. He also included what he had heard about the two men's escape in the car wash outside of Denver.

"Those bastards got away?" Robert asked. "How's that possible?"

"I asked the same thing. I don't have any details. Officer Parsons got word from her detective friend in Albuquerque." Alan made sure the conversation did not include Robert's name. Robert was dead, according to the Albuquerque police, and needed to remain so in their eyes.

"They drove all the way to Denver," Robert said. "I'll bet they're going to fly out of there. I'm not letting this go, Alan. They went after you and Cathy and that was their first mistake."

"I'll help when I can but most of this will have to be on your own. I'm just happy to get Cathy back. The money means nothing."

"To me, it's more than that. Tell the police that the men probably were headed to the airport and that any sketches should be checked out with the security cameras there. I still think they had this setup and were planning on flying out of Denver before they even made the grab. Let's use the police as much as we can to find these men. If they go overseas I'll take it from there. This is now personal." Robert was pissed.

"Will do. We should be home in about ninety minutes. Officer Parsons is going over 100 mph with one of those portable flashing lights on top of the car. She wants to be home as much as we do. She must have a hot date."

"Alan, I'm glad your both safe. We'll talk in the morning and see if any leads turn up with the police. This is my main case right now. I'll let Julia and Peggy handle the small cases, but this one is on me." Robert was in his vendetta mode, and there was no turning back once he kicked into gear.

*****

Barry and Dawg's flight to Quebec City was scheduled to land in ten minutes. Dawg got a passport before the kidnapping, in case they went to Canada. Barry still had his old one for another year before it expired. Neither man had traveled to the country north of the U.S.

Each man carried a small suitcase, while Barry kept his computer in a bag over his shoulder. Their wet pants from the carwash were now dry and both men changed their shirts in the restroom.

After boarding the plane, Barry checked the second Cayman account and saw the new deposit. The money was now secure.

"We need to open an account for you, Dawg," Barry said. "You may not want to leave Canada for a while, but I'm going to Paris as soon as I can."

"Why Paris?" Dawg asked.

"I've never been there and I hear France is famous for its food. I'm never coming back to the States. I know you've never been out of New Mexico, but I'm telling you Dawg, you'll be arrested if you return. Several people have seen our faces, and sketch artists are pretty good at what they do. Our pictures will be all over the Albuquerque Tribune in a day or two."

"How do we set up the account, Barry? If you leave for Europe and I stay, then I want to start celebrating soon. We're now rich and I need to unwind."

"I'll have your account set up in a few minutes. We better separate when we get off the plane. If we are traced to Canada the police will be looking for two men traveling together. There is less attention walking through security alone."

The kidnappers settled into their seats and ordered the best drinks the flight offered. Barry set Dawg up with his own account and had him insert a password to get money when he wanted it. They were two-bit crooks with a lot of spending money. Barry was leaving North America and never returning, while Dawg had no idea what he was going to do.

The Air Canada flight from Denver landed in Quebec City around five p.m. After going through customs, Dawg and Barry met in the car rental parking lot. They didn't appear in any surveillance camera footage together while getting their passports stamped.

"Meet me outside the lot, Dawg," Barry said. "I'll get a car, and pick you up out of the terminal's camera range. We need to plan where to go and what you'll do when I'm gone."

Dawg had a dazed look on his face and said nothing. Many of the signs surrounding him were in English as well as a language he couldn't read and many of the people spoke French. He felt like he was on another planet. He proceeded to the end of the parking lot and waited. Barry arrived ten minutes later and stopped the car.

"Get in, Dawg. I don't see any cameras, but hurry anyway."

Dawg got into the Ford Fiesta and felt cramped immediately. "Why didn't you rent a big car, Barry? We have the money, so let's start spending it."

"Let's not draw any attention to ourselves, Dawg. If

the cops ever trace us to Canada, they're sure to look for two guys spending money like crazy. Time to celebrate comes later."

"Is this place anything like France? They mostly speak French here. If that's the case I don't want any part of Paris or Europe." Dawg kept looking around for something familiar.

"I kind of expected this from you, Dawg. Going to Europe is my thing. You have your account and can get your money anytime you want. I'll drop you off at a decent hotel and you can decide what you want to do. Please don't return to Albuquerque, Dawg, at least for a while. You're safe here for now." Barry kept pounding Dawg with his advice.

"That's the hardest part of this whole situation, Barry. I'm a homeboy and I don't like foreigners. Even this place freaks me out. I have no idea what they're saying. At least they have McDonalds." Dawg pointed at a Golden Arches sign a block away. "Let's pull into that one and get something to eat before you drop me off."

"Okay, Dawg. We'll have one last meal together, courtesy of Ronald McDonald. Let's do the drive thru and go to a park and eat."

"Fine with me," Dawg said. "Order me two double Macs, two fries and a chocolate shake. Nothing on that flight tasted good and I'm starving."

The two newest millionaires from Albuquerque were living it up in Canada. Barry already booked a flight to a part of the world where some of the best food in Europe was served, but decided to share one last meal with his partner. He really didn't think Dawg would last long on his own. It had been a good run together and the payday was worth the effort.

After the men ate their meal in a nearby park, reminiscing over a few of their past jobs, Barry found a decent hotel for Dawg. He walked him to the front desk and shook his hand goodbye.

"Thanks for everything, Barry," Dawg said. He knew without Barry none of this was possible. He now had the money to do whatever he wanted. Tonight he'd start celebrating the only way he knew how. He'd go to an expensive nightclub and get real drunk. He hoped the hookers in this town knew how to speak English because he planned on hiring two of them at the same time.

*****

Robert waited two days before he made his next move. He'd learned to hack into police files when Alan worked for him and he now had the latest information on Cathy's case. Several sketches in the file appeared after Cathy gave the police artist the kidnapper's description. One picture was a close match to a local man who grew up in Albuquerque.

"I've downloaded this picture and information on this man named Doug Miller but nothing yet has come up with the second sketch." Robert was talking to Julia in the kitchen. "He may be in the system but not in any New Mexico files. There's even an address for Miller and it lists the high school where he went."

"Are you sure you want to continue this manhunt. Cathy and Alan want to get past the whole mess and move on," Julia said as she brought a plate of French toast to Robert in the office.

"Here's the thing for me, Julia. Two guys come along, nab Cathy, and get away with two million. It sets up a precedent for all two-bit crooks that this town is easy pickings and anyone can do it. You could have been a target just as well."

"Robert, you're probably right and I'll help as much as I can. Maybe this will be good for you to do on your own. Just take me along if there is any travel involved. I love going places with you."

"Deal. I'm making some calls, and see if I can talk to someone who knew Miller, either from his school or his job, if he had one."

"Good. You do that. Cathy and I are going to a spa today. She needs me to accompany her with some pampering. We'll be back this afternoon and meet here for dinner."

Robert finished his French toast and took the last sip of coffee. He knew he might be spending a lot of time finding the kidnappers. He wouldn't stop until they were behind bars.

*****

A week after the kidnapping, Robert found two friends of the suspect named Doug Miller. They played football with him at Highland High School and told Robert their old friend went by the name Dawg.

"He wasn't the brightest player on the team," said one of the teammates, "but his size took us to the city finals twice in 2003 and 2004."

Neither man had seen Dawg since the ten-year reunion, two years ago. One of them had his last known address.

Robert arrived at the apartment address and found the manager. He told Robert that Dawg rented the apartment until now.

"I got a call from him two days ago and he told me there was a family emergency and he wasn't coming back," the manager said. "Dawg wired $300 to pack up his possessions and put them into the apartment storage shed. He said he'd come back later to get everything and send another check to cover the storage cost."

"Have you packed up the apartment yet?" Robert

asked.

"I have a team in there right now boxing his stuff up. I need to get another renter in as quickly as possible. Why are you interested in Dawg?"

"I'm a private investigator doing research on a case Dawg is involved with. He may be a fugitive and one step ahead of the local police. We think he's caught up in a kidnapping and forced to leave the city. Do you still have the call log when he phoned you?"

"Yes, I believe I do." The manager reached into his pocket for his phone and found the call number. He then handed the phone to Robert.

Robert could see the call was international from the area code. Dawg must have called from a phone other than his cell, thought Robert. He wrote down the number, handed back the phone, and thanked the manager. He had to move quickly if he was going to catch this guy.

On the drive home, Robert called Peggy and told her to pinpoint the location of the call after giving her the number. By the time he reached the office, Peggy handed Robert the name of the Hotel Palace Royal in Quebec. She confirmed the call came from the hotel lobby.

Robert was positive Dawg wasn't the brains in this two-man team. Finding him was too easy. Robert had to catch a flight tonight and find Dawg before the police did. Questioning him might lead to the second kidnapper.

"Julia, I'm off to Canada. Do you want to go or stay here?"

"Where exactly are you going?"

"Quebec City."

"Of course I want to go. How soon?"

"About an hour. I have a location on one of the men, and if we can get there tonight, we have a chance to catch him. I'll book a room at the hotel where the suspect named Dawg, made a call."

"Are they both there?" Julia asked.

"I don't know. All I have is a picture of Dawg and a sketch of the other man. If they're still together we may close this case quickly."

"How are you going to arrest them? This is Canada. Do you think we'll have to get the local police involved?"

"Yes. I don't know anyone in this region of Canada and my French is minimal. How's yours?"

"Fluent. When I lived in New York, Quebec was a fun place to visit. I love the area. I also took French in school."

"I'll get our tickets. There is a flight at eight p.m. tonight. That means we can arrive before midnight, get some sleep and be ready in the morning."

"Can I put some clothes in a suitcase for you while you're on the computer?" Julia asked.

"Please do. We'll grab a sandwich at the airport before boarding the plane. Canada here we come."

Chapter 11

Paula and Marco left Paris on the same day but in different directions. Poppy was busy covering up the mess after Miss Monroe's bodyguard died. This was the first time someone was killed while making a grab for Poppy and he was clearly upset. Anyone connected to this kidnapping would be an accessory and he made sure nothing led back to him.

At the apartment, the Monroe woman was awake and struggling to get her hands out of the metal cuffs that attached her to the bed.

The woman hired to watch over her, spoke in broken English, "When you calm I bring food. Not before."

"Don't you know who I am, you bitch? My father will have you killed for doing this to me," Miss Monroe screamed.

"I only watch you. Do nothing to take you. I no care who you are. They pay me, not you. Calm down and I bring food."

"I'd rather starve first," Miss Monroe yelled, still pulling on the handcuffs.

"Okay with me. I go now and come back in ten minutes. We see later."

Just then, the guard's phone rang. It was Poppy.

"How is the woman, Frances?" They spoke French. "Has she eaten anything yet?"

By now, Frances was in the hallway. "No Poppy. This one is a real bitch. She has not settled down since she woke up. I'm checking on her every ten minutes, waiting for her to shut up but no luck so far. She yells at me as soon as I walk through the door. Are you sure I can't slap her around a little to straighten her out?"

"No, just leave her alone. We want her in good shape when her daddy gets her back. I sent the ransom letter to her father an hour ago."

"Where are Marcos and Paula? Are they coming back or am I on my own?"

"I'll send Jacques in an hour. After that, you get some sleep. If this takes more than ten hours, I'll need you to take over for Jacque. Maybe by then she'll relax and eat something."

"This one I don't care about. These rich Americans are the worst, especially the women. Other nationalities are ready to eat right away. She deserves to be roughed up."

"One more hour, Frances. When we're paid we can all take a vacation."

Francis knew Poppy was right. She was tired and this hysterical woman did not make the job any easier. If the woman was still a captive when her shift came up again in ten hours she'd punch Miss Monroe in the stomach so it wouldn't leave a mark. She hated the entitled bitches of the world.

"Just tell Jacques to hurry up. I'm on my edge with this one and might not last an hour."

"Fifty-eight more minutes. You can do this." Poppy hung up and went to his computer. The ransom money was set up for deposit into a French account and automatically transferred to several other banks to avoid electronic tracking. After paying everyone involved, and locking up his apartment, Poppy planned to take a week off in Florence.

He loved spending time visiting the museums in that city and never tired of seeing The David. He was gay and especially attracted to the statue Michelangelo created. Several miniature creations of this work were in his apartment. He also had the phone number of several men who'd go out with him while in Florence. He had the money and they had the time.

Three hours later, a message came through from the bank. The money arrived. Poppy checked the balance and saw that five million Euros was deposited and transferred to other banks. He then spent the next thirty minutes paying the different people who helped with the job. Two million Euros was now added to his personal account.

Poppy called Jacques.

"Hello, Jacques. Time to go. Your money is in your account and everyone's been paid. Wipe the place down and leave the woman cuffed to the bed. Has she eaten anything at all?"

"No, and she refuses to allow anyone near her. We should have tied her feet as well."

"Go out the back and don't let anyone see you. The police could be there soon. I just let them know your location, so hurry. She's a handful, but daddy paid for her right away. These damn Americans can be the most difficult but their loved ones pay the ransom without much hassle."

"Can I give her a slap before I go?" Jacques asked.

"She really must be a pain in the ass," Poppy said. "Francis asked the same thing. Get out of town for a while and take a break. Leave her alone. I'll call you in a few months in case we have another job."

"All right, Poppy. I'll talk to you later."

Twenty minutes later, Jacques walked out the back door and headed up the alley to Boulevard de Sebastopol. It was a short walk to Notre Dame and his favorite café across the river. A train for Spain left in a few hours and the warmer weather was a good alternative until Paris warmed up.

*****

The Paris police now had an address. When they arrived, they found Miss Monroe still cuffed to the bed and she was hysterical. She threatened the police and blamed them for her capture in the first place. The chain was cut to remove her from the bed and the cuffs snipped off her wrists.

By the time Miss Monroe arrived at the station, the police wanted to slap her as well. *Capitaine* Le Cure told her to return the next day to make a statement. A sketch artist would help her identify the kidnappers.

"If you refuse to cooperate, Miss Monroe, you will be charged with hindering an investigation," *Capitaine* Le Cure said.

"You'll hear from my lawyer," she screamed as she walked out of the police station.

"Maybe we will, Miss Monroe, but you need to be here by ten a.m. or I'm sending an arresting officer to your hotel. Your lawyer can talk to you in the holding cell."

This last comment drove Miss Monroe over the edge. She pushed an older man out of the way as she stomped off to her waiting car.

"If she is not here by 10:01, make out an arrest warrant and bring her in," *Capitaine* Le Cure told his

Sergent. I really don't like that woman."

"*Oui Capitaine,*" *Sergent* Bruno answered. "It would be my pleasure to bring her in myself. She is one crazy American for sure."

Capitaine Le Cure wanted this case closed. If the bodyguard lived, the file might be in the unsolved cases cabinet. Murder changed everything. Kidnapping for ransom was a regular occurrence in Paris and criminals from all around the globe came to the French capital to cash in. Sometimes the victims were young women, sold as prostitutes, or as sexual gifts to rich Arab businessmen and never seen again. In the case of Miss Monroe and other wealthy families, large sums of money ensured their return.

"What have we found out about the dead bodyguard, *Sergent*? Do we know what killed him?" *Capitaine* Le Cure asked.

"There were some burn marks on his neck and ribs, which suggests a stun gun. The examining doctor thinks the blast in the chest area stopped his heart."

"Didn't we have a case a few months back, involving one of these stun guns? No one was killed, but the victim was grabbed after being shocked."

"Yes, the Marlow case. The head of some bank in California vacationed in Paris and disappeared outside some high-end whorehouse in the Moulin Rouge district. I think the kidnappers demanded three million Euros for him. The money was transferred to some local bank in Paris and then transferred to another bank overseas. The same thing happened with the Monroe woman. In this case, the kidnappers got five million Euros."

"It sounds like we have a pattern, *Sergent*. Did we ever come up with any leads involving the Moulin Rouge case?"

"Not one. Only the fact that a stun gun was used."

"Go back a few years and see if there are any other kidnapping cases using a stun gun."

"It might take me an hour or more so I'll talk to you after lunch, *Capitaine*."

"Take your time and find all the cases you can. Stick to the kidnapping ones. We could have a group who's making a good living off of victims right here in Paris."

The *Sergent* went back to his computer to start his research. Murder changed the importance of the case, and now he and *Capitaine* Le Cure needed to investigate thoroughly to bring the killer to justice.

*****

Barry's flight landed in Paris around eight p.m. He didn't book anything online because he didn't want anyone tracking him through the Internet. The cab driver took him to a nice hotel along the Seine River.

"Welcome to the Hotel Eiffel Seine. We are happy to have you visit us," the receptionist said in English, as Barry walked into the lobby

"Thank you. How did you know I wasn't French."

"The way you dress. Your clothes are American and so is your luggage."

Barry loved the hotel's location, which was walking distance to the Eiffel Tower and right on the river. The hotel was simple but elegant. A stone fireplace was blazing on one wall and comfortable chairs and couches filled the lounge area.

Barry presented his passport to the front desk when he checked in. He paid for the room with cash, which was unusual for most travelers.

"Do you have any rooms overlooking the river, Miss?" Barry asked. "I plan on being here for a week while I look for an apartment."

"I'll see what I can do, Mr. Cobb. Since you'll be here for a week, and we're in the offseason, I think I can find the perfect room for you."

"Thank you, Genevieve." Barry read her nametag. "I appreciate all your help." He then laid a ten Euro note on the counter and walked over to the couch in the reception room to wait for his room. Five minutes, later Genevieve called Barry back and told him to follow the bellboy. His room was ready.

Barry loved Paris so far. If he stayed for a while he'd have to learn the language, but other than that, he felt it might work for now.

The elevator arrived on his floor. Room 407 overlooked the Seine with a small balcony used to sit and drink wine when the weather warmed up. The simple, double bed and bathroom were basic by American standards but more than adequate. The tourist season was still two months away and the places Barry wanted to visit were more accessible without crowds. He'd look for an apartment, but mix business with pleasure and take his time. This was living and Barry was not in a hurry.

*****

Robert and Julia landed at Jean Lesage International Airport just after twelve p.m. and took a taxi to the Hotel Palace Royal. Robert had no idea if Dawg was still there but he'd find out. After checking in, Julia went to the room with the porter while Robert remained at the front desk.

"Ronald, hello again. I have something to ask you." Robert said. He then pulled out his Albuquerque police badge, he purchased five years ago, for special situations like this.

"I'm a detective from New Mexico and I believe this man," he pulled out a picture of Dawg, "checked into your hotel a few days ago and may be still here."

Ronald looked at the picture and then at the badge in Robert's hand. "What's he done?" Ronald asked.

"We believe he and a partner are involved in a kidnapping and flew here to escape the authorities in the States. If you can help us in any way, we'd be in your debt." Robert pulled out all the stops in the manners department, hoping the desk clerk wouldn't make any phone calls to Albuquerque and check on his credentials.

"Let me see if he's still with us. I believe he arrived with another man a week ago but the gentleman accompanying him didn't stay. I was on duty at the time. Yes, here it is. His room is reserved for three more days. I haven't seen him walking around in the lobby today. He seems lost and only comes down for meals in the dining room before going out to drink."

"Is he here now?"

"I believe he went back to his room after dinner and hasn't come down since. Shall I call security to accompany you?"

"No, Ronald. All I want to do is ask him some questions. Can you tell me what room he's in? It's too late tonight so I'll wait till morning to talk to him."

"Our hotel has a policy of total cooperation with the police so we'll do our best to help in any way we can. His room number is 324. I believe he sleeps in and comes down for breakfast around ten."

"Thank you for your help, Ronald. If this is the man we're looking for, and we make an arrest, I'll be sure to add your name to the report for helping us."

"Thank you, Mr. Forrester. I won't be on duty tomorrow morning so I hope you're successful."

Robert turned and headed towards the elevator. He had the drugs needed to complete the questioning process. The 'truth serum' arrived in a false tube of toothpaste and a syringe from a local twenty-four-hour pharmacy was now in his pocket. Robert had to show his badge for the purchase. The chloroform made it through customs in Julia's make-up bag.

"This is a nice room, Sweetheart," Julia said after Robert entered the apartment. "What took you so long? They even have a parlor."

"I used my best behavior to earn the trust with the desk clerk. He saw my badge, but never questioned my motives or tried to interfere. Shows what a little police pull can get you when you need it."

"You found out Dawg is still here?" Julia asked.

"Not only that, but the clerk gave me his room

number. He's on the third floor, right above us. We can either wait until tomorrow or surprise him tonight and get it over with."

"Since we're going to have him arrested let's wait until the morning. I need some sleep and it's almost one-thirty," Julia said, her eyes starting to droop.

"You're right, Julia. How about first thing in the morning? The front desk clerk told me Dawg doesn't get up early, so we can do our job and check out by noon."

"That works for me." Julia was already out of her clothes and headed towards the shower. She'd be asleep before Robert took his shower and got into bed.

*****

Around nine a.m. Dawg woke up, suffering from another hangover. He partied the first few nights he was in Quebec City but didn't feel like going out on the town after that. The words 'Oui' and 'no' were the extent of his French vocabulary. Because he was unable to return to Albuquerque, he was depressed and alcohol kept him that way.

Dawg had just stepped out of the shower and was almost dressed when a knock at the door startled him. He hadn't ordered room service, and the maids didn't clean the room until he was downstairs. He slipped on one of the new tee shirts he purchased after arriving in Canada and opened the door. Dawg had the size to ward off most attacks, but the element of surprise was still an advantage for anyone.

The cloth, soaked in chloroform, accompanied by a strong shove backward, sent Dawg to the ground. He reached up for the hand that held the cloth but the sharp jab in his arm told him he was too late. Blackness engulfed him.

When Dawg woke up, he was cuffed to a chair behind his back. Any movement he made and the chair went with him. In his fuzzy state of mind, he saw a man and a woman sitting across from him.

"What do you want?" Dawg asked.

The Sodium thiopental, or truth serum, took effect as Robert began his questioning.

"Are you alone, Dawg?"

"Yes. Who are you, and how do you know my name?"

"That doesn't matter, just answer the questions."

Dawg had a confused look on his face. His eyes darted back and forth as he tried to make sense of everything around him. His answers came easily.

"Did you and another man kidnap a woman in front of a yoga studio in Albuquerque ten days ago?"

"Yes."

"Were you paid a lot of money before she was released?"

"Yes."

"Did you know the woman you took?"

"No. She had a rich boyfriend. That's all we knew."

Julia taped the conversation. The recording was made for the police in Albuquerque.

"What is your partner's name?"

"Barry Cobb.

"Do you know where he is?"

"Paris, France. He left several days ago."

"Do you know how to get in touch with him?"

"No, we split up. We probably won't see each other again."

"Why not?"

"He's not coming back, and I'll never go to France, so our paths won't cross. He has his money and I have mine."

"Don't you mean Alan Hogan's money?" Robert asked.

"Not anymore. It's in a bank in another country where no one else can touch it." Dawg gave Robert a smile.

Robert thought that this last statement was possibly true. He could get the name of the bank from Dawg, but the account was safe in a foreign country.

"You might be right, Dawg, but here's the deal. You're going to prison in the States for kidnapping. The only way you'll be able to reduce your sentence is for you to return the money. Can you understand that?"

"I earned that money," Dawg said. "I'm still sore from where the bitch kicked me and I'm not going to give it back. We never used any weapons or hurt the girl. Barry told me the courts would go easy on us because we weren't violent. We just grabbed the girl, got paid and returned her in one piece."

"Dawg, you made one fatal mistake. You crossed a state line and now the crime is a Federal one. You'll be really old by the time you're released. You grabbed a good friend of mine, and I'll be waiting for you when you get out of prison. I'm going to make your life miserable. You messed with the wrong people and you're not going to benefit from it." Robert was bluffing but thought he could scare Dawg into giving up the cash for a reduced sentence.

Dawg had a blank look on his face. He didn't want to go to prison and he didn't have Barry around to advise him. Maybe he should have gone to France, he thought. He might not like Europe, but it was better than prison.

"Let's wrap this up," Julia suggested. "We still have to call the police in Albuquerque and have them connect with the local authorities in order to take him into custody. We have enough information on the tape for the Albuquerque police to use. We now know where his partner went."

"You're right, Sweetheart." Robert and Julia didn't use their names around Dawg. "You call the police and ask for Detective Louis. Just tell him we've captured one of the kidnappers and give him our location. The local authorities can hold Dawg until they arrange to fly him back to New Mexico."

"What do I say when he asks who I am?"

"Say you are the one who helped crack the Ian case. I believe he'll take you seriously. Also, tell him not to try and find out who you are. You have to remain anonymous, to be effective."

"That should work," Julia said.

Dawg was listening to the conversation, but none of it made any sense to him.

While Julia made the call and talked to detective Louis, Robert injected Dawg with another compound, reducing him to a putty-like state of being. He then moved the big man from his chair to the bed. Robert taped Dawg's arms and legs together to make sure he'd be in the same location when the police arrived.

Julia closed her phone after talking to Louis in the bathroom. "Detective Louis was surprised, to say the least. He's calling the local police right now so we have to get out of here. I think we should check out, as though nothing happened. Our name Forrester is only connected to an address in Arizona, and we both have undergone enough facial changes to hide our identity. This part of the job is over."

"I agree. Good work, Sweetheart. When we get home, we need to come up with a plan to find this Barry character. He may be a little harder to track down because he's definitely smarter than this one. Dawg was easy to track down but Barry went to Paris a week ago and that could be difficult."

Robert and Julia left Dawg's room, walked down the stairs to their room, packed and checked out twenty minutes before the local police arrived. They caught a flight to New York and spent two nights in The City so Julia could get her New York fix before returning to New Mexico. There was more to do, but a little down time, before getting back to work, never hurt.

Chapter 12

After four days of exploring Paris, Barry found an area where he wanted to live. A renting agency located an apartment for him near the Montmartre district with a view of the city below. He made a deposit and signed a six months lease. After the lease finished he might travel to another part of Europe and live there as well. He had nothing but time on his hands.

*****

While Barry was settling into the Paris lifestyle, Robert found out what he could about the man. Dawg revealed Barry's last name in the hotel interview and eventually a picture matching the sketch he had from Cathy came to light. Footage of flights that flew to Paris from Quebec City, on the day Barry left, was also examined. Peggy provided Robert with the airlines Barry used and video of him getting into a purple taxi in Paris.

Robert needed the help of the Paris police in tracking down this two-bit crook. He wrote a detailed letter and sent it to Detective Louis describing the second kidnapper in the Alan Hogan case. In the letter, Robert promised to continue his search for Barry in Paris.

"Do you think he'll go along with your plan? Julia asked. "I think he's taking a huge risk by giving you so much leverage with the Paris police."

"That's where you come in. We all have to work together to find Barry. Louis knows the mystery investigator is a woman because you called him to give Dawg's location. If he gives us the green light, then you're the one who talks to the Paris police to see what they can do for us. This could get a little tricky, but if Louis is happy with us feeding him leads, then we can create a working relationship with him. He's the one chalking up the credit while we get the satisfaction of taking down the bad guys."

"I hope you're right about this, Robert. I'm ready to go to France and catch Barry as fast as we can. It's going to get warm here in a few weeks and the weather in Paris will be perfect. Let's hope Detective Louis sees our contribution the same way we do."

*****

Louis sat at his desk pondering the letter he just received from his mysterious crime-solving ally. He knew he couldn't send anyone to France to investigate the second kidnapper. At the same time, it was a huge risk to allow this person to represent the Albuquerque police. He decided to talk it over with June. Getting a woman's perspective was always a smart thing to do and Louis needed someone else to weigh in. He walked over to Officer June's desk.

"I've got something to talk to you about, June. Can we meet for lunch?"

"Sure. Let's go back to that burger place where we first had a lunch date," June said. "We haven't been there in a while."

"Okay, but we need to find a table where we won't be disturbed. This is a touchy subject, and I don't want anyone overhearing us."

"Does it have anything to do with the Yoga Ease kidnapping?"

"Maybe, but we can't let anyone else in the office know about this, especially Martin. He'd have my ass if he found out about this."

"Don't worry about me telling him anything. He's still eating those jelly-filled donuts and thinks he's getting fruit in his diet, right? No way would I tell him anything, even if he is our boss."

"Good, then I'll meet you there in an hour. This could be big and I need your input."

"Louis, I'm flattered. Wait till we get home and I'll really show you my appreciation," June added.

Louis knew she meant sex. When she said it using a certain voice tone, he knew it would be special. She might dress up in the Catholic schoolgirl outfit or even the French maid get-up. Both really turned him on. He had no idea June had this wild side to her when they first started dating.

*****

Lunchtime found the couple sitting in the back booth of the Burger Barn.

"What's this important information, Louis? I bet it has something to do with the kidnapping, doesn't it?"

"Yes, and that's why I need to talk to you because you're the smartest cop in the office."

"You're sure it's got nothing to do with me being your girlfriend?" she smiled.

"Well, that too, but seriously June this could change how we do things."

"Let's order first and then you can tell me the whole story," she said.

Louis placed the food order as the lemonades arrived at the table. Louis looked around the restaurant making sure other members of the police department weren't having lunch in the Burger Barn.

"Remember the Ian McClure case and the mystery headphones you used to tape Ian when he confessed his crimes?"

"That was the most bizarre case I've ever worked on. Did we ever find out who was responsible for sending those earphones and breaking the case for us?"

"No, but guess what. The same person called and gave me the location of Dawg in Canada. It was a woman and she admitted she gave us the Ian clues. Now she has another request."

"Really. What does she want?" June asked.

"She says she wants to find the other person who escaped to France. We know the partner flew to Paris. She wants to work with us again, and needs our help."

"This is crazy. A woman is helping us solve cases." June was definitely intrigued.

"We still don't know who she is or if she's working alone. She wants to keep it that way and continue to help solve cases. Here's the pill I'd have to swallow. She wants us to give her authority to represent the Albuquerque police department and present a letter to the Paris police. In other words, she needs a 'get out of jail card' so she can find Barry, the other partner."

"And she knows Barry's in Paris?"

"They got Dawg to talk," Louis said. 'The information is on the tape we received in the mail the day after we picked up Dawg. Barry is staying in Paris. All they have to go on is the sketch the Hogan girlfriend gave us and a surveillance shot of him buying a ticket at the Quebec City airport when he went to France."

"Do you think Martin will go along with this?"

"No. Do you?"

"Not at all. If anything goes wrong, he could lose his job." June said.

"Whoever this person is, she's batting a thousand so far. She gave us The Company names, the Ian confession, and now the Dawg conviction. What do you feel about teaming up with her but on the quiet? This mystery woman wants this to be a covert operation and continue the same way in the future."

"What's your gut feeling, Louis? You don't think this is a setup do you?" June asked. She was interested, but June knew Louis was sticking his neck out if this plan backfired.

"We got credit for all the times she helped before. I'd say she's earned our trust. This is a big step. We'd have to tell the police in Paris that she has our backing, but the operation has to be covert and no communication with us. I can get official stationary with a seal but I can't have any phone calls getting back to Martin. If that happened we'd be cooked for sure."

"I'd say we go for it. This is what I love about you, Louis. You have this mad streak that comes out every so often and it really turns me on. Let's give it a try. If we can nab this other person in Paris, and bring him back to New Mexico, you could get a promotion."

"I don't care about that. I'm happy with what we have right now. Having a silent partner is an added plus."

"How do you get in contact with this silent partner?"

"She sent me a PO Box number and location to pass on any information back and forth. All I need to do is write the letter, send it to the address and she'll call when the case is solved. We can't go wrong with that setup."

"This is really a dream come true. A private citizen solving cases and giving us the credit." June was all in.

"Let's finish these burgers and get back. The sooner I type the letter and have you proof read it, the faster this person can get to Paris and hopefully catch our man."

"Fine with me, Detective Louis. Isn't this fun, running a covert operation within the police force? Don't forget, we have a special date tonight. I may even have something you've never seen before."

Louis could not believe he had hooked up with such a creative woman. He felt she needed to act out her fantasies after working day after day around criminals. It was a release for her and usually a wild ride for him. She did all the prep work and Louis just needed to show up.

"Works for me," Louis said. "I plan to be there. Anything I can bring?"

"German beer. This'll be a Bavarian surprise."

Man, I love the Germans, thought Louis.

Chapter 13

Marcos arrived back in his Stockholm apartment two days after Poppy sent him his share of the ransom. He made sure the money was secure in his Cayman account, and then transferred what he needed for the next few months. His girlfriend, Bridgette, was expected home in an hour. He always brought her a nice gift when he returned from any of his business ventures but this time Marcos, outdid himself.

Marcos purchased the Russian Sable coat in an exclusive fur store in Copenhagen. The animal fur market was nearly extinct and only a few of these high-end stores existed. The prices alone kept most of the world population from purchasing these luxury items.

The coat lay on the couch for Bridgette to see when she walked in the door. Marcos was on his second drink when she came through the door.

"Marcos," she screamed as she entered the apartment. "Is that for me?"

"Of course, my Swedish Pancake. Who else would it be for?"

"It's so good to see you. I missed you." She ran over and gave Marcos a kiss. She knew how to make Marcos feel good, and he loved every minute of it.

"Take it into the bedroom and try it on," Marcos told

her.

Bridgette grabbed the coat and hurried into the bedroom. Five minutes later, she came out with the coat buttoned up to her neck. She spun around to show it off. On the second turn, she undid the buttons and pulled the coat open revealing her naked body. Full, 40-inch D cup pink breasts, a twenty-two-inch waist, and perfect bell shaped thighs stared Marcos in the face. Bridgette was the reason he lived in Sweden. The Swedes were not hung up on sex and were famous for their free spirit attitudes towards making love.

"Come over here and get your 'thank you gift', Marcos."

Marcos did not have to be asked twice. He approached Bridgette while unbuttoning his shirt. He felt her hands undo his belt and pull down his trousers. His underwear was next and then the warm feel of her mouth engulfed him below the waist. Marcos was not in a hurry and allowed her as much time as she needed to get him to the point of orgasm.

She could tell he was close, so she pulled away, allowing Marcos to control himself. She wanted to be satisfied as well, so she threw off the coat and bent over the couch to receive him. Marcos started with slow thrusts and timed her moans with the speed in which he worked. The noises coming from her increased in volume, and when she starting screaming, "More, more,

more," he knew she was close. Marcos felt her body shiver as she reached climax, and then he exploded in her. He hadn't had sex in weeks and this was the highlight of his return home.

Bridgette relaxed and waited for Marcos to back away from her. She then turned and gave him a long, passionate kiss. More sex later that night would happen but now she was hungry and wanted to go out to dinner. The evenings were still cool enough for a warm wrap and she wanted to show off her new coat.

"Where should we go for dinner, Marcos? I want to wear my gift. When we come back, let's pick up where we left off. I really missed you."

Marcos buckled his belt and reached for his shirt. He thought for a moment and said, "You choose the restaurant. This is your city and I don't know many good places to eat."

"Ralphos has good Italian food. We haven't been there in a while and its only ten minutes from here. I'll get dressed and be right out."

*****

Forty-five minutes later Marcos and Bridgette sat near a window with a view of the street outside. The night lights were on and lit up the sidewalk.

The host, after seating them, asked, "Can I take your

coat, madam?"

"No thank you. I want to hang it over my chair and feel it on my back. It's brand new and I don't want to be far from it."

The couple ordered wine and one of the specials for the night. Bridgette then asked, "How was work? I know I don't talk to you much about your job, but I was wondering how everything went?"

"My team did well. We persuaded a man to invest in his family's welfare, and there was only one setback. We took care of that, and now my team is spread all over Europe celebrating our success."

"That was the best description of telling me exactly nothing about what you do. I still have no idea."

"All I can tell you is this. We find clients, find out what their needs are, and then present them with a package. They then invest in our ability to get them a good return. After they agree, we present the package, and they're usually happy with the results. It's boring work, and that's why I don't like to talk about it."

Bridgette realized no new information was coming from Marcos. She had a beautiful apartment she shared with him. He brought her nice presents when he returned and she had the place to herself when Marcos was away on business. Most women her age would kill for that lifestyle. Also, Marcos was well endowed and kept her satisfied when he was home.

Halfway through dinner, a tapping on the window startled Bridgette. A man stood outside the glass holding a sign and pointed at her fur coat. It read 'Animal Killer'. The man had a snarl on his face showing his dislike for the act of killing animals for their fur.

Marcos looked at the man carefully, memorizing his face. He remained calm as he reached into his pocket making sure he had his stun gun with him. It was there.

"Just ignore him, Bridgette. I can't do anything about it right now because we're in a public place. I'll call the host and have the man removed."

Bridgette, visibly shaken by the encounter, turned white as the blood drained from her face. By now, the host arrived at the table and could see the man outside with the sign. He quickly sent his biggest busboy to scare off the intruder.

Marcos made a mental note, remembering which direction the man walked away. The blood was boiling in his veins but he kept cool. This was not Paris where he could leave the next day after taking care of business. Dealing with this man discreetly, without being seen, was his only option.

Bridgette wanted to go home. No dessert or after

dinner drink for the couple. The man with the sign had ruined the mood.

The attendant brought the car around to the front of the restaurant and Marcos asked Bridgette to drive. She agreed but gave Marcos a puzzled look because he always drove. He asked her to go in the direction he saw the man with the sign walk. About three blocks later Marcos spotted him, a block away. He still had the sign in his hand and held it up when he spotted anyone with fur covering their body.

"Pull over and drop me off. I'll meet you back at the apartment," Marcos said.

"Why, what are you going to do?" She could tell Marcos was upset and didn't want to argue with him.

"Please, just do what I say. I'll explain later." Marcos said firmly.

Bridgette pulled the car over and let Marcos out. She knew the situation at the restaurant upset him and thought he might want to walk around to calm down.

Marcos waited for Bridgette to drive away before following the man with the sign. Marcos felt anger take over his reasoning abilities. He knew he had a temper, and when he got mad he turned into the Hulk, and couldn't hold back.

After following his target for a block, the man with

the sign crossed an alley street. Marcos quickly came up behind and zapped him in the neck with the stun gun. An instant later he pulled the man into the shadows. The sign fell from the man's hand as both men disappeared into the darkness.

I think he saw my face, thought Marcos. Suddenly a blow came from someone standing behind Marcos in the alley. Whoever it was, they saw the attack and now tried to help. Marcos bent at the knees but had enough strength to deliver a zap to the leg of his assailant, taking him to the ground.

Marcos had to make an instant decision. Two people saw him commit a crime. He couldn't take any chances. He set the gun to full power and applied a shock to each of the men in the center of the chest. He checked their pulse, making sure their hearts stopped. Marcos killed people before, but this was only the third time he used his stun gun to do the job.

An hour later Marcos returned to the apartment. He had a knot on the back of his head but no blood came from the injury. Bridgette sat on the couch waiting for him. The frightened look on her face told him he needed a good excuse for disappearing after dinner.

"What happened? Where did you go? I was so worried."

"I had to take care of a few things," Marcos said.

"You went after that man with the sign, didn't you?"

"Bridgette, the man embarrassed you in a restaurant. He may have an issue with furs, but attacking others like that was unacceptable. I saved your honor."

"What did you do? I hope nothing serious."

"No, nothing like that. I just roughed him up a bit," Marcos lied.

"I don't like violence, Marcos, but I do respect you for standing up for me. Next time, if anything like that happens, just walk away. I'll get over it."

Marcos nodded his head but at the same time, he knew he couldn't walk away from someone who attacked him or anyone he loved.

By now, Bridgette had come over to Marcos and put her arms around him.

"Now that that's over, let's take up where we left off."

Her lips locked onto Marcos' mouth as her right hand reached down his pants to his groin. He was already hard as she stroked him. He then picked her up, cradled her in his arms, and headed to the bedroom. Bridgette only had on a nightgown and it quickly came off. Marcos was soon in the same naked state as the two bodies came together in passionate penetration. Marcos rolled over on his back and let Bridgette work her magic on him. She knew how to keep him erect and make the evening of lovemaking last a long time.

*****

At two a.m. the Stockholm police received a call regarding two male bodies found by a street sweeper making his rounds. Both corpses were positioned sitting up against an alley wall between two large trash containers. After the bodies were brought to the police morgue, an autopsy showed burn marks on the neck, leg and chest areas, indicating the men were killed with a stun gun of some kind.

"Is there any more information regarding the two men?" Sergeant Hanson asked the coroner.

"Nothing so far. This is my first case involving a stun gun. Both of these men were in good health and the killer shocked each victim twice. There was no need to kill them. One shock was enough electricity to take each man down. Maybe our suspect lives in the neighborhood and was afraid of being identified," the coroner speculated.

"I have someone investigating to see if a connection between the two men exits but so far, nothing," Sergeant Hanson said. "It wasn't a robbery because both men had their wallets, and nothing was taken."

"Have you notified the families of the victims, Sergeant?" the coroner asked.

"Yes, we have. Both men are from middle-class families and had jobs. One of the men was an activist and warned several times to stop bothering women wearing fur coats. We also found a sign in the alley that said 'Animal Killer'. Maybe that man pissed off the wrong person and paid with his life."

"What about the other man?"

"The only thing I found on his body was a bruised right hand across the knuckles," the coroner said. "He might have hit his attacker before he was killed."

"I'm sending the families down here to view the bodies. After they arrive, let them stay as long as they like. This is a total shock, and they need to grieve."

"I'll have the bodies ready to view in ten minutes," the coroner replied. "If I find anything else I'll let you know."

Sergeant Hanson returned to his office. He had no real leads and only an unusual weapon used to kill the two men. Finding the make and model of the stun gun could help in finding out if any other similar cases existed. The police in different cities in Europe used a communication hotline to pass on information to each other.

"I'm writing a letter to other police headquarters in major cities throughout Europe," he told his secretary. "I'll give it to you when I'm finished and have you send it out to all the departments using the law enforcement hotline. If anyone has a case involving a stun gun, maybe we can make a connection."

Chapter 14

"The letter arrived, Robert. I just picked it up and we're a go," Julia said as she walked through the front door.

"Pack your bags, Julia. We're going to Paris. With this letter, we now have a chance to find Barry."

"Do you have any idea how we're going to do this? Paris is a huge city and we don't know if he's still there." Robert knew their chances were slim but he had to at least try and find Barry.

"We'll have a lot of leg work but we now have a decent picture of our man. The sketch matched a police profile and they came up with a Barry Bartlett from Phoenix, Arizona. He spent ten months in a low-security prison for breaking into warehouses. After he served his time, he left the state, moved here and changed his last name. I bet Barry hooked up with Dawg to get some muscle on his team. Barry's not a big man and you can see he has a scar on his face. Probably some bigger thug cut him and he needed Dawg to back him up when he got into trouble."

"That's quite a theory, Mr. Forrester. Did you come up with that all by yourself?"

"Just putting pieces of the puzzle together. What do you think happened?"

"He was probably cheating on his girlfriend and she

had enough. She gave him a parting gift. Something he would always remember her by," Julia said with a smile on her face.

"Is this your way of telling me what might happen if I ever messed around?"

"Maybe, but it did get your attention," Julia laughed.

"I guess I know where I stand. It's a good thing you married one of those straight-laced husbands who doesn't like his face rearranged by a knife."

"Except when it comes to having your appearance changed."

Julia referred to the facial surgery both she and Robert went through before their wedding. The Albuquerque police had pictures of Robert Woods from eight years ago when he first moved to New Mexico. The changes were not drastic but enough so that both she and Robert didn't look like any older photos.

"Enough of the knife stories," Robert said as he glanced at the letter. "This is meant for you. All Detective Louis knows is that a woman talked to him on the phone when you gave him the location of Dawg and he used the name you gave him in the letter. It looks like you'll be contacting the police in Paris. I'm now your backup. You have the lead on this, Sweetheart, so strap on your belt and pull up your pants because we're off to

Paris to get our man."

"Where do you get these metaphors, Robert? You do remember I walked a beat in New York before I met you. Also, my dad was a detective before he died so I think I can handle the Paris police. Anyway, my French is much better than the four French words you know, so keep your Oui, no, Dijon mustard and Bistro vocabulary to yourself."

Robert knew he'd married the right woman to go into the investigation business with. She didn't take crap from anyone, especially him.

"All right then, Frenchie. I think that should be your nickname while we're in Paris. I don't want to blow our cover and call you by your real name," Robert said.

"You start calling me that and sex will terminate immediately. That's how strong I feel about nicknames."

"All right, you win, Julia. You can have the last word."

Julia knew the 'no sex' comment would put Robert in his place. She was relieved he didn't call her bluff and go without sex while they were in Paris. After all, she thought, isn't Paris the World Capital of Love?

*****

Two days later the team of Robert and Julia Forrester landed at Charles de Gaulle airport in Paris after a one-night stayover in New York. The eight-hour night flight touched down at seven a.m. and they were in their room at the Hilton Paris La Defense by eight-thirty.

"I think we both need a few hours sleep, Robert. I can't function after long flights."

"I agree, Julia. Shall we eat some breakfast later?"

"Let's get room service when we wake up. Jet lag messes me up for a day at least."

Julia jumped into the shower while Robert unpacked his suitcase. He'd wait until he woke up to make his phone calls. By the time Julia was out of the shower, Robert was asleep on the bed. She flopped down next to him and within minutes, she was out.

Two hours later Robert felt Julia move on the bed. She reached for his groin area and made it obvious she was ready to start their stay in the City of Love with her own ritual. Phone call or not, when the hand calls the body answers.

"Shall we put an order in for breakfast first, Sweetheart," Robert asked.

"Shut up and focus. Just don't call me Frenchie or this

is all you'll get the whole time we're here."

Robert knew when to keep his mouth closed and this was one of those moments. Breakfast could wait.

*****

Half an hour, later the two lovers stood in the shower preparing for the day. They ordered room service after drying off. During breakfast, Robert took out his personal phone that couldn't be traced.

"I'm calling the Police Nationale on Boulevard Bourdon where Detective Louis addressed the letter. You should do the talking and make an appointment to speak to a Capitaine Le Cure. Louis said in a separate letter that the police stations are connected and the picture of Barry can be sent to each command post quickly."

"Do we know if the police will cooperate? I know the French don't care much for Americans."

"I really don't know, Julia, but I'm glad you're doing the talking and not me. Your French is good and you're a gorgeous woman. If you meet the Capitaine, both of those facts could work in our favor."

"Oh, Monsieur Forrester, you are just trying to butter me up and get laid tonight, aren't you?"

"Yes and no. I think you being the lead on this is a distinct advantage because the French are famous for appreciating beautiful things."

"Let's get this done. I'd love to find Barry as easily as we did Dawg. Then we can really take a look around this city and have some fun," Julia said.

"The difference between the two men is that Barry has a brain. I know that's not saying much," Robert said. "He's not going to make the same mistakes Dawg did and he's been here for more than a week."

"Go ahead and place the call. I'll make an appointment for tomorrow. I'll be over jetlag by then. Tonight we find some quiet café and lose ourselves in Paris."

Robert dialed the number he had for *Capitaine* Le Cure and handed his phone to Julia.

"Bon Jour, my name is Julia Forrester," she said. "I need to speak to *Capitaine* Le Cure *s'il vous plait*."

"*Oui*, Madame. I will see if he's available. Hold on please."

"I'm on hold, Robert. This may take a minute."

Suddenly the phone clicked and a male voice was heard. "Bon Jour. This is *Capitaine* Le Cure. How may I help you?"

"*Capitaine* La Cure, my name is Julia Forrester and I have recently arrived in Paris representing the police in Albuquerque, New Mexico. I have a letter of introduction from a detective, Louis Marshall, allowing me to follow up on a fugitive who has escaped to your city. I would like to meet with you tomorrow and go over the case if that is possible."

"I would love to help you if I can Madame Forrester. Are you a police officer as well?"

"No, I'm a private investigator. The police in Albuquerque don't have the funds to go after the suspect in Europe. The case is personal because the victim was a close friend of mine. I'm pursuing the fugitive on my own."

"I would love to hear more about the case. How about tomorrow morning around ten? Will that work for you?"

"*Oui, Capitaine* Le Cure. Thank you for taking the time to meet with me. I realize you must have a busy schedule."

"I'll see you tomorrow morning, Madame Forrester."

"Thank you again." Julia hung up.

"Well that's done," Julia said. "I'll meet him at ten. I have an idea, Robert. Let's take a taxi to a famous part of the city and just walk around. No plans or reservations for anything, just Paris and us. When we get hungry, we can find a place to eat and walk around some more. Let's just get lost."

"What part of the city did you have in mind, Sweetheart?"

"How about the Moulin Rouge? You know the area that has that famous windmill on the roof of some nightclub. I believe that's where the Can-can originated."

"How do you know all this stuff?"

"Robert, I read a lot. Also, I've been here before. I know this is your first time in France, so let me be the tour guide."

"Fine with me. Let's don't lose our focus on why we're here, Julia."

"Robert, we have business to do but it doesn't mean we can't have fun. What did you do before I came into your life? I know you didn't travel much so let me educate you about the world and what it offers. Let's enjoy Paris as well as solve the case."

"All right, Julia. I'll do my best. You're right about me not traveling much. That trip last year to China and Tibet was definitely out of my comfort zone but looking back on it I'm really glad we went."

"Okay, *Monsieur* Forrester, we are going to have fun and still get our man, so hang on to your hat."

"First I better go out and buy one," Robert said smiling.

Chapter 15

Poppy arrived in Florence after wiring his employees their share from the last kidnapping job. He hooked up with a male friend who lived in the city so he had company. The friend knew Poppy from a previous visit and met him in a gay bar. They were safe within the walls of their special brotherhood where the straight community left them alone.

Poppy ran another business none of his coworkers knew about. He made money from the kidnap victims but also brokered guns for sale on the black market. Germany, Russia, France, China and the United States were the biggest manufacturers of automatic rifles and side arms. The gun industry really didn't care who bought their product but they had to cover sales with a paper trail indicating a legitimate business bought their product. Profit was the bottom line and wherever there was a war or military uprising, the industry made sure their people got there and sold what they could.

France was Poppy's country of choice when dealing with arms. He was tormented when he was a boy in Ireland and swore he'd get back at the world for abusing him. He had guns put in his mouth and threatened with his life because he was gay. He had no allegiance to anyone. Poppy sold French weapons because of his connection with a certain executive.

"Hello, *Monsieur* Norman, this is Poppy."

"Poppy, it's been a while. How are you? This is a secure line, right?"

"Yes it is and I'm fine. I've been busy getting more cash together. I needed a vacation as well."

"Do you have any buyers lined up?" *Monsieur* Norman asked. "I have a truckload of assault rifles ready for delivery but they have to be picked up in Austria. I have to cover my tracks and make out a bill of sale to the Austrian police department. If you're interested, you have to go to Salzburg for delivery."

"They're still the same price we agreed upon, right?" Poppy asked.

Poppy had a Congo group ready to take delivery of the rifles in Naples and transport them through Egypt. That route was the best way to get them back to their country. He had his people already in position for the transport to take place.

"Yes, the price we agreed upon is what you pay. I don't change the way I do business, Poppy. I'd lose customers if I did that."

"You're a good man to do business with, *Monsieur* Norman. E-mail me the information where I need to go in Salzburg and who to pay. I'll make sure the weapons get to Naples and the Purple Army Congo group receives the shipment. They're nuts but their money's good and that's the bottom line, right?"

"I don't care who you sell to. We can't have any connections coming back to me, or we can't do business anymore. I'm too involved with the top administration."

"As long as there is war, we make money," Poppy said.

"That's one way of looking at it, Poppy. The problem is keeping up with the other producers. The Chinese are making their guns with cheap labor and that lowers their price. Most of our production is automated but we still have higher costs. We are focused on making the best product and shooting the most rounds per second. The faster you can kill seems to be what these groups are looking for."

"I really don't care much about any of that," Poppy said. "We have an overpopulation problem in the world and I sometimes think we are helping to deal with it. Small wars are good in many ways because it beats going nuclear with all that radiation floating around in the atmosphere. That wouldn't be healthy at all."

"I'll send you the information," *Monsieur* Norman said. "You'll pay for the guns upon delivery. The seller wants cash for this sale. Call me when you're ready for another shipment. I heard a couple of those groups in the middle-east might be looking for some more fire power."

"Sorry, *Monsieur* Norman. I'd rather stay with the fighting in Africa. Those groups in Iraq and the Middle East are crazy and can't be trusted. If they ever found out I was gay, they'd have my head on a pole in a second and take my guns, no questions asked. The African groups are nuts as well, but they pay for what they get and could give a shit who I sleep with."

"You're right. Poppy. Religious fanatics are the worst and they always have a holy book of some religion backing up their actions. What's this world coming to? Anyway, I'll talk later. Good doing business with you."

Poppy hung up and made plans to drive to Salzburg. He'd been there before and knew his way around the city. It was the birthplace of Mozart and the second largest cultural city in Austria besides Vienna. He might even take in a concert while he was there. He was an educated man and needed to connect with the world of art and musical expression.

Chapter 16

Julia arrived at the police station ten minutes before the meeting with *Capitaine* Le Cure. She wore the perfect outfit, tightly covering her body and still showed she was a woman underneath. She wanted to use her female attributes to get the *Capitaine* to help her find Barry any way he could.

"Please wait here, Madame Forrester and I'll see if *Capitaine* La Cure is available right now," the desk officer said.

Two minutes later he returned.

"He's ready to see you, Madame," the *Sergent* told her.

Julia followed him into the office of the *Capitaine* and sat in front of his desk after they shook hands.

"Madame Forrester, I'm happy to meet with you. Your French is quite good. Not many Americans speak French. They seem to think the world should learn English."

"My father was a detective in New York. When I attended college he told me if I learned any other language, then French should be the one. Along with English, I could travel the world easily. So far he's been right."

"A smart man indeed. Even though English seems to

be more popular, it is good to know a few languages, especially living in Europe. Anyway, what is the situation you're in and how can I help?"

Julia handed the *Capitaine* the letter from Detective Louis. After he read the letter, Julia spent the next twenty minutes telling *Capitaine* Le Cure about the kidnapping that took place in Albuquerque and how one of the men escaped to Paris.

"I have a picture of him and wondered if you could get it out to the other stations in Paris?"

"How do you know he's still here?" the *Capitaine* asked.

"We captured his partner and he told us Barry moved to Paris. He has plenty of money and will probably find a nice apartment to live in. Also, can we get his picture out to the different renting agencies throughout Paris and see if anyone recognizes him? My partner and I will do the legwork on this and only use the Paris police to make the arrest."

"Really? You don't want any recognition if you find your man?"

"The kidnap victim is a close friend of ours. My partner wants to make sure this man is put away for his crime."

"I think I can do what you asked, Madame Forrester.

Is your partner with you in Paris?"

"Yes, but he doesn't speak French and rather stay anonymous until we've captured this person. We are a married investigation team." Julia felt she needed to set some boundaries with the *Capitaine* from the start.

"I'll get this information out to the *'Commissari at de police'* located in Paris as well as the *'Agence de location centrale'* for the city. They have their own network and handle everything rented in the city. If they know that this man is a person of interest, they'll let me know right away. How do I get in touch with you if anything comes up?"

"We're staying at the Hilton Paris La Defense. We'd appreciate any possible leads and can do all the follow-up work. If there is an arrest to be made, I'll call you personally and let you take over."

"This is an agreeable arrangement in many ways. I wish more law enforcement groups would see the benefit in working together with each other, instead of wanting all the credit for themselves," Le Cure said.

"We do too. If it works out the way we want it to, then maybe we can start a trend with law enforcement," Julia added.

"That would be a nice change, Madame Forrester. I'll call you if I get any leads. I don't know if we'll find him but we may get lucky. Computers can help in many ways."

"Thank you again for your time, *Capitaine* Le Cure. I'd appreciate anything you come up with. I'll look forward to your call."

Julia walked out of the office and headed to the café where Robert waited for her.

"How did it go, Sweetheart?" Robert asked after taking another sip of his second espresso. "I have to say this coffee has me wired. I may never go back to regular coffee again."

"We better get some food in you. The coffee in France is much stronger than anything you get in the States. They do sell espresso machines in the Albuquerque if that's what you like."

"I do, but let's go eat. How about the restaurant on the Eiffel Tower? We have to go there at least once."

"Fine with me. I hope we can get a table. It's only eleven a.m. so we might have a chance."

Robert and Julia caught a taxi to the famous 986-foot erector-set tower and caught the elevator to the restaurant. They only had a twenty-minute wait. The view was worth every minute.

After they were seated, Robert again asked Julia how

the meeting went with *Capitaine* Le Cure.

"Actually, I was a little taken back by his eagerness to help. Le Cure said the organization that rents apartments might turn up something. They'll have the picture of Barry. Because he is an American, it'll narrow the field down rather quickly. Also, if he rented something in the last week a red flag should go up."

"Le Cure said he could do all that? Maybe he can help."

"Well, Sweetheart," Julia said, "I think fun is on the schedule for a few days while we're waiting for the picture of Barry to make its way around town."

"I'm fine with that. Take a sip of your wine. Is that not the best Boudreaux you've ever tasted?"

"It is good, Robert. I guess we better drink what the locals produce. Paris is not known for their beer so we might become winos by the time we leave."

*****

Barry settled into the Paris lifestyle and having a million dollars made the task much easier. He wondered about Dawg but didn't give him much of a chance to make it on his own. He knew his ex-partner wasn't smart and his inability to stay out of trouble put his chances of remaining free at a low percent. Barry knew any connection with Dawg was over in his life.

I might as well get some culture since I'm living here, he thought.

"One ticket for the museum please," Barry told the woman at the window.

"Is this your first time here?" she asked. "If it is then I suggest you take a tour with an English speaking guide. The Louvre is quite large, and the tour will help you understand the history of the art and give you some background."

"*Merci*. I think that's a good idea. When is the next English speaking tour starting?" Barry asked.

"In about ten minutes. Go over to the seating area and I'll call you when it's about to begin."

"Thank you for your help." So far Barry was impressed with the French population and how helpful they were. He'd found a nice apartment without much trouble and even his neighbors were friendly. Most of them spoke some English but not enough to carry on a conversation.

Barry planned on finding a French class so he could start learning the language. He had to learn some basic sentences in order to get around Paris and the lessons would help. Maybe he'd meet some other Americans living in Paris and develop some friendships. He planned on making his life in Europe work and becoming a part of the culture would be a start.

*****

Three days after arriving in Paris, Julia received a phone call from *Capitaine* Le Cure. A possible lead had turned up through the agency that handles rentals in the city. The picture of Barry was identified by one of the agents. She thought the picture looked like the American who rented an apartment in the Montmartre district of Paris. It was over a week ago and he paid for the apartment in cash.

"If this is your man," Le Cure said, "you are the luckiest investigator I've ever met. Finding him in two days could be a record."

"*Capitaine,* this is great news," Julia said. "Give me the address. My partner and I will go there and make sure it's him. After that, we'll notify the Albuquerque police. They'll send you any needed paperwork, and you can grab him. This is fantastic news."

Le Cure told Julia the address and the apartment number. He also offered a backup officer to go with them but Julia declined.

"If this is our man, we don't want to spook him with someone in uniform. We won't try to grab him, and he doesn't know what we look like so we should be fine. I don't think he's violent and carrying any weapons because his partner told us he doesn't use them. He should be easy to pick up after the warrant arrives from New Mexico."

"I'll wait for your call after you've made a positive ID. Have the police in Albuquerque send any papers directly to me and I'll handle the arrest."

"We will, *Capitaine*. I'll call you when we have everything lined up. Thank you for your help, you've been wonderful and we appreciate."

"I'm glad to help you. I'll be waiting for your call."

Julia hung up and looked over at Robert. "Did you hear all that?" she asked.

"I can hardly believe we might have found Barry in just a few days," said Robert.

"Compared to Albuquerque, Paris is huge. Anyway, we have an address and a possible match with the picture. We should make sure it's Barry before we call Detective Louis and get that warrant. We may develop a working relationship with the police in New Mexico after all."

"I love it, Sweetheart," said Robert. "I don't think Alan will get his money back if it is hidden in the Cayman Islands but the same things goes for Barry as it does for Dawg. We'll have someone waiting for them when they get out. They'll make it difficult for them to touch that cash."

"Let's get over to this address and start snooping around," Julia said. "I'll show the picture to the neighbors and ask if he's the same man renting there. If we get a positive match with the picture we should call Louis tonight."

"Maybe we can stick around for a while longer after we wrap this up. The wine is excellent and those espresso coffees are addicting. I stay buzzed until three in the afternoon every day."

"Get on your shoes and let's call a cab, Robert. I'm looking forward to a nice dinner afterward so we can celebrate."

*****

The afternoon went by quickly. Julia was able to make contact with a few neighbors who lived in the same apartment complex as Barry. They confirmed from the picture it was the same man living at the address.

"He is such a nice man compared to other Americans I've run across," one neighbor said. "He doesn't speak French but I believe he's taking classes because he plans on staying here for a while."

"Thank you for your help, Madame," Julia said. "You've been extremely helpful."

That evening a call was made to Detective Louis on his private cell. "Detective Louis, this is your contact in

Paris. We have your man," Julia said.

It was five a.m. in New Mexico and Louis was barely awake. "You have him all ready? How in the hell did you pull that off so quickly?" he asked.

"*Capitaine* Le Cure was most helpful. He suggested contacting the central renting agency in Paris. They showed the picture of Barry and made a match two days later. I've confirmed he's the one in the apartment. We now need a warrant and extradition papers sent to *Capitaine* Le Cure so he can make the arrest and get credit on this end. I'm sure the transfer papers to the States can be obtained easily. You can pick Barry up when he lands in New York. You get credit and the case is closed."

"I don't know how you did this without my boss knowing but I want to thank you. This could turn out to be a great way to do international police work."

"Let's don't get too far ahead of ourselves, Detective Louis. We've broken two cases together so we should take it one crime at a time. Send the papers and let's get Barry back to the States. I'll call if anything else turns up or if I need you in another investigation." Julia said.

"I'm going into the office right now and get the warrant. Thank you again, whoever you are."

Louis closed his phone next to the bed. June was

awake by now and heard the conversation because Louis had it on speaker.

"They caught the guy already?" she asked.

"Can you believe it?" Louis asked. "We may have our own private investigation team helping us solve cases. They use us and we use them. The best part is they don't care about getting credit for the bust, and we show up on the front page of the local rag with our man in tow."

"This is good for the Albuquerque police image," June said. "I'm glad we took a chance and decided to support this woman. We still have no idea who she is, do we?"

"No, we don't. If that's the way she wants it and it's working, then why mess up a good thing.

"Sort of like us, Louis. I never knew we'd work out and now look at us. We're running an inner department investigation network, working at the same police station and practically living together."

Louis thought for a moment and then said, "Why do we still keep separate apartments. If we bought a house together we could easily afford that. More room for both of us and more privacy when we want it."

"What are you referring to, Louis? Our special parties we have every so often? By the way, I never asked you how you lived Bavarian night? Was that outfit fun for you?"

The last outfit was that of a Munich beer frau in a revealing short skirt and low cut blouse. June had her hair done in pigtails and entering the bedroom holding two large beer steins.

"I think the Bavarian night was my favorite so far but the French maid is a close second. How many of these outfits do you have?"

"I make them up as I go, Louis. I have as much fun putting them on as you do taking them off. Wait until you see what I have planned next time."

"I can hardly wait," Louis said. "Since we're awake why not practice for next time. I'm getting excited thinking about it already."

June reached over and felt Louis with a full erection. "That works for me," she answered in a seductive voice. "After sex, I would like coffee in bed."

Louis felt her continuing to stroke him and knew she could get him to agree to anything at this moment. "No problem, June. Coffee coming right up."

The two lovers embraced and came together. Living in the same house, fighting crime and getting paid for it was the ultimate lifestyle for Louis. He couldn't tell if June was open to the idea but right now he didn't care. That would be a discussion for another time.

Chapter 17

Poppy arrived in Salzburg on Sunday evening and checked into the Bristol Hotel on Makarplatz. He stayed in the best because he could afford the best. His appointment to pick up the guns was set for Monday evening at midnight when the roads would be clear, and not many people walked by the warehouse. He arranged for a delivery truck to carry a load of hops for making beer. The eight cases of automatic rifles would be buried under the hops and driven to Naples. All the paperwork was in order and the hops would actually be used in an Italian beer factory.

The weapons were worth three million Euros on the black market and would cost Poppy 3/4 of a million Euros. Expenses for delivery was another 250 thousand Euros so after the guns were sold, two million would be in Poppy's account. All the border guards were paid off so nothing would hinder the shipment into Italy.

Poppy was not a big time gun runner. Many weapons, like the ones he was delivering, were sold throughout the world supporting revolutions and uprisings. These groups wanted the latest and best. The more firepower the better so the manufacturers were constantly improving on their product to give the buyer what they wanted. It was almost like the latest in new cars. New features were added to the recent models and the price continued to climb.

"Hello, Herr Krimm. This is your buyer, Mr. Gustoff." Poppy never used his real name when doing business with people he didn't know.

"*Ya*, Mr. Gustoff, I've been waiting for your call. Is everything ready for delivery tomorrow night?"

"Yes, it is, Herr Krimm. The truck will be there at 11:45 p.m. As soon as the crates are loaded and inspected, you'll get paid. Are you making the transaction yourself or is someone else handling the payment?"

"I handle all the financial deals myself. Have the cash in one hundred Euro notes and in a duffle bag. I trust I won't have to count it."

"I wouldn't be in business long if I shortchanged anyone. The correct amount will be in the bag."

"Good, then I'll see you tomorrow night, Mr. Gustoff."

"Yes, Herr Krimm, tomorrow night. I'll see you then." Poppy turned off his cell phone and returned it to his pocket.

Poppy saw that the William Shakespeare play, The Comedy of Errors, was playing in town tonight. He wanted to see a Mozart production but nothing was playing until the Festival in July and August. He needed to unwind and a cultural production from the world's best playwright would do the trick.

Poppy drove into the center of town and found the concert hall. The play was sold out but there were always a few scalpers around who had tickets to sell at twice the price. Poppy didn't care. He purchased a 200 Euro ticket and returned to his hotel. He had time to change clothes, take the cable car to the Festung Castle above the city and have dinner. He'd enjoy a meal in the courtyard overlooking the city and return to the center of town in time for the play.

"Will you be staying with us another night, Herr Gustoff?" the hotel manager asked.

"Yes, I think I might stay two more night. I going to a play tonight and have business tomorrow night but I need one more day to look around your beautiful city. Wasn't The Sound of Music filmed here?"

"Yes, back in the early 60's. There are still people in town who remember Julie Andrews walking the streets between takes, as well as a few of the children used in the movie. It was a great accomplishment for Salzburg at the time."

"I saw the movie when I was ten and loved it," Poppy told the manager. I better get moving. I have to eat before the play begins. Maybe you can give me an idea of someplace special to see on my last day."

"Of course I can, Mr. Gustoff. Salzburg has lots of places to visit. Enjoy your dinner and evening. I'll talk to you tomorrow and give you a list of places to see."

Poppy thanked the manager. He then caught a taxi that took him to the tram carrying people to the castle restaurant above the city. After the gun exchange tomorrow night, he'd breath easier. The only risk for Poppy was during the exchange and so far his contacts held up their end of the exchange. No one wanted to mess up this lucrative business, especially the gun manufacturers.

*****

At 11:30 p.m. Poppy arrived at the warehouse and waited in his rented BMW. The truck, used to haul the weapons, arrived twenty minutes later and pulled up to the loading docks. Herr Krimm came out a side door at the same time Poppy got out of his car.

"We have to do this quickly," Herr Krimm said. "We have a thirty-minute window so let's move."

The guns were loaded into the truck by a two-man crew, inspected by Poppy and then resealed. The nine cases filled the bottom of the truck and a tarp was placed on top to seal them from the hops that would be loaded within the next hour. Poppy handed Herr Krimm the duffle bag of Euros and shook his hand.

"It's a pleasure to do business with you Herr Gustoff. The hops should cover the crates with four feet of grain and get you through any checkpoints without any problems."

"Thanks. If I have to use Salzburg again for a pickup location I might see you again." Poppy kept his business private and said nothing to Herr Krimm about how he planned to get the guns to Italy.

The truck left the warehouse and drove half an hour to the loading dock where the hops were loaded. The early morning crew was paid a bonus for their effort to show up and cover the crates with the beer-making plant. The driver of the truck then headed south towards Innsbruck and Italy.

Poppy could now relax. He knew all his people were in place, making sure the shipment made it to Naples and into the hands of the Congo rebels. He had a man in Italy making sure everything went smoothly on that end. Money had to be in the account Poppy used before the weapons were transferred. There was no negotiation when it came to payment for guns. Dealing with radical revolutionary groups meant one had to be extra careful or insane. No weapons dealer would hand over guns to fanatical revolutionaries before they were paid.

Two days later Poppy received a call from his contact in Naples.

"The crates are loaded and on the way to Egypt, Mr. Gustoff. I see you sent my payment. I'm calling, like you asked, to tell you everything is completed. You are smart to not deal with these African soldiers yourself."

"Why is that?" asked Poppy.

"I had two bodyguards with me when we made the transfer and I still didn't feel safe. If I had to try and collect money from them I'm not sure how it would have played out. These are some hardcore people for sure."

"If I use you again for any group out of Africa. Continue to keep men posted and armed. Because the deal is completed in Europe there is less chance they won't pull anything with us. I don't supply groups in the Middle East because those assholes believe they have Allah on their side. There's no telling what they'll try to do in the name of their religion. I'll call you when I have another sale leaving Italy. Ciao."

One more day and Poppy was finished visiting Salzburg and started the drive back to Paris. He rented a car for the trip because he loved the roads through Germany and the French countryside. He'd take several days with stops at a winery or two on the way. He had research to start in Paris to line up his next nab victim.

The kidnappings gave him the extra cash to set up the next arms deals. Poppy knew he had to be careful with Marcos because he had botched the last job and killed the bodyguard. Murder changed the case and gave the French police an incentive to solve it. This kind of mistake could not happen again.

*****

The arrest warrant arrived by fax. *Capitaine* Le Cure was pleased everything had gone smoothly. He sent two squad cars to pick Barry up and bring him back to the station. His men were stationed a block from the apartment, and waited until Barry returned and was inside. After he returned to his apartment they sat in their squad cars twenty minutes before knocking on the door.

"This is the Paris police, Mr. Cobb, open the door."

There was no answer. Sergeant Block knocked again. "Open the door, Mr. Cobb, we have some questions for you."

A window was found open in the back of the apartment when the police finally broke down the door. Barry was gone.

"He won't get far *Sergent*, we have a car parked at the end of the street and they'll pick him up."

"Call them right now. This American is not getting away."

The three officers returned to the street and were pleased to see the two rookie officers who were parked outside. They walked Barry towards them with his hands in cuffs.

"He didn't get far *Sergent*. He saw us and tried to run down this alley but the twelve-foot wall stopped him. There was no fight in him, and he gave up right away."

"Good work, men. Let's get him back to the station, and hand him over to the *Capitaine*. Officer Blunt, you and Pierre search his apartment and box all his belongings. He won't be coming back, so tell the landlord they can keep his rent and clean it for another tenant. This guy is returning to the States."

*****

Barry was returned to the station and handed over to *Capitaine* Le Cure.

"The American has not said anything to us the whole time we drove him here, *Capitaine*."

"I don't think he understands French or speaks it," Le Cure said. "Let me try talking to him."

Le Cure spoke excellent English so he started asking Barry questions. "Do you know why you're arrested, *Monsieur*?"

"Oh, someone does speak English, Barry said. "No, why am I here?"

"It seems there is a warrant out for your arrest back in the States. The paper says the city is Albuquerque in the state of New Mexico. What do you know about that?"

Barry didn't answer. He was going over in his mind how he messed up and they found him.

"The warrant also says you took someone and were paid a lot of money to return that person. We found five thousand Euros in your wallet when we picked you up so you must have more of the cash in some bank. Is that right?"

The *Capitaine* planned on keeping the money and put it in the budget to cover the cost of the arrest. If he could get any more out of this American, he would spread it around with the arresting officers and keep everyone satisfied.

Barry knew his money in the Cayman Islands was safe. If he played along and didn't put up any resistance, he'd be out in five years. He figured by now that Dawg told the police in Canada that he had flown to Paris, but how they caught him was still a mystery.

"I don't think he is going to tell us anything else, *Capitaine*," *Sergent* Bruno said. "Maybe get him on the next plane to New York and be done with this case."

"I think you're right, *Sergent*. I still want to talk to the American woman who brought us this case. They did the legwork in bringing him to us and I now have a favor to ask her."

"I'll call the detective in Albuquerque and tell him

their man will be on the flight to New York tonight. They'll need to have someone pick him up," the *Sergent* said. "I'll get an air marshal to escort him and after they reach New York he's all theirs."

"Thank you, *Sergent*. Good job by the way. I'll call the American woman and see if I can get her cooperation on one of our cases."

"Which one is that, *Capitaine*?"

"Remember that bodyguard that was killed in the nightclub two weeks ago? He was guarding that rich American bitch who gave us such a hard time."

"You mean the one I wanted to slap? She was a crazy one for sure. What about her?"

"I received an international request from Stockholm," Le Cure said. "He has an unsolved crime involving a stun gun. They were able to determine the type and model of Taser used on both of their citizens. It's the same model used on the bodyguard here in Paris. We could have a connection."

"Really, a break in the case? Not many criminals, I know, use a Taser to kill people so you could be right. What do you want the American investigator for?" Bruno asked.

"We helped them get their man, and as far as I'm concerned she owes us. I want her to help us get this

Taser killer. She has a partner and they're not police, so they could investigate as undercover agents."

"Are you sure this is a good idea, *Capitaine*? If they catch the killer they'll get the credit."

"No, that's the best part. They don't take credit for any crimes they solve. All the crime solving for this last case goes to us, as well as the police in Albuquerque. They're some kind of team that solves cases and lets the police clean up the mess and make the headlines."

"That's my kind of citizen, *Capitaine*. Good luck getting her to work with you on this one. Catching the Taser Killer would give our station a big plus in the eyes of the international police. It's worth a try."

"I thought so too, *Sergent*. I'll let you know if it works out."

Bruno went back to his desk to make the arrangement to send Barry back to the States. At the same time, *Capitaine* Le Cure made a call to Julia Forrester. He hoped she'd stay around in Europe for a while and assist him. It'd be a huge feather in his hat if he could solve this case.

"Hello, Madame Forrester. This is *Capitaine* Le Cure again. I wanted to tell you that we picked up your man, and he's being processed as we speak."

"This case went smoothly, thanks to you and your

department, *Capitaine*. My partner and I are in your debt."

"Good, and that is partly why I'm calling you, *Madame* Forrester. I have a rather large favor to ask you."

"What's this about, *Capitaine*?"

"We have an unusual case in Paris that involves a kidnapping and murder with a stun gun. It happened several weeks ago and we may have a lead. I was wondering if I could meet you somewhere in private to discuss the situation. I don't want to talk about it at the station because it's not official."

"Where do you want to meet, *Capitaine*?"

"How about the lobby of your hotel. I'll come to you."

"We are at the Hilton Paris La Defense. I'll bring my partner so we both can hear what you have to say. We'll do what we can and maybe extend our vacation a while longer."

"Let's meet this afternoon around three. I won't be in uniform. This has to be a private meeting. Will that work for you?"

"We'll make it work. You've been most helpful in finding our man. I don't think we could have done it without you. We're in your debt."

"I'll see you at three, Madame Forrester."

Capitaine Le Cure closed his private phone and turned to *Sergent* Bruno. "Get me all the paperwork on that killing in Stockholm. I want a copy of everything they sent us and a copy of the case regarding the bodyguard killed in that nightclub. Put them in a file for me right away. I'm meeting that American investigator and will see if she can help us find our killer."

"Right away, *Capitaine,*" Bruno said. "I'll put this in a folder and lay it on your desk."

Chapter 18

"June, they have Barry. I just received a fax confirming the Paris police picked him up this morning, their time, and are putting him on a flight with an air Marshall to New York within the hour. We have to tell Martin and get someone to meet the plane Barry is on."

"What'd I tell you, Louis? We did it. Whoever that detective woman is, she pulled through. How are you going to break the news to Martin?"

"I have no friggin idea. What do you think?"

"Just tell him we sent out an APB to the Paris police, along with Barry's picture, and got lucky. Martin doesn't have to know anything about our investigator at all," June said.

"I'll have to tell Martin about the warrant. The rest I'll make up," Louis said.

"Yes, but don't get technical, Louis. Tell him we just got lucky. You sent a warrant for Barry's arrest when the cops in Paris found Barry. Martin better be excited about that and not get pissed because you acted on your own."

"He's a glutton for recognition," Louis said. "This arrest will be another plus for all of us so he shouldn't be too worried how we pulled this off."

"Louis, we did it," June repeated. "I have another idea.

Get that detective friend of yours in New York to meet the plane and transfer Barry. You know, the guy who helped us with the Ian case."

"Oh, you mean Bates. I'll call him right now. What time is that flight from Paris landing? Also, the flight number would help."

"It's right here in the fax. Get him to make the exchange and we'll get another Air Marshall to escort Barry back here to Albuquerque."

"Will do," Louis said as he reached for his phone.

After the call to detective Bates was made, Louis prepared himself to face Martin. He made his way down the hall and knocked on Martin's door.

"Come in Louis. What can I do for you?"

"Hold on to your hat boss. We're about to make the headlines again."

"What do you mean headlines. Did we get a break in the kidnapping case? I thought the second guy disappeared in Paris?"

"Guess where he is right now?"

"How in the fuck should I know, Louis? Between you and officer Parsons, you're not around much anymore. I'm happy for your love life, Louis, as long as it doesn't interfere with our work at the station."

Martin was jealous of Louis and his new connection in the office. Before, he and Louis were close, but now Louis spent his spare time with Parsons and Martin got his information about his friend second hand.

"Barry is on a plane with an Air Marshall and will be in New York in a few hours."

"He what? How in the hell did this happen? I thought we lost him for good?"

"So did we," Louis answered.

"We. You mean Parsons and you?"

"Yes. We took a chance and sent a BOLO to the Paris police. We were not expecting anything to happen. I thought Barry was gone, but his picture turned up and the police captain in Paris asked me for an arrest warrant at five a.m. this morning. I came in the office, made one out and sent it. I wasn't going to say anything to you until an arrest was made. I didn't know anything else until just now. The police captured Barry, questioned him and stuck him on a plane."

"Next time let me know what you're doing, Louis. If this thing had backfired it could have been my ass. We need to get the press in on this and have some video taken of us picking up our man at the airport."

Martin was pleased the BOLO turned up something and Barry was arrested. Martin was too excited to question Louis regarding how the Paris police tracked Barry down. The headlines would read that his police officers had wrapped up the kidnapping case involving the girlfriend of Alan Hogan, the Internet billionaire. There would be another candle on his cake of fame for sure.

"How is Barry getting here from New York?"

"I'm having my friend, Detective Bates in New York, pick him up and put him on a flight back here."

"You mean the one who helped us with the McClure case in New York?"

"Yes, the same one. We scratch his back and he scratches ours."

"All I can say is you and Parsons deserve to be at the airport for the photo opp. I'll be there as well so let me know when the flight is expected to arrive. I'll need to put on a clean shirt and my dress uniform. I suggest you and Parsons do the same. We have to look good for the cameras."

Louis went back to June's desk to give her the news regarding Martin's reaction.

"He seemed to be more concerned about wearing his dress uniform than finding out more about the case. I think we're in the clear."

"He wants us both at the airport for the arrival of

Barry?" June asked.

"That's what he said. He's including both of us in the capture of this kidnapper."

"I think this calls for another celebration, Louis. Pick a country you like and I'll do the rest."

Louis was starting to see a pattern with June. When he picked France she dressed up as a French maid. Germany gave him a Bavarian beer maiden to undress. He was not going to say any cold countries because she might show up in too many clothes and it would take too long to undress her.

"How about some South Pacific Island. Will that work?"

"I'll see what I can do. You provide the drinks from that part of the world and I'll get what I need."

There are a lot of countries in the world, thought Louis. This ongoing game with June could take a lifetime and he was in no hurry.

*****

The New York flight touched down at five p.m. after the stopover in Atlanta. The three Albuquerque police officers were at a special gate to meet the Air Marshall and take the prisoner off his hands. Detective Martin took the paperwork, thanked the Marshall and shook his hand.

At that moment the press came into the room where the exchange happened and began filming for the five o'clock news.

A microphone was placed in front of Martin and the first question was asked. "Is it true this is the second kidnapper in the Cathy and Alan Hogan case?"

"Yes, it is," Martin answered. "I would like you to meet Detective Louis and Officer Parsons. They were more involved in the case and were the ones who sent the information to the Paris police. They can answer any questions you may have."

"Detective Louis, how did the Paris police find the second kidnapper in a large city like Paris? Did you have any leads to give them?"

Louis paused for a second. He couldn't give up his source so he had to word the answer so no one would find out anything about his source.

"We got lucky. We knew Barry flew to Paris because of a confession by his partner. He had a record so we found his full name, a recent picture and sent the information to the Paris police. As far as I know Barry might have been picked up for a minor misdemeanor and his picture was with the police already. We're still following up on this information. All we know is that the Paris police called me to get an arrest warrant. The rest is history. Barry was arrested, questioned and put on a plane this morning."

"That sounds like the luckiest break in a case I've ever heard," the reporter from CNN said. "If Barry didn't get picked up in Paris he could be still on the loose."

"Call it what you want," Louis said. "I call it international cooperation. I admit a little luck was in play. We now have both men and they'll be in prison for a few years."

"Mark Thompson from Fox News. Did any of the kidnap money get returned? We heard two million dollars was paid out for the return of Cathy Hogan."

"We're still trying to track the money down. We'll let you know if we get another lead as to where the cash was transferred."

Louis knew Cathy wasn't married to Alan and didn't share the name of Hogan but he decided the news people didn't need to know that. The 'Religious Right' would get a hold of that information and judge Alan as living in sin. What a bunch of fucking hypocrites, thought Louis.

"One last question for officer Parsons. Alison Waters from Woman's Weekly. How does it feel to work with a police force with 90% men on the job? Have you had any problems in the office?"

June thought for a moment and glanced over Martin, who was staring intently at her. She knew she had to be careful with her answer.

"I'm not sure how that question has anything to do with this case," she said. "I've been in the office for over a year now and have helped with several big cases. Every rookie gets the same treatment and is put on assignments that may appear boring. I've completed my year, and I now get assigned to help with important police work. This case is a perfect example. Last year I helped in the Ian McClure case. The station treats me fairly and with respect so I have nothing to complain about."

A sigh of relief came from Martin. He didn't see that question coming and he was pleased with Parson's answer. Maybe Louis ended up with a smart girlfriend after all, Martin thought. I wonder if she is in line for a promotion soon?

"If there are no more questions about the capture of the second kidnapper and our international work with the Paris police, then I would like to get back to the office and start the paperwork. Thank you for your time," Martin said as he wrapped up the press interview.

Louis whispered in June's ear, "Good answer. There always seems to be some reporter who is trying to create a different story from the one in front of them."

"Let's get out of here, Louis," June said. "I wasn't expecting that magazine reporter to be here and ask me something like that."

Martin approached the couple and held out his hand to June. "You did a terrific job handling that question that had nothing to do with the case. You made us look good and to me that's important. Good teamwork."

June gave a sigh and thanked her boss for acknowledging her.

"I did my best, sir. That woman came out of nowhere with that question." June knew she'd need Martin's recommendation down the road because she planned to start taking the detective classes in a couple of years. One step at a time, she thought.

*****

Robert and Julia were sitting in the lounge area of their hotel when *Capitaine* Le Cure walked in. He was in slacks and coat without a tie, wearing dark glasses.

"Hello again, *Madame* Forrester. Thank you for meeting me. This is your partner?"

"Yes," Julia said in English. He doesn't speak French so we better keep the conversation in the Queen's tongue."

"But of course," Le Cure answered. "I'm *Capitaine* Le Cure." He shook Robert's hand and sat down in the chair across from the two.

"My name is Robert Forrester," Robert said. He decided not to try and hide his identity with a French police captain who had just helped him and Julia solve a case.

"Good to meet you, Mr. Forrester

"What do you have that demands a secret meeting?" Julia asked.

Capitaine Le Cure thought for a moment before answering. He wanted to make sure this was the right team to help him solve the Taser murder case.

"It seems we have a killer in Europe who does not use a gun, so he shocks his victims to death with a Taser device. He killed the bodyguard of an American woman a few weeks ago using one of those weapons and escaped. The ransom was paid for the release of the woman but the killer was never found. We think he left France."

"Any idea where he might have gone?" Robert asked.

"We may have a lead. The Stockholm police sent out a request to the major police departments in Europe, asking if they had any unsolved cases involving Taser killings. A week ago two bodies were found in an ally in Stockholm with Taser burn marks on their necks and chest areas. We made a match with the pictures of the burn marks on our victim to those in Stockholm. The photos are in this file I brought with me."

"And you're telling me it's the same model of Taser in both cases?" Robert asked.

"We believe so. A burn on the neck to knock out the victim and a jolt to the heart area to shut the person down completely."

"And the Stockholm police don't have any leads?" Julia asked.

"Not as far as we know. We think it's the same person. More than likely he may live in Sweden and is hired as a strong arm to kidnap victims. We had another case six months ago where a wealthy American was shocked while coming out of a whorehouse in the Moulin Rouge district of Paris. He never saw his attacker. He paid his ransom, through his lawyer, before he was released. We feel now the person is getting off on killing people and uses his weapon to deliver several shocks to victims at full charge."

"Have you let the police in Stockholm know you have a similar case?"

"Not yet. That's where you come in. I have a request."

"What do you mean request?" Julia asked.

"I can't send anyone from my department to Stockholm. I would like you two to do some investigating for me, and see what you can find. If the killer does live in Sweden, and he gets wind of police from Paris snooping around his city, he may take off and disappear forever. If you two show up and work undercover for a few days, we may have a chance to catch this guy. I don't have a lot of confidence in the Swedish police. They don't have a lot of crime in their country compared to France or the United States. I don't think their detective skills are up to par in a case like this one."

"I guess that says a lot about high crime countries. The more crime you have the better the investigation skills. I don't know if that's a positive or negative," Robert added.

"Whatever the case, I feel you two could do a better job. I'll pay for any expenses and make it worth your time. You could look at it like a little vacation in Scandinavia and take in the sights as well."

"How long do you want us to try looking for this Taser Killer, *Capitaine?*" Julia asked. "I would love to visit Sweden but we can't be gone from our cases in New Mexico for too long."

"How about a week. If nothing turns up, then let me know and I'll take it from there."

"We appreciate what you did for us, *Capitaine*. A week sounds doable. Can you write us a letter to present to the head of the police in Stockholm so we can view any clues regarding the case?" Robert asked.

"I'll give you anything you need. You won't have trouble with the language because the Swedish speak English better than many Americans I've met in Paris. No one in Europe other than Swedes, speak Swedish, so they have to learn several languages to get by in the world."

"We'll have to let our people back in New Mexico know what we're doing. When do you want us to start?" Julia asked.

"I'll write the letter of introduction and copy all the information in this file by 2 p.m. It's not a long flight so if you wanted to leave tomorrow, that would be fine."

"Tomorrow works for me," Robert said. "We can use the afternoon to check out that famous museum everyone raves about. The Louvre, right?"

"Yes, please use the rest of the day to enjoy Paris. I really appreciate you taking the time to help me in this case. My feeling is that the killer is starting to warm up and he may kill again, only next time he may kill the kidnap victim. That's how cereal killers get started."

"Wow, a Taser serial killer. That's a new one," Julia added. "We better get going if we want to check out the museum, Robert. It's huge and we'll never see the whole thing in one day."

"We'll come back and see more of the museum some other time. I want to thank you again, *Capitaine,* for your help in our case. We'll do our best to help you find this Taser killer." Robert stood up and shook Le Cure's hand.

"I'll send a courier back here to deliver the letter and the file. It will be at the front desk. Keep track of your expenses and everything will be taken care of."

Capitaine Le Cure shook Julia's hand as well, replaced his sunglasses and turned to walk out the front door. His driver appeared a few minutes later and drove him back to the police station.

"Wow," Julia said. "I wasn't expecting that. What do you think, Robert?"

"Are we ready to go international?" Robert said. "If we can help track this Taser killer, we just might get a name for ourselves and visit Europe involving other cases."

"I wouldn't mind that at all," Julia answered with a smile on her face. "This is as exciting as dropping in on New York every so often for dinner and a show. I've never been to Stockholm so this will be new for me as well."

"Let's get a move on. The museum, dinner, and off we to the land of the summer sun."

"Not only that, Robert, but the people are friendly and

open-minded in Sweden. I've read about them and I'm really looking forward to visiting their country."

Julia and Robert went back to their room, put on some walking shoes and casual clothes. Tomorrow was a new day in the continued international investigation life of Robert and Julia Forrester.

Chapter 19

The flight touched down around ten a.m. at Arlanda International Airport. The Hilton Stockholm Slussen was booked for Robert from their hotel in Paris. Julia wanted a top floor so she could look over the city from up high.

"Isn't this exciting, Robert? This has been a fun work vacation so far and we're not even done yet."

"We have the phone number of the police officer in Stockholm, right?" Robert asked.

"Here it is," Julia said. "The police officer in Stockholm is a Sergeant Hanson. He sent out the information regarding the two killings in the city last week. Do you want me to call him and set up an appointment, Sweetheart?"

"Would you, Julia? You're good at talking to strangers."

"I'll call him now and then maybe we can go for a late breakfast."

"Perfect."

A call was made to Sergeant Hanson.

"Hej," Sergeant Hanson said as he answered his phone.

"Do you speak English?" Julia asked.

"Yes, of course. This is Sweden. How may I help you?"

My name is Julia Forrester. *Capitaine* Le Cure from Paris sent me to your city. I have a letter of introduction regarding the Taser murders that took place last week. He should have sent you a message telling you we were coming."

"Yes, he did Miss Forrester. I received it this morning. It says you may have some information regarding the murders and the letter asks for my cooperation in the case. You and a partner are investigators and are working on the case for *Capitaine* Le Cure. Is that right?"

"Yes. Actually, my partner and I are married and work as a team. We would like to meet you today, go over any evidence, and help you and *Capitaine* Le Cure find this killer. We believe he murdered someone in Paris and from the evidence we have so far the same Taser model was used."

"This is good news. We're not making much progress with the case and would appreciate any help we could get."

"What is a good time to visit you and go over the case file?"

"Can you be here in two hours? I have some another case I need to focus on this morning. Noon would work for me."

"My partner, Robert, wants you to do something for us before we arrive."

"Yes, what is that?"

"Can you find any incidents in the past year that have anything to do with a stun gun. Our killer seems to use this weapon on a regular basis and he or she may have used it in another incident. It would help in our investigation."

"I'll assign one of my men to look into this right away. I'll bet this type of murder doesn't happen too often."

"Probably not, but if you have anything it will be a start."

"I'll see you in a few hours, Mrs. Forrester. Just tell the cab driver the address. They'll have no problem bringing you here."

Julia hung up the hotel room phone and turned to Robert.

"Sergeant Hansen seems cooperative. He and *Capitaine* Le Cure really want to solve this case. He'll see if there are any other cases involving a stun gun of any kind and we can start from there."

"Good work, Julia. You make our job so much easier. Shall we have an early lunch before the meeting or wait until after?"

"How about we get some snack food to get us through the meeting and then go out to some nice restaurant near Gamla Stan. I've read it's the old town of Stockholm and worth the trip."

"You plan the vacation part and I'll keep focused on the case. I'm sure there's a lot to see in this city," Robert said.

*****

The taxi dropped Julia and Robert off in front of the police station in the center of Stockholm five minutes before twelve. The policeman at the front desk directed them to Sergeant Hanson's office.

"Right on time Mr. and Mrs. Forrester. So glad to meet you." Sergeant Hanson rose from his chair and shook Julia and Robert's hand.

"You have a lovely city, Sergeant Hanson. We hope we can see some of it before we return to the States," Julia said.

"I hope you can as well. Please sit down."

Julia and Robert sat in the two red upholstered chairs positioned in front of Hanson's desk.

"Here's the file on the two killing a few weeks ago in the city. Also, we have an incident report that may interest you." Sergeant Hanson handed both files to Robert. "I don't know if the incident report is connected to our killer but it may be worth a follow-up. I never thought of doing such a search. When you suggested it, I found the paperwork and I thought we might have something to go on."

Robert glanced at the file and saw that it had been translated into English for him. He read it quickly and looked up.

"The report says a couple was jolted with a stun gun while boarding a tour cruise boat. The male was seriously injured while the woman was dropped to the ground with a jolt."

Sergeant Hanson added his own interpretation of the incident. "I talked to the officer who took statements from the people who saw the situation unfold. It seems one of Sweden's third-rate television stars and her bodyguard tried to push their way onto the boat without waiting in line. None of the witnesses gave a good description of the person who used the stun gun. The officer believes the crowd sided with the man and several said they would have done the same thing as he did."

"Did the officer interview the television star and her bodyguard?"

"He did manage to get a rough sketch of the man from the actress. Her bodyguard suffered some serious head trauma. He did not remember much after he fell off the dock and into the water."

"Can we interview the actress and see if we can get more information from her?" Julia asked.

"I believe so. We better do it here at the station. She's not a pleasant person and tried to blame everyone else for her behavior. I don't think we could get any of the witnesses to testify against the man with the stun gun.

"'This looks like a good place to start. I see you have photos of the stun gun marks on her and the bodyguard. I have photos of the murder victims in Stockholm and the man in Paris. If they all match up we may have a lead in finding this guy," Robert said.

"You two investigators are good. I can see why Capitaine Le Cure sent you. Maybe we can catch this guy."

"Let's hope so," Julia said. "Call us when you get the actress to come down to the station. I'll probably do the interview because women react less when talking to another woman."

"Good idea, Mrs. Forrester. I'll call you when we get Helga down here. I'll probably have to threaten her but she'll come."

Robert and Julia thanked the sergeant and took the files with them. Their first job was to visit the boat dock where the incident happened several months ago. Lunch came first in old town with a walk around the plaza. So far the clues were falling into place.

*****

Marcos was back in Stockholm, enjoying his life. His girlfriend, Bridgette, worked during the week, so he had the days to himself. He still hadn't taken the tour of the Stockholm waterways after his attempt two months ago. There were several locations where he could catch a tour boat. He knew he couldn't return to the dock where he had the previous incident. Today was the day he would try another tour and avoid pushy people.

"How long does the tour last?" Marcos asked the ticket vendor at the tour boat harbor. He used his basic Swedish but it was still obvious he was not a native of the country.

"About three hours," the guide answered in English. "All the special sights of Stockholm are covered in the tour. Take notes and visit a few of the locations after the boat docks. You won't be disappointed."

"Thank you," Marcos said. "I need one ticket."

Marcos boarded the boat cruise and sat in the deck chairs at the rear of the boat. He was doing his best to stay away from people. The Taser C2 was in his coat pocket but the power was off. He needed to get through the trip without zapping anyone.

*****

When Robert and Julia arrived at the cruise ship dock, the first thing they noticed was a security camera aimed at the parking lot.

"Julia, do you see that?" Robert asked as he pointed to the camera. "We may have our suspect on tape. I bet the police didn't even try to access the video. Let's put in a call to Sergeant Hanson and see what he can do."

"I agree," Julia nodded. "I'll do that and question the crew to see who was on duty that day. The date is in the files, but I bet they'd remember the incident."

"Fine with me. You call and I'll start with the ticket booth."

Julia reached for the number of Sergeant Hanson in her purse, while Robert walked over to the building that sold the touring tickets for the cruise ship.

"I'm sorry to bother you, but first I have to ask if you speak English?"

"Of course. In this job I have to speak German and French as well. How can I help you?"

"My name is Robert Forrester and I'm an investigator for the Stockholm police on a special assignment. My partner and I are trying to find out anything we can regarding an incident on April 11."

"I was working then so maybe I can help."

"I'm sure you would remember the stun gun incident with two people attacked on that day."

"Of course I do. That was the topic of lunch conversation for several weeks."

"I would appreciate it if you could fill me in on anything that would shed light on the case. We believe the man is also involved in the death of two Swedish citizens two weeks ago and another man in Paris."

"Really? In this case, the so called victims seem to have it coming."

"What do you mean?" Robert asked.

"The woman involved is a known television personality. She appears on a daytime show titled *Stockholm Lies*. I believe you have shows like this in the U.S. called soap operas. The acting is usually bad and if anyone has any talent they eventually move on to movies."

"Yes, I have her name," Robert said. "Helga Alman. She had a boyfriend with her named Olaf Gunter and he's some kind of athletic. Does that information check out?"

"Yes, it does. He had to be taken away in an ambulance, and she went with him. Whoever used a stun gun on the two really did some damage."

"Did you see the incident?" Robert asked.

"Part of it. I was here in this window selling tickets and heard Helga screaming at the man with the stun gun. The next thing I saw was her falling to the deck of the ship and the man walking away to his car."

"You saw all that?" Robert asked. "Did the police ask you any questions?"

"No, they talked mostly to the crew who were near the incident. It took three men to get the boyfriend out of the water and breathing again. He hit his head on the dock and was lucky he wasn't crushed by the ship."

"How about the man with the gun. Did you see him drive away?"

"Yes, I did."

"What can you tell me about his car."

"It was a Volvo, one of those expensive models. I even wrote down the license number just in case anyone interviewed me."

"And you said no one did." Robert was amazed by the lack of police follow-up.

"No, they didn't. After I heard what happened I decided not to give them any information on the man. The story was that Helga and her boyfriend were trying to muscle their way onto the ship and bribe the crew just so she could get a deck chair and work on her tan."

"Why are you telling me now what you know?" Robert asked.

"Because you said he may have killed some people. He was justified in taking out Helga and Olaf but killing someone in Sweden does not happen often."

"I have a rough sketch that Helga gave the police after the incident."

Robert pulled the picture out of the file and showed it to the attendant. "Does this look anything like the man you saw?"

"Yes, but his face was a little fatter. Other than that, the sketch is close. I did sell him a ticket so I got a good look at him."

"Do you have his license plate number with you?" Robert asked.

"Yes, it is in my purse."

The woman turned and retrieved her handbag that hung on a peg on the back wall. After digging around for a few minutes she returned with a piece of paper in her hands.

"Here you are, Mr. Forrester. I wasn't going to give it to the police but if he's a killer then he should be arrested."

"Thank you so much, Miss Olsson." Robert read her nametag on her uniform. "If this clue leads to his arrest, do you want me to tell the police your name and that you helped in the case?"

"You can. Just remind them that they need to do a better job interviewing people who witnessed the incident. Like I said before, they never approached me. Probably had something to do with the behavior of the television woman. Most witnesses thought she deserved what she got."

"Well, I want to thank you again. You've been helpful, to say the least. If there is a reward posted for the capture of the man then I'll add your name to the list of people helping to take him off the streets."

"Thank you, Mr. Forrester. You're a gentleman. I have enjoyed our conversation."

Robert turned around and headed back to where Julia was waiting for him near the parking lot entrance.

"Did you find anything out, Robert? I just finished my conversation with Hanson and he said he was not aware of the camera viewing the parking lot. He is going to interview the officer who handled the case as well as get the footage for us."

"How about the make of the car and a license plate. So far I think the officer who investigated this case did a piss-poor job. He didn't even question the ticket booth woman and she saw more than anyone."

"How's that possible?" Julia asked.

"I think it has something to do with the people who were zapped. Everyone close to the incident said the bodyguard and the television actress deserved it. I'll bet the officer dropped the ball on purpose and hoped the case would just go away. The people who witnessed the incident said they would have done the same thing if they were in the shoes of our suspect."

"In other words, the public took the case on themselves and sided with our zapper. Now that he's a murder suspect they're willing to come forward."

"I believe so," Robert said. "If the lead from the ticket person helps solve the case, we have to make sure she gets a reward if one is offered. Maybe we can get the actress to cough up some cash."

"Let's work on her when we do the interview," Julia said. "The sergeant mentioned he persuaded her to come into the police station. We have a two o'clock meeting planned."

"Maybe we can get to the bottom of this case faster than we thought. I really hadn't given us much hope, but now that I see all this evidence popping up, we might get our man if he's still in Stockholm."

"We have what we need from here so let's go back to the room for a rest. We can visit some special sights in town and have dinner on the water somewhere. This is a beautiful city and all the women are so gorgeous," Julia said.

"Sweden is famous for beautiful women. Remember, Peggy is Swedish and she is really cute," Robert said. "I think her grandparents came from Stockholm."

"That's right. We better send her a postcard. Also one to Cathy and Alan."

"Here comes our taxi, Julia. We're done here."

*****

The Stockholm tour of the waterways was uneventful. Marcos knew he had temper issues but he couldn't take his anger out on the general public in Sweden. He loved living here and his girlfriend was everything he wanted in a woman.

"We will be docking in ten minutes, sir," the waiter said to Marcos. "Can I get you another beer before we land?"

"No, I'm fine. This has been a wonderful tour. I've lived in Stockholm for several years and I finally got to see the city and its waterways for the first time."

"Stockholm has a long history. I'm happy our cruise

has been up to your expectations."

"Thank you again," Marcos said.

After docking, Marcos made a call to Bridgette. He said he'd pick up dinner and a bottle of wine before heading back to the apartment.

"You are so thoughtful, Marcos. I've had a long day at the office and I'm ready to be pampered when I get home."

Bridgette worked as a paralegal at a law firm in Stockholm and was studying to be a lawyer herself. Her relationship with Marcos was perfect. Expenses were minimal, and when he was in town he bought everything. She knew they would not be together forever, but for the moment the relationship suit her needs.

"I should be there in an hour," Marcos said. "Get ready to be pampered."

Chapter 20

Poppy was back in Paris looking over the information his informants sent him when a rich American was expected to arrive in Paris. The target could not be someone who flew in and out within days. They had to be a person who'd be in the city for a while, create a pattern of behavior as to where they went and have minimal backup. One bodyguard was doable, but two or more was more than Poppy cared to deal with.

Poppy had plenty of money to do what he wanted because of his two businesses. The thrill of getting away with crime was what he was addicted to. Fooling governments and getting ransom from stupid billionaires was like a fix. He couldn't get enough.

"Hello, Marcos. This is Poppy."

"Yes, Poppy, I'm surprised to hear from you so soon. Something has come up I'll bet."

"Only if you're interested. I can get someone else if you need more time off."

"Tell me what you've lined up and I'll let you know if I want to do it."

"A hotel owner is in Paris for a month negotiating a deal with the city to build an office building and a five-star hotel in Paris. I just found out that he brought his family with him."

"Who's the target?" Marcos asked.

"My informant tells me the wife is the easiest person to isolate. She has a regular schedule and seems to stick to her routine."

"You said, family. How old are the kids?"

"They're in their late teens. I don't think they would make a good target."

"Why not?" Marcos asked.

"That is a difficult age for most children. They don't have a regular schedule and each child has two bodyguards following them. My informant also says they are a pain in the ass and treat everyone around them like their servants."

"How about the wife? Does she have more than one assistant?"

"So far my informant has only seen one bodyguard. The wife goes to a yoga studio three times a week and at the same time on Monday, Wednesday, and Friday."

"When do you want me there, Poppy? I haven't been home for long and now you have another job."

"Only if you want it, Marcos. The family is expected to be here for three more weeks. I have to either use you on this grab or another man I use as a backup."

"If I do this job I won't be available for the rest of the year," Marcos said. "I'll fly down tomorrow and case the yoga studio. Give me the address and the times she takes the classes."

"91, rue du Faubourg, St Martin. The studio is called Yoga Iyengar and she takes the eleven a.m. class on those days. The woman's name is Gwen Towers and she is married to Ralph Towers of Tower Industries. I'm shooting for a quick 5 million for her and don't expect any delays from the husband in getting her back."

"I'll call you after I look at the yoga studio and make sure there's a good escape route. Are you calling Paula to help with this job?" Marcos asked.

"Only if you want me to. She can be here by tomorrow and she's available."

"Same driver as well?"

"Of course."

"I call in a few day. Talk to you later, Poppy"

Marcos returned his phone to his pocket and looked around the apartment. He had to leave today and write a note for Bridgette. He hated to leave like this, but facing her and saying goodbye for a week was always hard. He'd have to get her another special gift on his return trip.

Marcos packed his bag and decided to take a taxi to

the airport and leave his car parked on the street. He left the keys to the car for Bridgette to use if she needed it. She usually rode a bicycle to work, but occasionally she would drive to the country on weekends to unwind from her busy job.

*****

"Sergeant Hanson called and said the license plate checked out. We now have an address to go with the car," Robert said. "Also the television actress will be in the police station tomorrow. She can't make it this afternoon."

"Who's going to check out the address? Us?" Julia asked. She didn't feel comfortable dealing with a man carrying a stun gun.

"We can have police backup when we stake it out. We better do so right away," Robert answered.

"Do we have a name that goes with the car?" Julia asked. "I'll make sure he is in the residence before we knock down any doors."

"And how are you going to do that?" Robert asked.

"I have my ways," Julia answered in a coy voice. "My charms worked on you didn't they?"

"You're really too much. If he's there, then what are you going to do?"

"I'm not going into the residence if that's what you mean. I'll leave and let the police take over."

"Any sign of trouble and we move in, Julia. Remember this guy zaps people for a living."

"Call Sergeant Hanson and have a squad car meet us at the address. Tell them to park down the street and wait for us. We still have to make sure he's there."

A call was made and the plan went into motion. When Robert and Julia arrived, the police car was already parked a block away. Robert walked over the vehicle to let them know the plan. As he walked towards the car he noticed a dark Volvo matching the description he was given by the ticket attendant at the docks. He looked at the license plate and it was a match.

"Officer, I'm Robert Forrester. My wife is making sure our suspect is in the apartment before we move in. That's his car parked down the street so get ready because we may have to move quickly if he's there."

"Here's a radio, Mr. Forrester. Call us by pushing this button. We'll be right behind you."

Robert took the radio and walked back to the apartment steps to wait for Julia. By now she had knocked on the door and could hear someone coming to answer.

Bridgette had just arrived home and held the note Marcos left for her on the kitchen table.

"Hello, my name is Julia and I'm doing a survey with foreigners living in Stockholm. I understand a Marcos Lent lives here. Is that right?"

"Yes, he does," Bridgette answered. "What kind of survey are you doing?"

"A basic one asking the person how they like Sweden and everything Stockholm has to offer."

"I can assure you Marcos loves everything Sweden has to offer. He's been here several years now and wants to make Stockholm his residence for life."

"Is he in? I have to ask him the questions that go with the survey."

"I just got home and picked up a note he left me. He goes away on business occasionally and from the note, he says he was called away again."

"When do you think he will be back?" Julia asked.
"It's hard to say with Marcos. These trips happen two or three times a year but he usually has a schedule. This trip seemed to have come up today and he's now gone."

Julia raised her hand and motioned Robert to come up the stairs to the apartment.

"Move in," Robert said after pushing the police radio button.

By now Bridgette knew something was not right, and

attempted to close the door. Julia's foot stopped it from closing and with Robert's help they pushed the barrier open.

"Please take a seat," Julia told the scared woman. "We're not here to harm anyone. We are on police business and have the support of the local department. Please tell us your name."

By now the police were entering the apartment.

Bridgette knew the law and was not going to be taken advantage of. She spoke Swedish to the policemen who had just entered.

"Do you have a warrant to come in?" she asked.

The officer in charge produced a paper giving them the right to arrest a Mr. Marcos Lent. He downloaded the arrest paper from his car printer.

Bridgette looked at the paper and gave a heavy sigh. "What's he done?"

"First of all, we need to know your name and your connection with Marcos. He's wanted for murder. If you hold anything back you will be charged with obstruction of justice."

"He what? Marcos killed someone? How's that possible? He's a businessman and works in Paris on occasion."

"And your connection with him?" Julia asked. She gave Robert a look that told him to let her do the questioning.

"My name is Bridgette and I work at a law office in Stockholm. I'm his girlfriend and have lived with Marcos for over a year. Are you sure we're talking about the same man?"

"Do you know what he does in Paris?" Julia continued.

"Not really. He usually has a schedule. This trip is unexpected."

"Do you know how to get in touch with him when he's gone?"

"No, he doesn't like to be interrupted when he's working. I find our living situation workable and I'm free to do what I want. I'm studying to be a lawyer so my time alone is perfect for catching up with school work."

"I'm sorry Miss but you're going to have to come down to the station and make a statement," the officer in charge said.

"My last name is Hoffler. It's German but my mother was Swedish. Am I in trouble?"

"Not if your story checks out. If you had no idea where Marcos Lent is, then you should be in the clear."

"What exactly is he accused of?" Monica asked.

"I'm going to let Sergeant Hanson at the police station tell you anything you need to know. He's handling the case." The officer turned around in the doorway and motioned for Bridgette to follow him to the police car.

"I have to lock the door so please can everyone leave." Bridgette was almost in tears after finding out her living arrangement and boyfriend situation were about to change.

"Yes, we're sorry about all this but the crime is serious," Julia said as she walked out of the apartment. "The police have a warrant to search the address as well. You can either come with us to make your statement or wait until the police are finished searching and come down with them."

"I'll come with you," Monica said. She then turned to the police and said, "Please be careful with my things. Marcos kept most of his personal items in the second bedroom in the space above the closet. Here is the key. Lock up when you're done and return it to me at the station."

She then turned to leave with Robert and Julia.

"Before we go, can you bring that picture of you and Marcos? We have a victim coming in tomorrow and we need a recent picture of him," Robert said.

Bridgette grabbed the picture from the table and put it in her purse.

After getting into the waiting taxi Monica began to break down again. "I can't believe this is happening. I have no idea what Marcos does in Paris. He was never violent to me or anyone else when I was with him. How serious of a crime is it?"

"All we can say is, if he is convicted you may not be seeing Marcos for a long time. There are three possible deaths connected with him and that's all we know so far."

Monica couldn't stop the tears and continued to sob. "I have to phone my job and let them know I won't be coming in tomorrow. I need some time off."

"Do you have a way to get a hold of Marcos or does he call you when he's gone on business?"

"Not really. We don't call each other when he's away. He left sometime today because he was at the apartment this morning. I have this note he left me so he's probably in Paris now."

"I know this is really a difficult time for you," Julia told Bridgette. "If there is anything you can tell us that will help find Marcos, it would be helpful."

"All I can say is we met over a year ago. I have my job and he travels to Paris for business three or four times a year. I was surprised he is gone so soon because he just returned three weeks ago."

The taxi pulled up to the police station and all three of the occupants got out and went inside. Sergeant Hanson was there to greet them. He directed one of his men to escort Bridgette to a room where she could give her statement. Robert and Julia then followed Sergeant Hanson back to his office for a briefing. When they arrived Robert spoke first.

"We don't think this woman knows anything about her boyfriend's activities. All we could get out of her was that Marcos flew to Paris sometime today and she has no way to contact him. If you can access the cameras for any flights going to Paris we may be able to get the name of the airlines he used."

"I can do that," Sergeant Hanson said. "Maybe we should call Capitaine Le Cure and have him do the same with the incoming flights from Stockholm. We can at least find out when he arrived. Maybe the cameras will show us which taxi company he used. With any luck, we might find out where he stays in Paris."

"The girlfriend has a picture of her and Marcos together. If you can borrow that, and show it to the television actress tomorrow, we can at least confirm he's the one who injured her and her boyfriend. Has she posted a reward for the capture of the person who zapped her?" Robert asked.

"I hinted that she should do this the last time I

interviewed her. I said that most of the people who witnessed the attack were not willing to give us much information because of her behavior. She decided to put up 10,000 kronor about two weeks ago."

"If we capture him I would like most of that reward to go to the woman who gave us the car make and license plate. Without that information we would have nothing," Robert said.

"I agree," Sergeant Hanson said. "Give me her name and I'll make sure she's rewarded."

"I don't know what else we can do here in Stockholm," Julia added. "Since Marcos is in Paris, I believe we would be better served to help find him there. You know where he lives and can stake that place out if he comes back. I don't know how loyal his girlfriend is, but that's something we'll find out. If she is able to warn him, he may never return to Sweden again."

"I can't arrest her if she has nothing to do with Marcos' crimes. I do have a few questions for her. I'll say goodbye to you now and look forward to working with you again. If we catch Marcos, he has murdered in two countries."

Julia and Robert stood up and shook hands with Sergeant Hanson. After they left, the sergeant went down to the room where Bridgette was writing her statement and answering questions. He first went to the observation room where he could watch the questioning from the one-way glass window.

"I don't have much else I can tell you, officer Krump. You have my statement. I still don't know what crimes Marcos is charged with."

Sergeant Hanson decided to become involved so he entered the room from the side door.

"Bridgette Hoffler, my name is Sergeant Hanson. I was told you brought a picture of Marcos and you together. Is that right?"

"Yes, it's right here." She reached into her purse and pulled out a small 5x7 inch photo of the two in front of their apartment. "I would like this back when you are done with it. This is the only picture I have of Marcos."

"I'll be sure it is returned to you. I understand you don't know what crimes Marcos is under investigation for, is that right?"

"I've been told nothing. I know I haven't been charged for a crime and I'm here because I'm cooperating with you. I work for a law office and I'm studying to practice family law so I know a little about the legal system."

"Good, Miss Hoffler. We appreciate your working with us and I will do my best to wrap this up so you can go home. My first question is where were you three weeks ago. It was a Friday night."

"That was the day Marcos came back from Paris. I'm really surprised he's been called back to Paris so soon. He is usually home for several months before he leaves again."

"Do you remember what you and Marcos did that evening?" Sergeant Hanson asked.

"Yes, we went out to dinner. He purchased an expensive coat for me and I wanted to wear it out that night to show it off. I also wanted to thank him for the present so we made love the rest of the evening when he got back."

"Did anything happen out of the normal when you were out having dinner?"

"Yes, but it was nothing. Some young man appeared by the window where we were eating. He held up a sign saying something about killing animals and pointed to my coat. The restaurant manager sent a large employee outside to chase him away."

"What happened next?"

"Nothing. We finished dinner and drove home. On the way, Marcos said he had an errand to do and gave me the keys to drive to our apartment. He showed up about ninety minutes later and that's when we went to bed. It was a great night."

"Do you think you would remember the person with

the sign outside the restaurant if you saw him again?"

"Maybe. He had a slight beard, but he was dressed in decent clothes. He could have been a student."

Sergeant Hanson put a photo of each man who was found dead in the ally that night. "Does he look like one of these men?"

Monica studied each photo and pointed to the one on the right. "That man could have been him. Did something happen to him?"

"He and this other man were found dead in an alley. Do you remember exactly where you were when Marcos gave you the car keys and he got out of the car?"

Bridgette gave Sergeant Hanson the street location. She now had a panic look on her face. She never did find out what Marcos did after their meal and now the pieces started to fall into place.

"The two men were found four blocks from where Marcos got out of the car. They were killed by a stun gun. Do you know what a stun gun is, Miss Hoffler?"

"I thought that was a weapon used by the police to take down criminals?"

"Yes, but anyone can get a hold of one. It's more difficult in Sweden but you said Marcos went to France regularly. He could have picked one up there on the black market and brought it into Sweden. They're made mostly of plastic, with few metal parts, so they're difficult to pick up on a body scan."

"So you think Marcos had something to do with the deaths of these two men. Were there any eyewitnesses?"

"We have an eyewitness of another crime involving a stun gun. It happened April 11 and we have the person who was injured. If she identifies Marcos as the one who zapped her and her boyfriend, then we have enough to pin him to the crime. Another witness saw him leave and drive away in the car parked out in front of your apartment with the same license plate number. That's a lot of evidence and even you can see there is enough to issue an arrest warrant."

Bridgette turned white and felt sick. "I think I going to throw up. Do you have something with carbonation to settle my stomach?"

Sergeant Hanson turned to his officer in the room and told him to get Bridgette a soda water. After the officer left he turned to Bridgette.

"We don't have any evidence to hold you, Miss Hoffler. I think you're starting to see the trouble Marcos is in. When my officers return from your apartment with their final report, you are free to go. It's not a crime scene, but anything we find will be used as evidence against Marcos. I also suggest you do not get in touch with Marcos. If you do, and we find out, we will arrest you for abetting a suspect. Are we clear Miss Hoffler?"

"Up until now I really thought you had the wrong man. If that man who held up the sign at the restaurant is dead, and Marcos killed him, then I'm through with him. I'll stick around until your men return. I think Marcos paid for the apartment for three more months. Is there any reason I can't live there until the rent is due?"

"You can continue to live in the apartment as long as you want. Like I said, it is not a crime scene."

"I'll start looking for another place in three months," Bridgette said. "Either that or I'll get a roommate. I can't afford that place by myself."

"Do whatever you need to do. My men who searched your apartment have returned."

Bridgette looked out the glass door and saw an officer walk by holding a small box.

"I'll be right back, Miss Hoffler."

Sergeant Hanson went into the next room and saw his men removing attachment pieces used with a Taser gun. They were the metal projectiles, which attached to a wire from the gun. These were used when the stun gun owner did not want to get close to someone.

"We found this in a shoe box in the guest bedroom, Sergeant. I think this proves we have the right man. The gun was not there so he still must have that with him."

"Good work, men. After I show this to Miss Hoffler, she'll know Marcos is our man."

Sergeant Hanson returned to the room with the Taser attachments in the shoebox and showed them to Bridgette. "Have you ever seen these before?"

"No, what are they?" she asked.

"These were found in the guest bedroom in this shoebox. They are attachments to a Taser C2 model stun gun, the same model used to kill the two men in Stockholm and the man in Paris. If you have any doubt about Marcos, and what he's capable of, don't. He's our man and we're going to arrest him."

"What if he contacts me?" Bridgette asked. "I can't control what he does.

"If he contacts you, don't let him think anything has changed. If you help us, there is a reward for his capture. He can't know we're on to him."

"I'll do what I can," Bridgette said. She was still torn between her involvement with Marcos and his crimes. He had been good to her, but she was going to be a lawyer and warning him would jeopardize her chances of ever working in that field.

"Am I free to go now? You have what you want from the apartment. I expect to get the picture back when you're done with it," she said as she pointed to the snapshot of her and Marcos.

"You can go. I just need to show it to the victim tomorrow to confirm Marcos is the one who attacked her. We'll keep in touch. Thank you for your cooperation, Miss Hoffler."

*****

Robert and Julia decided to catch the next flight back to Paris. They checked out of their hotel and made a call to *Capitaine* Le Cure to let him know they were heading back to Paris. They decided to meet with him the next morning and see where the investigation was now headed.

Chapter 21

Marcos made a phone call to Poppy as soon as he was

settled in his hotel. He wanted to finish the job and get back to Bridgette and Stockholm as soon as possible. He didn't like being in Paris so soon after a job and the last one was only a month ago.

Unknown to Marcos, Poppy received a message from his informant in the police station regarding a dragnet posted two hours ago with all the police stations throughout Paris. A picture accompanied the bulletin describing the suspect and his possible connection with the stun gun murder of a bodyguard in a Paris nightclub. Also included was the account of the two murders in Stockholm, which were also connected to the same model of Taser gun used in the Paris killing.

"Marcos, thank you for calling. I have some bad news for you," Poppy said. "Your life in Paris and Stockholm may be over."

"What do you mean over. I just got here."

"From what my informant tells me, you might have escaped Stockholm hours before you were to be arrested for killing two men in that city with a stun gun. Your picture is in all the police stations here in Paris and you may only have hours before the hotels will have your photo."

"How in the hell did this happen? I have my apartment and girlfriend in Stockholm. Now you're telling me I can't go back."

"I'm telling you to get out of France right now. I'm still getting information from my informant and should know more tomorrow. All I know so far is a couple of Americans have been working on the case and may have been the ones who found out who you are when they went to Stockholm last week."

"This can't be happening, Poppy. What am I going to do?"

"Right now you need to leave your hotel. Don't check out at the front desk. Just leave. Catch a taxi and pay the driver to take you to the next city. I suggest you head west to Le Havre where you can catch a ferry to England. You're English so you'd blend in. I'll call you when I have more information. Do it now and we'll talk later," Poppy said. He then hung up.

Marcos was in shock. He trusted Poppy and the information he received from the informant and now his life in Sweden was over. Someone was going to pay for this, Marcos thought.

Marcos didn't even have time to unpack his suitcase. He grabbed it and headed down the stairs, avoiding the elevators and front desk. He found an emergency exit to an alley and walked to the main street where he hailed a taxi.

"I have an emergency meeting in England and can't get a flight in time," he told the driver. "How much would it cost if you drove me to Le Havre?"

"That is almost 200 km *messier*. I would have to charge you half the distance back as well."

"It doesn't matter. Can you do it?"

"Of course. I just have to radio into the office and let them know I'm out of Paris for a few hours."

"Fine, let's get on the road and phone them on the way. I'm in a real hurry."

Marcos threw his bag in the back seat. The driver drove past the hotel and maneuvered the roads leading to the A13 and the *Autoroute de Normandie*. As soon as the driver was on a street where he didn't have to dodge traffic, he called in his destination and estimated time he'd be back in the city. The dispatcher took down the information.

"When you're near the city on your return let me know," the dispatcher said. "I may have a fare coming into Paris."

"I'll call after I drop off," answered the driver.

Marcos gave a sigh of relief. He didn't have to give any personal information to the driver. He reached over and handed him a 500 Euro note to put him at ease. He knew the fare would be twice that but right now he felt he'd dodged a bullet. Poppy would call him with more information when he was safe in England. He needed to find out who did this to him. His life was completely ruined and he'd never see Sweden or Bridgette again.

*****

The second day back in Paris a call from *Capitaine* Le Cure came through to Robert and Julia.

"We might have missed Marcos," he told Robert. "We sent his picture around to different hotels and we got a hit on one. Hotel Moliere is a five-star hotel and they said Marcos stays there when he's in Paris. He checked in two days ago and then disappeared. He wasn't in his room and nothing in the hotel was used. We think someone tipped him off and he got away."

"Did his picture make it to the bus, train and plane stations? Robert asked.

"Yes, and we found the cab driver who picked him up at his hotel and drove him to Le Havre. We think he took a ferry to England. Right now he's gone."

"Who could have tipped him off? It had to be someone with access to the police notices. Has this happened to you before?"

"Since we sent the information to all the stations throughout Paris, it could have been from any of the locations."

"You could have an informer working for the police,"

Robert said. "Every country has one or two bad apples within their ranks. I think Julia and I have taken this investigation as far as we can. With Marcos getting away both times is somewhere in England, it's now out of our hands. We may stay another day to see more sights and head back to New Mexico on Saturday."

"I understand. You have done the police in Paris and Stockholm a great service. We may not have caught our man, but we know who he is and what he looks like. We'll make sure the English police have a picture of Marcos and have them try and track him down."

"I do know a trick you can try," Robert said. "If you want to find the informer within the ranks of the police, send out misinformation and isolate the news. I have a feeling Marcos was working with someone in Paris who set up the kidnapping. The informer might have fed the boss the information the police obtained and gave him the heads up."

"What do you suggest?" Le Cure asked.

"The note to the stations said two American investigators were the ones who found Marcos, right? What about adding different names for us and include the same address in New Mexico. I know a place where I can set up cameras and see if Marcos attempts to come after us. My feeling is the man has anger issues and will attempt to take out those who ruined his life in Stockholm. He lost his girlfriend and a safe place to live because of us. That would be enough to put him over the edge."

"What about our mole in the police force. Can we use this false information to capture the mole?"

"Make sure to use different names for us and send them out to each station. Tell them it is top secret and not communicate with other police. Each name will represent a different station. If we capture Marcos I have my methods to make him talk."

"I thought your country outlawed water boarding?"

"Who said anything about waterboarding?" Robert asked.

"What then?"

"I'd rather tell you after we capture Marcos. Because I'm a private investigator I can use other ways of finding things out. When we get home I'll send you the address after we set the trap. If Marcos shows, and we capture him, I'll find out what he knows and then send him back to you. He's all yours."

"You have an interesting approach to law enforcement, Mr. Forrester. I'll be expecting your email, and get this notice out as fast as we can. This crazy idea just might work."

"A lot depends on Marcos. If he's as angry as I think he is and comes after us, then we have a chance. If he decides to remain hidden then we've got nothing," Robert said.

"Have a good flight and let's keep in touch after the case. This has been a good experience working on an international case with an American. Just tell your government not to try and change the name French Fries into American Fries again. That is our food and we were right about Iraq as well."

"I have no argument with you on that one. I don't agree with what the US government does around the world in many areas. My focus is to catch the bad guys. If my government wants to make blunders and fall on their face then so be it. I try and stay neutral and go about my business."

Robert closed his phone and turned to Julia. What do you want to do on our last night? I suggest dinner on the Eifel Tower again and a walk around the Moulin Rouge."

"I've been here before Robert and you haven't, so that sounds fine with me. I'll call Peggy and let her know we're heading home. You jump in the shower first and I'll join you in a minute."

"Fine with me. I think we've had a great experience working with Le Cure but I'm ready to be home."

The evening proceeded as planned. Robert booked for two on the tower and the couple took a walk in the

Moulin Rouge district after their last dinner in Paris .

The flight the next morning placed the investigators in New York around 1 p.m. and the connecting flight to Albuquerque landed them at 5:30 p.m. Their car was waiting in long-term parking and the 30-minute drive placed them home by dinner. Chinese pickup and a couple of glasses of wine helped them sleep while they adjusted to jet lag and the time difference.

*****

Poppy received a phone call from his police informant three days after Marcos made his escape from France.

"What did you find out?" Poppy asked. "Is the information how they discovered Marcos available."

"There's a memo I received telling my *Sergent* all about the private investigators from New Mexico who traced Marcos in Stockholm. It seems they are a married team who went there to investigate the two murders in Stockholm."

"What do two murders in Stockholm have to do with Marcos?"

"Both victims were killed with a Taser gun. The marks on the bodies matched the marks on the bodyguard in Paris that died in the kidnap case. These investigators found a second case involving a stun gun and again matched the burn marks on the victims. The Stockholm police didn't tie the two cases together but these two investigators did. They came up with an eyewitness, a car, and license plate. Everything led to Marcos."

"You mean the police were coming after Marcos at the same time I asked him to return to Paris for another job?"

"The report says the police missed him by a few hours. The surveillance cameras at the airport gave the police the taxi company that picked Marcos up. From there they were able to trace him to his hotel. Your warning him to leave France was not more than an hour ahead of my office making an arrest."

"Do we have names of the Americans involved? I'm sure Marcos would like to know the people who ruined his life in Sweden. From what I understand he was planning on retiring there."

"Not only does the report include their names, it also includes the city where they came from. Albuquerque, New Mexico."

"Is that usual? I mean why would they include the city as well as their name?" Poppy asked.

"It's just a part of the report. It seems the police in Albuquerque worked with the Paris police on one case and then sent these investigators to help get their man in Paris. The person was a kidnapper and flew here from Canada. The police here were able to catch him through the city-wide rental agency."

"The what?"

"Paris has a central agency that tells the police who rented a building or apartment. In this case, it was fairly easy because he was an American. With the picture of the man, he was captured within a few days after these investigators showed up."

"Well, that was convenient. How did they get involved in the Marcos case?"

"From what I could get from my *Sergent* it was a favor. They were sent to Stockholm because of a murder case happened there recently and it had to do with a stun gun."

"Why send these two and not the Paris police?"

"*Capitaine* Le Cure wanted someone undercover. He also thought they would do a better job because murder cases in Stockholm are not that common. The police don't have the same skill as American police do. There are many more killing in America than in Sweden."

"That makes sense. Does the evidence ties Marcos to the killings?"

"The police think so. His girlfriend was questioned, and it turns out one of the victims harassed her because of a fur coat she was wearing. Something about eating dinner and her wearing a coat made of animal skins. Marcos was with her. The man was found dead the next morning with another man, in an alley about five blocks from the restaurant. The girlfriend told the police Marcos had her drive home alone. He had to finish up some business. He arrived home several hours later."

"How do they know Marcos killed the men?"

"All the burn marks from the stun gun matched. There were two murders in Stockholm, the murder here in Paris and the attack on a tourist cruise ship months ago in Stockholm. The cruise attack was the only place where a positive ID was made. Nobody saw who killed the bodyguard in Paris, but one of the waitresses at the nightclub identified Marcos from a picture a couple of days ago. He was there at the club, so any court would put him away if he ever went to trial."

"*Merde!*" Poppy said. "I had no idea Marcos had made so many mistakes in Stockholm. That's why my people don't use guns."

"Marcos is no longer a good asset on your team, Poppy. He's a liability now. If they ever catch him, he may lead back to you."

"Your right. I may have to tie up some loose ends. It's too bad because he was dependable."

"Whatever you do, Poppy, get it done right away. I'm sure there's an arrest warrant out for Marcos in England. If they catch him, there's no telling what he'll do to save his own ass."

*****

Marcos checked into a modest hotel near the East end of London. He knew he might be spotted in a five-star hotel because of the security cameras. The cheaper hotels did not have heavy security. By now he'd made some changes to his appearance. He shaved his head and found a skin dye to make him look like a Jamaican with without the dreadlocks. Dark glasses and a baseball cap with the picture of Bob Marley on the front completed the makeover.

His phone rang and Marcos saw that the call was from Poppy. "Where have you been?" he asked. "I'm so far underground even I don't recognize myself in the mirror."

"You are in a lot of shit, my friend," Poppy replied. "It seems the Swedish police, with the help of some American investigators, found out who you are from the two pranks you pulled in Stockholm. That television star and her boyfriend have a reward out for you, and the Taser gun you used matches their wounds as well as the two bodies found in an ally several weeks ago. How come you never told me about any of this?" Poppy was angry but kept it in check for now.

Marcos was silent. He was going over in his mind how the two deaths were connected to him. "How did the woman at the ship identify me? I left right away and went to Paris. I never saw any names connected to that incident in the Stockholm papers."

"It seems the two Americans, working for the Paris police, found an eyewitness in their follow-up. The woman, who identified you, saw you get into your car and drive away. They police traced you through your license plate. You left Stockholm hours before they came to your apartment to arrest you."

"Now what?" Marcos asked. "I'm fucked. I'll need to get another passport and get out of England as well."

"Probably. Let me get a passport made and send a man to you. Wherever you go, let me know. Maybe I can get you some work in another country."

"First get me the passport. Did you get the names of the investigators from the States?"

"Their names and the city where they came from was in the report. They are a married team from Albuquerque. A Mr. and Mrs. Blackwood. That was all they had in the report. No address, just the city.

"I think my first country to visit is going to the United States. I have some business to take care of over there. I'll send you a photo of me from my phone. I've changed my appearance and the passport needs to show what I look like now."

"Give me two days to get this done, Marcos. Tell me where you are so my man can deliver the passport personally. After you take care of your business in the States, let me know where you're headed. We may branch out to some other countries."

"Just get your man here soon. I'll send the photo in ten minutes. I can only do one thing at a time, Poppy. Call me when you man is on his way."

"Keep your head down, Marcos. The English police have your photo so don't hang out where there are any cameras." Poppy did not want Marcos arrested or he might be indicated as well.

Poppy hung up. He was sorry he had to have Marcos killed. He decided to go ahead and have the passport made in case something went wrong. Marcos was usually a careful man to work with but when he got mad there was no telling what he would do.

Chapter 22

Robert set the trap. He sent his list of fake names to *Capitaine* Le Cure three days earlier. Each police station in Paris would have a different name for the two American detectives. Whoever showed up in Albuquerque looking for Brown, White, or Blackwood would tell Le Cure which station contained the mole. An investigation into each officer working at that station would expose the informant.

"Laura, hi, it's Robert."

"Robert, hi. Jeff and I haven't heard a word from you since the Cathy kidnapping. We read both men have been captured and the second man got all the way to Paris. Did you have anything to do with that?"

"Julia and I are working with the local police but only with a few of them. We're undercover and only use Julia to talk to them. We got lucky with the second man and the Paris police were cooperative. We now have a new international case and I need your help."

Laura and her fiancé, Jeff, lived in Albuquerque. She used to work for Robert when she resided in New York and played a huge part in taking down Ian McClure and the Company.

"You need me to do what?" Laura asked. She was a wedding photographer and did private work on occasion for Robert.

"Actually I've set a trap and need a residence to draw the person in. I'll understand if you don't want to get involved so let me know and I'll find someone else."

"Are you kidding me? You practically bought this house for us. What do you need, and I'll run it past Jeff when he gets home." Laura was referring to the cash amount Robert rewarded Laura for helping him solve the Ian case.

"We have a possible suspect who may come to the States looking for Julia and me. All we have is his picture, and we believe he's English.

"What'd he do and does he have a picture of you. Jeff looks nothing like you and I'm not even close to Julia. What if he cases the house first and sees us. What then?"

"He only has a name and no pictures of us. Also, he has no idea we are setting him up. We plan to surround your house with security cameras and watch you like a baby in a crib. If he shows up we'll know before he knocks on the door."

"Is he dangerous. I mean does he want to kill you or something like that?"

"He may not even show up. His last place of residence was Sweden and he escaped to England a week ago. We have his picture so we'll know if he's around."

"You didn't answer my question, Robert. Does he

want to kill you?"

"I can't answer that. I can assure you he's not happy that we caused him to lose his home and girlfriend in Sweden."

"I'm not too excited about a possible killer showing up on my doorstep. Don't you have another way to get this guy?"

"You're right Laura. I don't even know if he will show up. It wouldn't be right to put you in danger."

"Hold on, Robert. Don't give up on us yet. Let me run this by Jeff. Is he known to carry a gun?"

"Not a bullet gun. He's a stun gun nut case. He zaps his victims."

"Oh, really! He zaps people. Does he get a charge out of that?" Laura laughed.

"You haven't lost your sense of humor have you, Laura? Run it past Jeff and see what he says. We're working with the local police on this so my belief is we can get this guy before he shows up at your door."

"I'll talk to Jeff tonight. If he is agreeable, I'll leave town for a while, and take a vacation while you take this mad zapper down."

"That's all I ask. I'll make sure the security systems are up and running and we'll have a squad car available just down the street."

"Call me tonight, Robert. I'll know by then if Jeff is as nuts as you are."

"Probably not but who knows. Maybe that's the reason you're attracted to him."

"You're cute, Robert. Call me tonight. Our love to Julia, the sane one in your life."

"Thanks for considering my plan, Laura. I'll talk to you later."

Robert turned to Julia. "We're going to have to wait for Jeff to give his okay on this. Laura said she'll talk to him tonight and then we'll know if they're a go."

"Robert, I completely understand why she's not interested in this. That's her home. Some crazy zapper showing up on her doorstep just might be a little more than she can handle. I know I would tell you to go screw yourself."

"When you put it that way I get it. At the same time, I'm confident we can set up enough security to make them safe. I guess it will come down to how Jeff feels. She wants me to call back tonight to see if it's a go."

"Don't be surprised if they say no. I know I would."

"We better come up with a second plan. No way can we ask Alan or Cathy. They live too close to us and she's still traumatized from that last ordeal."

"Plus the fact that a couple of investigators couldn't afford a house like theirs. They already have so much security around that place our suspect wouldn't even attempt to get to the front door."

"Anyway, I'll call Laura and Jeff tonight."

"Fine with me. I'll help Carla with dinner. It's Mexican night and she likes me to grade cheese and cut up peppers. Do we have Negra Modella in the refrigerator? If not, I better get a few bottles from the pantry and cool them off."

"We need more from the pantry. Thanks, Sweetheart."

Robert had no idea if Jeff would be interested in using his home as bait. He'd have to wait and see if the wild side of this real estate finance boyfriend of Laura's kicked in. Robert still held out hope.

*****

"Marcos, the passport is on the way to you. When is a good time for my man to meet you?" Poppy asked.

"Is he in London now?"

"Yes, he can be at your place in an hour. Will that work?"

"No, I rather meet in a public place and he can give it

to me then," Marcos said.

Merde, thought Poppy. His man couldn't take out Marcos in a public place. He might have to follow Marcos back to his apartment and kill him there.

"All right. Give me an address and he'll be there in an hour."

Marcos gave Poppy the name of a fish and chips restaurant in his neighborhood. He said he'd be wearing a black French Barrette and dark glasses.

"Have your man bring the passport wrapped in a newspaper. He can slip me the paper, say goodbye, and be on his way. We don't need to have a conversation."

"All right, Marcos. As you wish." Poppy could tell Marcos had his guard up, and taking him out might not be as easy as he thought.

Marcos closed his cell phone and put it in his pocket. He also put his Taser gun in the other pocket. He didn't want to meet some stranger without protection, even if the man was sent by Poppy. He took no chances.

An hour later Marcos sat at an outside table eating a plate of fish and chips. His back was to the wall of the restaurant, making sure no one could sneak up behind him. A man came into view, with a newspaper under his arm, and approached Marcos.

"Masseur Marcos, I assume," the stranger said.

"You assume right. Sit down." Marcos eyed the man carefully.

"Poppy wanted me to make sure it was you. What do you want me to do? Hand you the newspaper and walk away?"

"That works for me," Marcos said. He saw no reason for small talk, especially with someone he didn't know.

"Very well, *Masseur* Marcos," the man said. He slipped the newspaper out from under his arm and laid it on the table. After that, he stood up and walked away.

Marcos didn't take his eyes off the man until he was a block away. He trusted no one at this time. He knew the police in three countries were looking for him and he needed to get out of England as soon as possible. He opened the newspaper and there it was. His new name was Alex Bloom from Sussex and he was listed as an owner of a pawn shop in the town of Tambridge Wells.

Where in the hell did Poppy come up with that occupation, Marcos thought? The picture was the exact one he sent to Poppy a few days before and everything else looked official. Poppy definitely had connections.

Marcos finished his fish and chips and drank the last of his beer. After paying the tab he placed the passport in his pocket and left the newspaper on the table. He then started to walk towards his apartment where his packed bags were waiting for him.

After two blocks he took a turn into an alley and waited behind a large trash container. He had the feeling he was being followed. He was usually right about his feeling when he was in survival mode. Three minutes later someone turned into the ally and picked up their pace after making the turn. When the person approached the container, Marcos made his move. Before the man could reach into his pocket for the gun he was carrying, Marcos gave him the maximum voltage shot into the neck and the stranger fell to the ground.

I knew something was up, thought Marcos when he saw it was the same bastard Poppy sent with the passport. Poppy wants me dead. I must be a liability to him. That was a big mistake, Poppy. After I'm done in New Mexico I'm coming after you.

Marcos didn't hesitate with his next move. He had to make it quick. The full voltage to the heart area stopped the life force in the man's body. Marcos made sure he didn't touch anything on the man and continued down the alley. He had to catch a flight within the hour before the police started looking for him at the airports. He had a new identity, and the makeover would get him through customs but be still couldn't wait around. Flights were leaving to New York constantly and he needed to be on the next available one.

*****

"Robert, I'm engaged to a crazy man," Laura said. "He loves your idea and wants to be a part of your investigation. I guess he felt left out with the Ian case and now he wants to make up for it."

Laura responded to Robert's return call and at the same time made plans to see her mother in New York. She didn't want any part of the 'house used as bait' plan and decided it was a good time to go home for a while.

"Laura, this is great. I'll get a crew out there tomorrow morning to put up the cameras and home security items. Tell Jeff I'm pleased he's on board with this. It's still a shot in the dark but at least a trap is set if he does show up."

"Robert, I appreciate all that you have done for us but I'm letting Jeff handle this on his own. I'll be at my mother's house for a week or longer. I never knew Jeff had this 'living dangerously' side to him. I don't know if I'm attracted to it or just had enough of the drama after the Ian case."

"Go and visit your mother, Laura. Tell Jeff about the security men coming, and give me his cell phone. I'll call him tomorrow after everything is set up and give him instructions. Thank you again for letting me use your home. After a few week, if nothing happens, at least you'll have a good security system in place."

"Yes, and if you take my mild mannered boyfriend, and turn him into a loony investigator just like you, what then. I may have to get some coping advice from Julia."

"Laura, I'm not that bad, am I?" Robert asked.

"Yes, you are, and I still love you. I just don't want Jeff to think that this is the lifestyle for him. I love the simple work he does and the fact that he comes home every night to me."

"Laura, I'm in your debt. Give Jeff the info and I'll call tomorrow."

Robert hung up and turned to Julia. "It's a go. Jeff wants to try living on the wild side, while Laura is going to visit her mother in New York."

"If anything happens to Jeff, she might not come back from New York." Julia said. "I know the Ian case took its toll on her. Believing you were dead, and thinking it was her fault, put her over the edge. I still think she's still recovering from that."

"We'll make sure Jeff gets through this. The cameras go up tomorrow and we'll monitor their house from here. I need to have you call detective Louis and tell him we may need backup. He knows nothing about this Marcos character and we can't keep Louis in the dark."

"I'll do that in the morning as well. Should we tell Louis he and his partner will get the credit if we capture the Stun Gun Killer?"

"Of course. You don't think we should be in the photos if he's captured. Using the police removes us from having to deal with weapons and gives us any inside information we may need in future cases. This is a win-win working with the local police."

*****

"Detective Louis, this is your partner in crime fighting. We have another case," Julia said.

"You what? You just got back from Europe and now you have another case? Don't you ever sleep?"

"Yes, I do, but the cases are connected. I went to France to capture our local kidnapper and in return, I'm in the middle of helping the French police find a person who also is wanted for kidnapping and murder. Let me tell you the whole story."

For the next ten minutes, Julia relayed the story of tracing the Stun Gun Killer in France to two murders and two assaults in Stockholm. All the details were included as well as the girlfriend's testimony, positive ID and the near capture of Marcos.

"The Swedish police missed him by several hours and the French police were late as well. The suspect is believed to be somewhere in England and could be heading our way."

"What do you mean heading our way? Is he after

you?" Louis asked.

"There is a possibility. There is a mole in the Paris police feeding him information so we're attempting to capture him and the mole at the same time."

"How are you going to do that?" Louis asked.

"False information was fed to all the police stations regarding my name. If and when we capture this guy, all we have to find out is the name of the person he was looking for. I used different names, one for each police station. Once we have the right station, all the French cops have to do is conduct an internal affairs probe and get their man."

"That is genius. How did you come up with that idea?" Louis asked.

"Can I call you Louis? We don't need to be so formal anymore." Julia said.

"Fine. What should I call you?"

"Julia works. Anyway I have a small team, and we put together a plan of action. As long as we remain undercover we can do our job."

"What's the plan right now. How is this Marcos person going to find you?" Louis asked.

"We've hired a person who is letting us use his address. All the names lead to the same address. We put the names in the directory yesterday. Also, we have the house covered in surveillance cameras and alarm systems. This person is at work during the day so if anyone shows up, and is caught on camera, we need to call a squad car and get someone there right away."

"What's the address? I can make sure we have a car within two blocks of the house at all times."

Julia gave Lewis the address.

"Will this capture go down as an international case like the last one? Louis asked. "My boss had to get another hat size for his dress uniform when he posed for the pictures. He's gone all Hollywood on us."

"What a perfect working relationship, don't you think?" Julia said. "My team lines them up and you bring them in. We don't have weapons so any rough stuff has to be handled by you."

"Perfect. Give me the address and I set it up on my end." Louis was ready to help

"1654 Rancho Road. It's in one of the new suburbs on the east side."

"I know the area. My girlfriend and looked for a place in a development there. Having two separate apartments makes no sense to us."

"Good for you, Louis. I'd ask who she is, but it's none

of my business."

"If we ever meet, Julia, look for the cute blond officer who is usually near me when we work. She and I are the only ones who know about you so we shouldn't have any secrets. Her name is June Parsons."

"I hope this relationship keeps working for a long time, Louis. You set up the car and I'll have you on speed dial. If this guy shows up, all I ask is for me to get the name of the person he was looking for. That tells us which police station the mole is working at."

"You got it, Julia. We'll talk later."

*****

Marcos landed in New York after the long overnight flight. He had no weapon with him and ditched his Taser gun in an alley in London, behind some loose bricks in a wall. Every safe deposit box or locker storage unit in England had security cameras. If he ever returned to England he'd retrieve the weapon. The gun had been with him for many years and he even gave it a name; Tess. The weapon reminded him of an old girlfriend who had a wacko personality and swore at him all the time.

Getting another stun gun was the first item on his list. Marcos felt naked without a weapon in his pocket. Tess saved him from many tight situations and now he was in one of the most crime-infested cities in the world. The only difference was, he shocked people, while everyone else shot them.

A gun store on Broadway had what Marcos needed. Because Marcos wanted a Taser C2 and not a gun. It was easier to obtain.

"Most people get guns in this city," the owner said. He really wanted to sell Marcos a pistol because the profit was much higher than a Taser C2. "Are you sure this is what you want?"

"Yes, I don't like guns. They're too noisy and heavy. I know the Taser model well and I feel safe with it in my pocket."

"Well, you're lucky we have a few in the store. Mostly older women buy them and carry them in their purse." The owner tried to embarrass Marcos into changing his mind. "Real men carry guns."

"How much do I owe you?" Marcos said without taking the bait and getting mad. At the same time, he thought he should give the owner a jolt of 50,000 volts and see how manly he felt after that.

"You got the Taser C2 platinum for $550 and the four pack cartridges for $155. $705 should cover it. Just be careful with the settings on the platinum model. The top voltage could take down a horse so be careful what you keep the setting at."

"Thank you for your help." Marcos walked out of the store and for the first time since he landed in New York he felt safe. Instead of flying to Albuquerque he decided to take the Amtrak train and avoid the tight security checks at the airport. It would also give him time to plan out his attack on the investigators who destroyed his life in Sweden.

*****

"Poppy, I just found out what happened to the man you sent to take care of Marcos." Bernard was the French police officer who worked at one of the precincts in Paris. Passing on information to Poppy enabled him to live well with a second paycheck.

"What do you mean happened? Is he all right?"

"Not anymore. The London police found his body this morning in an alley. Because he had a Paris address with his driver's license, the police called the main headquarters and this notice arrived at all the stations. It has his picture from the license and what he looked like when they found him. The cause of death is a stun gun. Marks on his neck and chest area."

"Merde. Merde, merde, merde," Poppy repeated. "This is not good news. Any sign of Marcos."

"Not at all," Bernard said. "Who ever did this must have caught your man off guard. There was no sign of struggle and no witnesses."

"If Marcos killed him after he got the passport, then Marcos is free to fly out of England. He looks different from the picture posted with the local police. I don't dare try to get in contact with Marcos. Now he knows I sent someone to kill him. I have to get Marcos before he comes after me."

"Poppy, I have an idea," Bernard said. "Why don't we send the picture of Marcos and his new passport name to the investigators in Albuquerque? Let them capture him. Then you're in the clear."

"Better yet, let's send it to *Capitaine* Le Cure who's handling the case in Paris. I know him and he's a pretty tough officer. Let him get the message to the people in the States. At least then we can be sure the information will get to the investigators in New Mexico."

"I'll e-mail you the address of Le Cure's precinct, and you can send it today. Marcos has two days head start on us. If he's going to kill the investigators he may be in New Mexico already," Bernard said.

"Send it right away and I'll have a currier drop off a package with the information to Le Cure this afternoon. Good work Bernard. Let me know if anything else turns up."

*****

The package arrived on *Capitaine* Le Cure's desk around 4 p.m. He opened it and read the letter accompanying the contents.

"*Sergent,* give me the Forrester phone number. Something just came up and I have to talk to one of them right away."

"I'll make the call and transfer it to your desk," *Sergent* Bruno said.

Five minutes passed before the call went through.

"Hello, is this Mrs. Forrester," *Capitaine* Le Cure said in French.

"Oui," answered Julia. "This must be *Capitaine* Le Cure."

"Yes, it is. I have some news."

"I figured you did. It's still quiet here but the trap is set."

"I received a package from an unknown source giving me a picture of what Marcos looks like now," Le Cure said. "It's different than the photo you have. I'll send it to you. Also, a letter accompanying the picture says he is traveling under the name Alex Bloom from Tambridge Wells, England. Whoever sent this to me seems to want Marcos captured. We believe it has something to do with the death of a man in London a few days ago. The Frenchman was found in an ally with stun gun burns on his neck and chest areas. The markings match the Taser C2 that Marcos uses."

"Does the victim have any connection with Marcos at all?" Julia asked.

"None so far. It seems the person is a known gun for hire and has served time in French jails for petty thief a while back. I'm sending this information on to the London police. I'll them if they have any record of Alex Bloom flying out of the country. I think he may be heading your way."

"Let me know if they find out anything in London. We're ready for him if he shows up."

"Have you contacted detective Louis?" Le Cure asked. "He may want to get involved. It's always good to have backup."

"I'm using him as well. Thanks, *Capitaine*. When we capture Marco we'll let you know right away and send him back to you. As long as he doesn't kill anyone in the States, you can have him. There might be a fight for him between three countries now but you should have first crack at him."

"Thank you, Mrs. Forrester. Whoever sent this gun for hire wanted Marcos dead. If we try to take Marcos alive, maybe we can get him to turn on whoever tried to kill him."

"Will do, *Capitaine*. Call as soon as you get more information." Julia hung up.

She turned to look at Robert. "We have to be ready. Marcos could be in Albuquerque right now. That was Le Cure with another murder to report. He's sending us a current picture of Marcos right now."

"Marcos killed someone else? He seems to get a charge out of killing people."

"Was that a joke, Robert?" Julia asked.

"Yea, but it didn't go over well. Let's call Jeff and Louis and tell them Marcos could show up at any time. First, we need to wait for the recent picture of him and then send that as well."

"At least Laura is gone. Jeff doesn't get home until after six so we have a few hours to wait. Le Cure wants us to take Marcos alive. We don't use guns so we better tell Louis to take Marcos down physically and not shoot him. Le Cure thinks the man Marcos worked for in Paris might have sent the picture of Marcos. He's probably trying to tie up loose ends."

"But if we capture Marcos alive he might turn on his Paris connection. This gives us more reason to have Marcos cough up some names."

"Maybe the person who gave up Marcos thinks we'll kill him. The police in America are getting a reputation for shooting first and then asking questions."

"I thought that had something to do with the color of their skin. Just let Louis know we need to get Marcos alive. He has information that could help take down a mole in Paris and maybe a kidnapping ring."

*****

Marcos arrived in Albuquerque and checked into a bed and breakfast near the college. He hoped there'd be no security cameras at a small family run business. The campus library was only a few blocks away and a computer there gave him access to Google maps and the address on Rancho Rd. He had what he needed for now.

"Take me to 1654 Rancho Road please," Marcos told the taxi driver.

"Yes sir," the driver answered.

Fifteen minutes later the green Prius cab was on Rancho Road and approaching the 1600 block.

"Just drive by slowly, please. I'm not sure if my friend is home so I may have to come back."

The taxi drove by the all stone, single story home at 1654. The garage door was closed and no cars were parked out front.

"I don't think they're home," Marcos said. "Take me back to the restaurant, where you picked me up, and I'll call tonight."

Marcos could see that the home was easy to walk up to. No gates or barriers to interfere. He thought his best bet was to come back in the evening when both occupants would be home and take care of business then.

*****

"Robert, I just noticed a taxi driving by the house on the monitor. No one got out, but it seemed to be checking out our target."

"Good work, Peggy. Could you get a license plate?"

"It was one of those green cabs. WTF 674."

"Maybe we can find out who was in that taxi," Robert said. "I'll have Julia call Louis and have him put a trace on the cab. If we can find out where the person was dropped off, and match the picture to the passenger, we can take this killer down before he goes after Jeff."

"Good idea, Robert. What can I do?"

"Keep an eye on the cameras. He may come back and we can't let this thug get a jump on us. I'll call Jeff and have him check into a hotel."

Peggy turned around and continued to view the monitor. She could stay for a few more hours before she had to get home. Robert would take over when she was gone.

Robert placed a call to Jeff. "Hey, Mr. Secret agent, this is Robert. We think the Zapper's in town and just drove by your house in a cab. You should stay in a hotel tonight just to be safe."

"What! I wanted to get in on the action. Don't you think the Stun Gun Killer might think something's not right if I don't show up?"

"Maybe, but if anything happened it could take a few minutes before a squad car arrived."

"How about a policewoman posing as Laura?" Jeff said. "I could pick her up and we'd arrive together just like a couple. If he was casing the house, he'd think we were just arriving home and nothing suspicious would stand out."

"At least she'd have a gun and could take him out. I'll have Julia call detective Louis and see if we can set this up."

"Get back to me right away," Jeff said. He was getting excited. "I'll drive by the police station and pick up whoever they send. I'll bet this guy will make his move tonight."

"I'll call you right back, Jeff."

Robert called home. "Julia, can you call detective Louis again. We need a plain-clothed woman officer to go home with Jeff. Be sure she has a gun with her. Marcos might make his move tonight."

"I just got off the phone with him and he's putting a call into the cab company and emailing the picture of Marcos to the driver. Maybe he has an answer by now."

"Things are speeding up and feeling a bit manic," Robert added. "It's crunch time and we need to be ready."

Julia made the call. "Louis, Julia again."

"Julia, I just got off the phone with the driver of that cab. It's the same guy. He must have cased the house."

"We just talked to the occupant of the house," Julia said. "His name is Jeff. He wants to swing by your station, pick up a plain-clothed woman officer and bring her home posing as his girlfriend. She needs to have a gun in case things get out of hand. We're almost sure he'll make his move tonight."

"I think so too," said Louis. "I have just the person. Officer Parsons will be ready so have Jeff swing by and she'll fill in. We're the lead on this case so she knows all about the killer. She'll blow him out of the water if it comes to that."

"Remember, we need to take him alive. He has information about a couple of bad men in Paris and Le

Cure needs that. Also, we need ten minutes with Marcos alone after he's captured. Officer Parsons should leave the room so she won't get into trouble but it's the only way we can get him to talk."

"What are you going to do? Slap him around?" Louis asked.

"No, that's illegal. The less you know the better. Just give me ten minutes with him and then he is all yours. He'll talk and we won't hurt him in any way."

"All right, but you need to be near the house to take over. After June captures him, she'll need to phone in the arrest. After that, the house will be swarming with officers. Get in and get out because my boss can't know you have anything to do with this."

"No problem. I'll be waiting in a car a block away. Have Parsons call me as soon as there's an arrest. I'll come in, get what I need and leave before a squad car arrives," Julia said.

"Deal. This just might work."

Julia hung up and Robert called Jeff. "Pick up the woman officer at the downtown station. 800 Louisiana Blvd. Officer Parsons will be in street clothes and packing a gun. She knows all about the case so you don't have to explain anything to her."

"Will do. Ten-four," Jeff said.

Robert rolled his eyes. "You're really getting into this aren't you, Jeff?"

"Are you kidding? Nothing exciting happens in a real estate office. This is the most exciting thing I've ever done. I can now see why Laura liked working for you."

"This is not an everyday occurrence, Jeff. There is a lot of waiting involved when investigation things. Stick to real estate because the money is steady."

"Maybe, but if Laura ever is called you for another job, I'm going along just to carry her tripod. My juices are flowing and I'll need a beer to calm down."

"You do that, Jeff. If we're going to fool this Stun Gun Killer you need to let officer Parsons do her job. Don't get in her way at all."

"I'll answer the door and let her do the rest," Jeff said.

"Pick her up in an hour and act normal. Park in the garage and turn on the porch light so this guy knows you're home. Turn on the TV as well. Good luck. Julia will be a block away and needs ten minutes with him alone after the takedown. After she gone, the police will arrive, but don't let anyone know Julia was there. The woman officer knows all about Julia."

"This is so fucking cool," Jeff said. "I'll pick up Officer Parsons in an hour. I have no idea why Laura wanted to miss this much fun."

"Be careful, Jeff. We don't know what Marcos is capable of and he may act quickly."

"Ten-four, Robert. Over and out."

Robert rolled his eyes again. Another citizen who watches too many cop shows on television, he thought. I hope Jeff doesn't get hurt.

*****

Marcos walked back to his room at the Bed and Breakfast and packed his bags. He decided to make the hit tonight and get out of town right away. The Taser C2 was charged and ready for action. He needed to act fast.

A city bus stop was two blocks from the 1654 address. Taking a bus to the house and walking for a few blocks before catching a taxi to the Greyhound station would ensure a clean get away.

The sun set in the west just as Marcos boarded the bus to the Rancho Road home. With suitcase in hand, Marcos made his way to the house he visited hours before. The lights were on and curtains partially close. The television was showing the expected weather temperatures for the next five days. Monsoon rains by 5 p.m. and 55% chance of showers.

The surveillance camera picked up Marcos as he crossed the street and walked to the front door. Peggy made a speed dial call to Julia in the car a block away.

She, in turn, made a call to officer Parson just as the doorbell rang. While June was answering the phone, Jeff answered the door.

"Hello, may I.........." he never got another word out. The Taser C2 went straight to his neck and Jeff folded like a sack of potatoes in the doorway.

"He's at the door," Julia told June as she started her car and headed towards 1654.

June came into the living room gun in hand, just as Marcos ducked into the hallway leading to the kitchen. He was looking for the woman investigator and didn't see June enter from the back room. Jeff lay in a heap at the door.

Marcos turned around at the entrance to the kitchen when he saw it was empty. Where is that bitch, he asked himself?

June came around the corner and now stood face to face with the Stun Gun Killer. Marco saw the gun but did not hesitate as he lunged at June. A shot went off from June's gun just as a jolt from the Taser grazed her. The bullet struck the fleshy part of Marcos' leg.

"You fucking cunt," he yelled. "You shot me."

June was partially stunned as the two bodies collided in the hallway. Marcos had the size and his weight knocked officer Parsons backward towards the living room. She kept her feet and managed to get a kick from her right leg, which connected to the groin area of Marcos. He fell to his knees in excruciating pain just as Julia arrived at the front door.

"Don't kill him," Julia yelled as she saw what was happening in the hallway. "We need to get some information from him before we hand him over to you."

By now June had regained her footing and had her gun leveled at Marcos. He was still on his knees holding his crouch area. His Taser gun was still in his right hand.

"Drop the gun or the next bullet empties your stomach," June said.

The stun gun fell to the floor. Julia walked over to Marcos, injecting his neck with the truth serum. She only had ten minutes to get some names before the squad car was called. She pulled him back to a kitchen and let him remained on the floor.

"You need to leave right now Officer Parsons. Here is the taser gun. I have to ask him a few questions before you get him."

June knew the drill. She turned around, went back into the living room and drug Jeff onto the couch. He was breathing and would come out of his stunned condition in a few minutes. She proceeded into the bathroom to fill a glass with water.

"We're going to make this quick, Marcos. We know who you are and what you've done. We need some names, now. Who do you work for in Paris?"

Marcos sat in a daze as the drug rapidly took over his thinking process. He relaxed into the moment and felt the answer flow from his mouth without hesitation. "Poppy ------"

"What's his address?"

"Don't know. I've never been to his house. I only call him."

"What do you do when you work for him?" Julia started the recorder after the first question. She looked at her watch and saw she had five more minutes.

"I grab rich clients and we get ransom for them," Marcos said.

"What is Poppy's telephone number?"

Marcos reached into his pocket and produced his cell phone. "I don't have it memorized. It's under Poppy."

"When do you plan on working for Poppy again?"

"Never. He tried to kill me in London. I was going back to Paris after I was done here and kill him."

Julia opened the phone and went to the frequent calls section. She wrote down the number for Poppy.

"Who were you looking for in this house?"

"Two investigators who ruined my life in Sweden. Mr. and Mrs. Blackwood."

June had all she needed from Marcos. Blackwood gave her the name of the police station in Paris where Le Cure could find the mole. She now had the phone number of the kidnapping ringleader as well.

Julia called down the hall. "Officer Parsons, can you come in here."

Jeff was waking up on the couch and would recover soon.

When June came into the kitchen with her gun in hand, Julia handed her Marcos's cell phone. "Here's his cell. I got the information I needed from him. The squad car should be here any minute. I'm going to inject him with this memory drug to erase any recollection of the conversation we just had. I don't need to be here when your fellow officers arrive." Julia injected another needle into Marcos' neck and turned to leave.

"He should come out of his stupor in another ten minutes. He may not remember much as to how he was even captured. Make it up if you need to. I have to leave." Julia turned and walked towards the front door.

"Thanks for your work on this case, Julia. Call Louis and tell him what you can. We've got it from here. I don't think Jeff remembers much. He should be fine in an hour," June added.

Julia walked out the door and got into her car. As she drove down the street the squad car was just pulling up to the house behind her. By the time the two officers entered the house, Parson had the cuffs on Marcos and was rechecking Jeff in the living rooms. She'd have a fun time writing out this report and telling Louis what really happened tonight. Maybe she'd surprise him with another special costume from some foreign country. She felt excited and sex would help her calm down.

Chapter 23

Capitaine Le Cure received the information regarding Marcos two hours after Julia returned home. The Albuquerque police were tying up the loose ends and were busy processing Marcos for transport back to France. The bullet in his leg passed through the flesh only and the wound was wrapped.

"*Sergent,*" *Capitaine* Le Cure yelled across the room. "Come in her quickly and close the door." He waited until his *Sergent* sat down. "Those American investigators did it again. They captured Marcos and we also have the precinct where our mole works. It's the one located at Place Mazas. I think I know who it is."

"Why do you say that, *Capitaine*? I've met a few officers from there and they seem to be good men."

"Yes, those who are on the street and not my concern. There is an officer who does the secretarial work. Everything that gets to the desk of Lieutenant Alain goes through his hands."

"Is that enough to arrest him on?" *Sergent* Bruno asked.

"No, we still have to do an investigation. Officer Christoph goes to the same sports club I do. I've met him two or three times, and he drives a Renault Megane RS Trophy. Do you know how much those cost?"

"No, but I'm sure you do."

"I'm a *Capitaine* and I can't afford one. How does a clerk in a police station have the income to buy such a car? My money is on Christoph. Want to make an in-office bet?"

"No, I believe you. Here's what I know," *Sergent* Bruno said. "If it's him we can get a hold of his financial records and prove he has been receiving kickbacks for passing on information. We'll then have grounds for confiscating his possessions as evidence. That includes the Renault. We sell that off and everyone in this office could get a nice Christmas check this year."

"I like the way you think, *Sergent*. Keep that thought. If he turns out to be our mole, then I'll let you do the honors and write out the bonuses in December."

"What's the first thing we have to do, *Capitaine*? Should we contact the internal affairs team and give them the evidence or conduct this investigation ourselves?"

"If we can get Lieutenant Alain to work with us we may be able to capture the mole ourselves. We'll have to interview every officer at the Place Mazas office. Let me talk to Lieutenant Alain first. The first thing I can do is look at everyone's cell phone. I have a phone number of the mastermind behind the kidnapping. If anyone has this number in their phone directory, then we have our man. I'm still betting on Christoph. He's too slick for his own good."

"You make the call, *Capitaine*, and I will start an investigation into the financial records of Christoph. If the phone number shows up, and unusual deposits have been made into his account then we may wrap this up in a week."

"Also, get a trace on this number. We may get lucky, and an address could be connected to it. All we know is that his first name is Poppy."

"I'll get right on it, *Capitaine*. There is nothing worse than an informant in the police force."

*****

Poppy decided he needed to go ahead with the grab of the billionaire's wife at the yoga studio where she went every other day. He hoped the police in the States killed Marcos because his old employee wouldn't give up without a fight. The police in America had a reputation for shooting first and asking questions later.

"Is this Paula? Poppy here."

"Poppy, it's good to hear from you. I understand you've run into some problems with Marcos recently."

"How'd you hear about that?" Poppy asked.

"In our business news travels fast. You know that."

"Marcos outlived his usefulness. Killing that incident

with the bodyguard made him a target for the Paris police. I bet you didn't know he killed two more people in Sweden and another in London. That, plus attacks on two others told me he liked killing people. He's out of control."

"Do you know where he is?" Paula asked.

"Either dead or in an American jail. I'm hoping for the first choice. We don't want any of his past actions coming back to haunt us, now do we, Paula?"

"Of course not, Poppy. I worked well with him but I had no idea he was on some kind of killing spree."

"I'm still waiting to hear some news about Marcos, but decided to go on with the grab and use someone else. Are you available?"

"I can be," Paula said. "What do you have lined up?"

"An American is in Paris and may not be here much longer. We only have a small window. Have you heard of Ralph Towers, the hotel builder?"

"No, but then again I don't read the paper much. Too much *merde* in the news."

"He's negotiating a business deal with the building commission in Paris. He wants to build another of his famous hotels in the city and a business complex as well. These are two huge construction projects. From what I've heard they're hired. He is using French contractors for all aspects of the job so the local government is pleased."

"Just give me the details, Poppy. The politics of business and government don't interest me at all," Paula said. "Are we grabbing him?"

"No, he's protected and is in meetings every day. His wife has only one bodyguard and is an avid yoga student. She's a regular at a studio called Yoga Iyengar."

"No kidding. Poppy, I know that place. I've been to a few of the sessions there. Some American woman named Anne owns it. I don't know her last name."

"Won't you be recognized?"

"No, I don't go there that often and I'll wear a wig and dark glasses on the job," she said.

"So you know the neighborhood. Good. I'll call you back after I line up another enforcer and get the exact time she gets dropped off. The best time to make the grab is before the class begins. If we try after the class, everyone is coming out at the same time. They arrive in small numbers so there are fewer people to deal with."

"Are we using the same driver as last time?"

"Yes, any problems with him?"

"No, not at all. I thought he was cute. Maybe he and I could hook up and go spend our money together after the job is done?"

"Paula, what you do with your spare time is your business. Just don't let your feeling get in the way of this job."

"You know me, Poppy. Business first, pleasure after."

"I'll call tomorrow when I have my new man lined up. You two should go over your escape route and how to get to the apartment we have lined up. The same people will be used to watch over the woman until the money is paid. I'm sending a photo of her and her yoga schedule to your phone. We need to pull this off soon before the Tower family goes back to the States."

"Okay, Poppy. Will the new guy be using a taser or a gun?"

"The man I might use is huge and only needs his bulk to get the job done. No weapon means you have to work fast before any police show up. It also means we won't have every policeman in the city looking for you."

"As long as this new guy can handle the bodyguard. I'm sure he'll have a gun so that needs to be neutralized quickly. That's the one good thing I liked about Marcos. He could drop anybody with one blast from his Taser, and be done with it."

"Marcos was good at what he did. If he hadn't killed all those people, he would be with us right now. Three countries are after him for murder."

"That is too bad. Call me tomorrow, Poppy. I'll be ready."

Poppy hung up and made a phone call to his contact at the weapons factory. Another shipment of guns was ready and another buyer turned up in another African nation wanting to overthrow the government. Poppy had already set up the deal with the rebels and this time the exchange was arranged for the French port of Marseille. Lots of illegal transactions passed through this port and it was easy to pay off guards to look the other way. Juggling two different deals at the same time was not wise, but both needed to be done soon.

"Monsieur Norman, this is Poppy. What is the exact time I need to pick up the crates?"

Oscar Norman handled all the paperwork for his company and made sure a legitimate buyer was on the other end. After the sale, he could care less where the weapons went. Revolutions around the world meant guns were always needed.

"Have your truck at the warehouse in three days. Midnight is still the best time for the exchange. The paperwork says the weapons are going to the Moroccan police. After you pick them up and sign for them, they are yours to do what you want. Just be sure to use the Moroccan stamp I sent you last week."

"My driver is doing the exchange. The cash will be in

the gym bag as usual. Until next time, *Monsieur* Norman."

"My pleasure, Poppy. Call me Oscar from now on but maybe not over the phone. Only when we meet in person. Contact me next month when you have another buyer lined up."

"Will do, Oscar. Ciao." Poppy hung up.

*****

"*Capitaine*, I think we have our informant," *Sergent* Bruno said. "That telephone number you gave me matches a number made several times a month on Christoph's phone records. We need to get this information to Lieutenant Alain and make him a part of this investigation."

"You're right, *Sergent*. The sooner we take down Christoph the sooner we can go after the person on the other end of this phone number. What time is Marcos expected to land at the airport? I would like you to be there when we take him from the Air Marshall. I'm trying to keep this out of the news and make the exchange in a private location."

"I did schedule myself to be there for the exchange. Sometime after two p.m. is what we have. We're using an ambulance to transport him to the prison hospital. He has a gunshot wound in his leg and he may walk with a limp."

"He has four murder cases against him in three different countries. Walking with a limp is the least of his worries," Le Cure said.

"*Capitaine,* getting him safely behind bars and keeping this quiet might be all we can do today. We don't want Christoph to hear about Marcos arriving in Paris, or he'll tell his boss and we might lose him."

"I'll call Lieutenant Alain and let him know what we're doing. He also needs to keep Christoph in the dark. A few phone calls are not enough to arrest him but his financial records are enough to start an investigation. We can hold Christoph for forty-eight hours while we track this information. We have to make the arrest soon. He'll eventually hear about Marcos going to prison."

"Make the call, *Capitaine*. I'll make sure we pick up Marcos without press involvement."

*****

The new man, hired by Poppy to assist Paula, met with her a block away from the yoga studio in a café.

"Dante, right?" Paula asked as she shook his hand. "Poppy said you were a man of size and you certainly fit the description."

Dante needed two chairs to sit at the small table on the front patio. He lifted weights twice a day and financed his lifestyle by providing muscle to anyone who met his price. He was not smart enough to plan any crimes on his own but he did know how to use his body size to get whatever he wanted.

"Just tell me what to do and I'll take care of it," Dante said with an Austrian accent. He didn't speak enough French to carry on a conversation so he used English to communicate with Paula.

"You are Austrian, right?" Paula asked. "You sound like the terminator."

"No jokes, please," Dante said. "I've been playing second fiddle to Arnold for too many years. Let's just focus on the job."

"Fine with me," Paula said.

"What day are we going to make the nab? Dante asked.

"Today is Friday. The yoga studio is a block away. We can watch the drop off of this woman from here and plan our escape route. We're shooting for next Monday so you need to be here at ten a.m. She arrives in ten minutes. Just look at the white sign on the left side of the street. The studio is across from that."

All of a sudden a black limo pulled up to the studio.

The door opened and a man in a dark suit escorted a woman from the car. She matched the photograph that Poppy sent to Paula.

"That's her. She's a little early today. I guess that tells us we have to be ready for her in case she is early on Monday."

Dante didn't say anything. He was studying the man who escorted Mrs. Towers from the car. Dante knew he could take the man out quickly. His problem was with the woman. Paula needed to handle her because she could run while he was occupied with the bodyguard.

"Can you manage the woman? We have to do this at the same time or she'll take off down the street if we're not careful."

"I'm going to use chloroform on her and our driver will help me get her into the car. We need to park right in front of the studio and get away in three minutes. We're lucky the street's not crowded so it should be fairly easy. The bodyguard may have a gun. Be sure and take that away from him first. We don't want anyone shooting at us as we drive away."

"No problem," Dante said. "I can see the bulge in his upper left coat pocket from here. That has to be his gun." Dante held a small telescope up to his eye as he made the observation.

"As long as you handle him, the driver and I will take care of the woman. Have a restful weekend and I'll meet you here Monday morning at nine. We should eat something first right here. I'll have the driver pull up to the studio before she arrives. When the limo shows up, we'll pretend to walk down the street together and make the grab just as she's getting out of the car. That way the bodyguard will be focused on her and you can grab him."

"Make sure she is out of the car before you try and knock her out. We don't want her driver to get involved so we need to get her into our car before he attempts to help. Two men at once could be a problem, even for me."

"Just neutralize the gun and tell the driver to get back into the limo. Dump the bodyguard in the back seat and stab the tires. Do you have a knife? I don't want a limo following us when we make our get away."

"I do. See." He reached into his pocket and pulled out a six-inch switchblade.

Dante agreed with the plan and got up to go. He had another workout at his neighborhood gym planned for noon with the focus on the legs and calves. Lots of squats and treadmill running would give him what he really lived for.

"I'll be back," he said as he winked at Paula.

Merde, she thought. Right out of the Terminator. He's

playing this Arnold thing to the hilt. Too bad he's so damn big. I'd get crushed under him if we ever hit it off.

Paula made a call to Poppy. "We're all set. Have the driver show up at 10:30 and park right in front. He'll need to help me get the woman into the back seat while Dante takes care of the bodyguard and driver. Where did you find this hulk, anyway?"

"Met him at a gay bar in Paris. There are a few of these gay bodybuilders working. Some bars pay a few of them to show up every night just in case a homophobic cowboy shows up looking for a fight. That happens occasionally in Paris but not as much as when I first came out. Twenty years ago it was a lot tougher to be openly gay."

"All right, Poppy. That is more than I want to hear." Paula knew Poppy was gay but she never talked about his sexual orientation.

"Then everything is a go," Poppy said. "I have the same driver and I've already emailed you the address where we'll hold the woman. Call me when she is secured and I'll start the negotiating process with her husband right away. This one should be fairly quick unless he wants to get rid of his wife."

"Talk to you Monday." Paula closed her phone.

*****

The Marcos exchange when smoothly except for one detail. It was impossible for the news of his arrival not to get out to the police stations in Paris. When the memo reached the desk of Christoph, he started to get nervous. He hoped Marcos was shot and killed in the States. Neither he nor Poppy knew what Marcos was capable of, especially after Poppy tried to have him eliminated.

"Poppy, a change in plans," Christoph said after making a call from his office desk. "The police from the Le Cure station picked up Marcos at the airport. He's in their custody. That's all I know."

"Double *Merde*. Marcos doesn't know about you, but he has my phone number. If he turns on me, I may have to take a permanent vacation to Italy and disappear. I'm right in the middle of two business transactions so let me know if you hear anything else."

"If you don't hear from me then that means I don't have any more information," Christoph said. "I have to go now. My boss is calling me in for a staff meeting."

Christoph hung up his desk phone and went into the main office. As soon as he walked in he was grabbed on either side by two officers, handcuffed and seated in the chair in front of Lieutenant Alain's desk.

"What's the meaning of this?" Christoph yelled at the officers. "Are you charging me with something?"

"Your first mistake is you used the office phone line to make calls to the person you informed for." Lieutenant Alain pushed a button and played the last part of the conversation Christoph had with Poppy.

"If you don't hear from me then that means I don't have any more information. I have to go now. My boss is calling me in for a staff meeting." Alain then pushed another button to stop the recording.

Christoph knew he was caught but he still tried to weasel out of it. "That was a private call. What right do you have tapping into my conversations?"

"Knock off the crap, Christoph. How long have you been passing on information from this office? We know you received deposits into your account. We have your financial and phone records. Here's the deal. You're finished here. How long you want to spend in jail comes down to how much you cooperate with us."

Sweat appeared on Christoph's forehead and began dripping into his eyes. He rubbed them with his cuffed fists but it only made it sting more. The length of his prison term depended on what he said next.

"What kind of deal can I make? The information I passed on to this man had nothing to do with National Security. I only followed the kidnap cases he was involved in."

"That's a start, Christoph. All the material benefits you purchased while working for him are now ours. That's the first part of the deal. The other part is this, ten years or five? It's up to you. Withhold information about Poppy and you will be a middle-aged man by the time you get out. Tell us what you know and you may be able to start a new life. Also, we'll make sure you won't get placed with the hardened prison population. They find out you were a cop and you won't last two months."

This last statement frightened Christoph the most. He knew Alain was right. Two officers, who didn't cooperate last year when they were caught keeping drugs after a bust, ended up dead in prison after six months. The hardcore population had ways of dealing with ex-cops and the outcome was usually the same, a short life.

"I'll tell you everything I know. First, if Poppy finds out I'm arrested he's gone and you'll never find him. You need to make it appear I'm still working here. He could have other informants throughout the police force that I don't know about. If they I'm gone, then word could get back to him."

One of the officers, who handcuffed Christoph, spoke up. "He's right, Lieutenant. If someone else is an informant, and they see us lead Christoph out of here in handcuffs, we could lose this Poppy character."

So far the ploy was working. Christoph had no idea if there was another informant but he needed to buy some time.

"First, I need a statement from you, Christoph," Lieutenant Alain said. "Write down everything you know about Poppy and what his plans are. We find out you haven't told us everything and the deal's off."

Lieutenant Alain was furious he had a mole working in his office. At the same time, he knew the car and extra cash from pay-offs would be a nice bonus for those involved in the case. It was one of the perks he and *Capitaine* Le Cure worked out before setting up Christoph.

"You're going on vacation. We'll leave when the building's almost empty. Then we'll go out the back and hold you in a private hotel room until Poppy is caught. We'll spread the word that you took an emergency vacation to see your sick mother in Brest on the coast. That way no one will miss you."

Panic filled Christoph. He knew he had to negotiate a better deal. "Poppy has another grab scheduled for Monday. Make it four years and you can stop the kidnapping and get three more of his crew. That information has to be worth something."

"Give me the keys to your car now and we have a deal." Lieutenant Alain knew how to make a counter offer and come out on top. Christoph would do anything to lessen his prison time.

"Deal." The keys to the Renault Megane RS Trophy came out of Christoph's pocket and laid on the table. He just bought a year out of prison for the price of an expensive sports car and it was worth it.

For the next hour, Christoph wrote out his confession including what he knew about the kidnapping scheduled for Monday morning in front of the yoga studio. He had the time and location but not the names of those involved. There were two more people involved as well at the apartment where the woman would be held but he didn't have the address.

By now all that remained in the office was the *Sergent* and Lieutenant. Christoph remained seated in the chair in front of the desk. The drawn shades allowed only one other officer besides the Lieutenant and *Sergent* to know what transpired in the office.

"I'm calling *Capitaine* Le Cure and let him know where we stand. If we let his team make the bust, Poppy will not know anything. We can also try to get an address from his phone number. I'll get a court order and tap the phone. I'd like to see what he does in his spare time," Alain said.

"Great idea Lieutenant. You pull this off and you may get your *Capitaine* bars." The *Sergent* knew how to brown nose his boss. He hoped Alain would take care of him as well. Another stripe on his arm meant a pay-raise.

"In an hour you and corporal Morrell take Christoph to the safe house. Make sure you're not seen. Use the back stairs to the parking lot and cover Christoph's head. We don't want anyone recognizing him. When this is finished, those involved will be compensated for their work and their silence."

Alain called *Capitaine* Le Cure. "Le Cure, we got him. Your plan worked and he fell for the bait. He called a man named Poppy and passed on the information about Marcos returning to France. We have the conversation on tape and a full confession."

"Good work, Lieutenant. What are you going to do with the mole?" Le Cure asked.

For the next twenty minutes, Alain laid out his plan. He would keep Christoph hidden until Poppy was captured and the three people were apprehended at the yoga studio. "We need your team to grab the three involved and keep it out of the police files. We may have another mole at our office. If Poppy finds out about the foiled grab on Monday, or Christoph getting caught, we may never see the creep again."

The information given to Le Cure included the address of the yoga studio, time and date of the grab but not much else. All Christoph knew was a driver and two people were hired to do the job. Alain told Le Cure he was getting a court order to trace Poppy's phone and see what else he was involved in.

"We also have the car and bank accounts of our man. Give me the names of everyone involved in the case on your end and I make sure everyone gets their fair share. I should get a good price for the car because it's practically brand new," Alain said.

"Did you know it was the car that gave Christoph away, Lieutenant? If he didn't have that car, I would never have suspected him. No way any police officer could afford a set of wheels like that."

"Good thinking on your part, *Capitaine*. That's why you have your rank. You broke this case and found the mole. This should work out well for all of us."

"Let's get these three on Monday and grab Poppy as well. Let me know right away if you get some information from the wiretap. If we can find out where he lives, we've got him."

"You're right, *Capitaine*. I'll call if I hear anything. Good luck on Monday."

Lieutenant Alain left his car in the parking lot and drove Christoph's car to his home wearing dark glasses, overcoat and a hat. He parked it in the garage where it would remain until it was sold. He'd get a ride in the morning with his *Sergent*.

*****

Sunday night the plan was presented to Anne, the owner of the yoga studio. After she agreed, *Capitaine* Le Cure assigned two officers inside her studio and two plain-clothed police in a car ten meters from the front of the building. Early Monday morning they were in place.

At nine a.m., Paula and Dante sat at the café a block from the studio eating a light meal. Dante had his telescope so he could keep an eye on the building. Several women and one man approached the stairs and entered the front door with yoga mats under their arms. The women dressed in multi-colored spandex pants, while the man wore loose fitting pajama type trousers, popular in India.

"Anything out of the ordinary?" Paula asked.

"Nothing yet. It looks like a regular yoga day," Dante said.

"I'm just being careful," Paula continued. "I don't like surprises. Eating prison food is not appealing in any way."

"It doesn't appeal to me either, Paula. If I get arrested I'll have a huge target on my back. Being gay is a difficult secret to keep in a prison society."

"Enjoy your quiche and coffee," Paula said. Jail was not a possibility she cared to discuss. "We have about thirty minutes left before Mrs. Towers arrives. Our driver is there already. We'll have three minutes to nab her when she arrives."

"You and our driver are responsible for Mrs. Towers," Dante reminded Paula. "I'll handle the bodyguard and her driver. I may have to use a sleeper hold to take out the guard but first I'll take his gun. Once she's in our car, I'll stab a tire on their car and we're gone."

Dante and Paula sat quietly for the next fifteen minutes, finishing their breakfast. A fake license plate was added to the escape car the night before, in case someone took down the number. Ten minutes later Paula and Dante began walking towards the studio, timing the arrival of the limo and their target. When they were ten meters from the entrance, the limo, carrying Mrs. Towers, turned down the street and approached the studio.

"This is it," Dante said. "We need to be right in front of the car when it stops."

The limo pulled up to the curb and the bodyguard got out of the front seat. As he reached for the handle and opened the door, Dante wrapped his powerful right arm around the man's neck and removed the gun from the holster under his arm. Paula placed the chloroform cloth over Mrs. Tower's face as she stepped out of the car. The driver for Paula and Dante stood ready to carry the Towers woman to his waiting car.

Coming down the stairs of the yoga studio, two police officers appeared, aiming guns at the three unsuspecting criminals. "Move and your weightlifting days are over," said the officer in charge. "Drop the gun."

The plain-clothes police, parked nearby, also arrived at the scene. Paula, Dante, and the driver hardly knew what happened.

"Place the gun on the ground," yelled the police officer coming down the front stairs. He could see the bodyguard grab the gun from the giant and knee him in the groin. The man then laid the pistol on the curb. He observed the woman dropping a cloth and raising her hands.

All of a sudden the driver of the getaway car made a dash to his vehicle. He had left the engine running and hoped he might get away. The officer on the stairs motioned for his man on the street to stop him. As the driver opened the door and started to get in, he received the full weight of heavy metal against his body. The blow from the door knocked him to the ground removing all the air from his body.

"I've got the driver," the policeman yelled back to his companions. "He's not going anywhere."

The officer in charge gave an order to his partner next to him.

"Shoot him in the legs if he tries anything, Maurice. I'm going to cuff him."

"I'm giveing up," Dante said as he stood near the limo. "No problems from me." He'd spent too many hours doing squats to want any holes in his muscles.

Within eight minutes all three kidnappers were in custody and loaded into the police van that arrived on the scene. Two officers lifted the driver into the back seat of the patrol car because he could not walk. The police cars drove away before any citizens in the area arrived on the scene.

"I'm the owner," Anne said, approaching the officer in charge. "Thank you for taking care of this attempted kidnapping."

"You're an American," the *Sergent* said. "I can tell by your accent."

"Yes, but I've been in Paris for thirty years. Is this going to be on the news?"

"Right now we need to keep this situation out of the news. We have another man to capture and this attempted kidnapping in front of your studio might not be the publicity you want."

"I think you're right. I'll talk to Mrs. Towers and smooth things over with her. I don't want to lose her as a client."

"You do that Miss.,…….what was your name again?"

"Anne, Anne D'Antonio."

"Oh, you are Italian-American. I'll have to come back later to get your statement, Miss D' Antonio. Curious people are starting to arrive from that café up the street."

"Here is my number," Anne said as she handed the *Sergent* one of her businesses cards. "Yoga is good for you no matter what line of work you're in. What is your name?"

"Paul Trudeau," he answered. He couldn't tell if she was hitting on him or just promoting yoga.

Within five minutes, Mrs. Towers was ready to leave. Anne complimented all her remaining classes while she was in Paris. The worst that happened to her was a cloth slammed into her face. She'd survive.

The Tower limo drove away and the last police car headed back to the station. *Capitaine* Le Cure met his men bringing in the three kidnappers. The bust would remain quiet until the mastermind was behind bars.

*****

Lieutenant Alain now had a court order for the wiretap on Poppy's phone line. He'd taped two conversations so far, regarding ten cases of military assault weapons ready for pickup at a warehouse in a suburb of Paris. Poppy never mentioned the name of his contact and the telephone number lead only to a burner phone number.

"It looks like Poppy has a few business ventures going. Kidnapping wealthy people and running guns," Alain said. "The rich held for ransom is one thing but the gun running is bad for everyone involved. Police are getting killed because of guns on the street and I can't stand for that."

The *Sergent* nodded his head in agreement. "Every policeman around the world should be concerned about gun runners. These people have weapons more powerful than ours. I would sure like to stop French-made rifles from getting into the wrong hands."

"Me too, *Sergent*. If we can catch Poppy, maybe we can nudge him a little into telling us who the seller is. It has to be someone working in one of the gun factories. If we stop a shipment, we'll be able to tell which factory manufactured it. We need to catch the seller."

"You want to use Poppy to catch the main man?" the *Sergent* asked.

"Poppy appears to be a small-time arms dealer," Lieutenant Alain said. "The person who is selling to him probably deals with other people as well. We cut off the tail of the lizard and it continues to live. We remove his head and he dies."

"How are we going to do this?" *Sergent* Bruno asked. "These gun makers are rich and carry a lot of clout with the military and the government."

"We have to get help from Le Cure and people he knows. Getting a team together is our best chance. Trying to do this alone would be madness."

"What are we going to do about Poppy? He'll find out eventually that his team is arrested."

"He has a weapons pickup to make tonight at that warehouse. I'm going to call Le Cure and get his input. If we let Poppy close the deal he might think he's safe to continue selling guns."

"We need to move on this fast because we only have a few more hours until the guns are transferred. Get a photographer at the site to get some pictures of who shows up. More than likely it won't be a boss but one of the men might flip when facing ten years for arms dealing."

Chapter 24

Julia and Robert returned to their job of working local cases now that the Stun Gun Killer was back in France. They received part of the reward posted by the Swedish television star but satisfaction was their biggest prize. Robert made sure a chunk of the reward went to the woman in the ticket booth who gave him Marcos' license plate number.

The phone rang just as Robert sat down on the couch with a beer in his hands.

"Who's this? It's an international call," Robert said as he looked at the numbers on his phone. "I think it's the number for *Capitaine* Le Cure."

"Well, answer it, Robert. Maybe something else happened with the Poppy case."

"Hello, *Capitaine* Le Cure. Good to hear from you."

"Bonjour, *Monsieur* Robert. How are you and Julia? Good, I hope."

"Much better now that Marcos is in your hands. You still have him, right?"

"Yes, of course. We even captured the mole thanks to your idea of using different names. He confessed and told us about the man he gave information to."

"Oh, you mean Poppy? Julia got that out of him

before he was arrested."

"Yes, Poppy. Here is our situation. We may have another international job if you're interested."

"What is it?" Robert asked.

"It turns out that Poppy is an arms dealer as well as a kidnapper. We think he's one of many supplying a French made rifle to different factions throughout the world. The real boss is someone working for a company that makes the weapons."

"Do you know his name?" Robert asked.

"Not yet. We taped a few conversations, but no names were used. We can't get a location. He may be using burner phones."

"What about Poppy? Is he still loose?"

"For now. We did break up his kidnapping team. They tried to grab the wife of a Mr. Towers who is in Paris negotiating a business deal. We arrested them last Monday. The woman attended a yoga studio in Paris and now all three kidnappers are in jail."

"You've been busy, *Capitaine*. Not much is happening in Albuquerque at the moment. We're doing follow-up work on a few cases."

"How would you like to be an arms dealer in the States? We're coming up with a plan to flush this person out but we have to be careful. He smells anything funny and we could lose him."

"The one problem I see is that guns are easy to get a hold of in the States. The idea that everyone should own a gun is still popular with many people and background checks are easy to get around."

"Yes, but what about those militant groups that live in the countryside waiting for the revolution to happen? We see stories about them on the French news. Don't you think they'd be interested in a military-style assault rifle to add to their firepower?"

"You want me to set up a deal to sell weapons to them? Those groups are so far out they make the KKK look like Boy Scouts."

"No, you don't sell to anyone. If the main dealer in France thinks you represent a group who want to purchase his guns, then we have a chance to find out who he is. Putting a plug in the flow of weapons would be a huge accomplishment."

"How would I get in touch with a group like this? This is not my area of expertise."

"We realize that. My team knows of an underground website for weapon sellers. You could come up with a group name and pretend to be a buyer. If we can make the number of guns look enticing to Poppy, and he becomes the go-between for the seller, you may have an in. The French government would put up the money for the purchase and back us in this bust."

"What do you want me to do?"

"If you agree to this, then all we need is a contact name, the name and logo for the militant group and a phone number that Poppy can call. We'll do everything else on this side of the ocean."

"I'll need some time to set things up," Robert said. "When will you be ready?"

"We already know about the website. Poppy and other dealers like him use it to find customers. There is a trace on Poppy's phone so if he calls you, we'll know it's him. You give us what we need and if you want to be a part of the bust, then you are welcome to come for another visit."

"Maybe we can make this work. I'll make up a group name and logo and send it to you. If I used a real group name, and they found out, I may have a few of them looking for me in New Mexico. I've already survived something similar a while back and I don't need that in my life again."

"Send the information, and we'll get this started. I'll call later after we've posted the information to the site."

"This could be a big bust, *Capitaine*. Let's do it right

and put Poppy and his partner away for a long time."

"*Au revoir*, Robert. Love to your beautiful wife as well." Le Cure hung up.

Julia was in the living room listening to most of the conversation. "Are we about to help in another French case?" she asked.

"It's more of an extension of the Marcos case. It turns out Poppy has several businesses. Gun running as well as kidnapping. Le Cure broke up the kidnapping ring, but now he's trying to bring down the gun seller Poppy uses. We could be his next customers."

"We what? You know how much I detest guns. Why would we get involved in this?"

"We're going to be involved in name only. We have to come up with a phony militant group interested in French assault weapons and the police will do the rest. If we can trick Poppy into selling us the guns, Le Cure might find out who the main seller is and take him out. We have some work to do. Let's get Peggy in on the research and see what she can come up with. We need a name, some kind of logo that represents the group and misinformation posted on an underground site. After that let's see if Poppy bites and we can reel him in."

"Okay, but no weapons in this house. Taking down the bad guys is one thing but getting involved in their insane ideas and guns is completely the opposite of what I'm willing to do."

*****

"What happened? Are you sure they're arrested?" Poppy asked.

"That's all the news I have, Poppy. So far the police are saying they just happened to be patrolling the block near the studio when the kidnapping attempt happened."

The information came to Poppy from another informant that worked at the Mondo Times newspaper. Poppy tried to call Christoph at the police department but was told he was on vacation and could not be reached. Poppy sent one of his employees to the apartment where Christoph lived to see if he was home. His car was not parked in the area where he usually kept it. The message on the private cell phone said Christoph would be in England for a two-week vacation. Something was not right, and Poppy had no idea what to make of the situation.

"So you're telling me the kidnapping attempt was broken up by a patrol car passing by the yoga studio and nothing more?" Poppy asked.

"That's the report we received. The paper doesn't know the victim and the yoga studio owner is not talking to reporters. Something about privacy and not wanting negative attention affecting her business."

Poppy had nothing to go on. With his police informant out of the country and his latest kidnap attempt foiled by a police patrol, this week was turning out to be a financial bust. His other business seemed to be intact and the pickup of the rifles went smoothly the night before. He received his payment before the weapons were loaded in Marseille and on their way to Africa.

"Thanks for the update. I'll make a deposit today in your account. If you hear anything else about my people arrested, let me know right away. Is there a bail amount posted for any of them?"

"No, the judge said they're a flight risk and were caught in the act so they're staying put."

"Can I get a message to the woman or is she cut off from any outside contact?" Poppy asked.

"I'll find out and let you know. That's it for now. It sounds to me like the police were lucky with this one and happened to be in the right place at the right time."

"You may be right. Thanks again." Poppy was still suspicious of the sudden departure of his police informant. He decided to concentrate on the weapons trade and leave the other business alone for a while. Guns were easier to deal with but the return was not as high. He needed to put together a new kidnapping team and that would take time.

None of his people knew where he lived and he kept it that way. He'd try to help Paula by hiring a lawyer. She'd been an employee for many years and he might use her again in the future. The Austrian body builder was less of a priority as was the driver.

I may have to set up another arms deal soon, thought Poppy. Losing three million on the Tower attempt is a big hit. I need to get another client and soon.

*****

"*Capitaine* Le Cure. *Salut*, it's Julia."

"*Salut*, Julia. It's good to hear from you so soon."

"Robert and I have the information you need for the underground website. We even have a logo we drew up."

"That was quick. You seem to have a good team over there working for you. Can you fax me the logo and the name? I'll add them to the site right away and hopefully, we'll get a hit. We'll do our best to screen out everyone except Poppy."

"How are you going to do that?" Julia asked.

"Any of the answers to your request are routed to a computer savvy citizen that works independently. We pay him well for each case he gets. He's an expert and can get what we need."

"We have a good computer person here as well," Julia said. "If your person needs help we have a backup."

"I'll remember that. What is the name of the group you made up?"

"The Brotherhood. Their logo has a Nazi flag and an American Confederate battle flag crossing each other in the background. Their ideas represent most of the hate groups in America today."

"What the hell is wrong with people who believe in that crap?" *Capitaine* Le Cure was getting angry. "We fought the Germans in WWII and never want to see the Nazis emerge in Europe again. We have small groups, but we keep a close eye on them."

"It's gotten pretty bad over here," Julia said. "Ignorance and the inability to think for themselves makes it easy for many of these groups to get followers and blame their problems on minorities. It's changing but slowly."

"Anyway let's get this setup. Fax me what you have and we will do our best. We'll set up the phone number and have it routed to us. We have someone here who can handle a call from Poppy so you won't have to."

"How many weapons are you asking for?"

"I'm sending that to you right now. The gun Poppy deals with is made in France. Somehow, he's able to get what he needs from the seller. If we make the shipment large enough it should take a while to get the order together."

"Let's talk in two days. That will give you time to add us to the website."

"Thank you, Julia. The French government will make this worthwhile for you. They want to plug this weapons leak permanently."

The *Capitaine* hung up and turned to his *Sergent*. "We should be getting a fax any minute from our American friends. Get the information to George so he can add it to the underground weapons site. The sooner we get this uploaded the better."

"You're right, *Capitaine*. I'll get the fax to George right away."

Chapter 25

"Leslie, hi. It's Anne."

Anne D'Antonio was calling from Paris to her sister in Tucson, Arizona.

"Anne, how are you? It's been a year since we visited. Are you ready for another adventure in Italy?"

Leslie was the wife of William Ray who played a part in Robert's biggest case so far, the collapse of The Company and Ian McClure.

"No, not yet, but you're not going to believe what happened in front of my studio three days ago."

"You better tell me cause I can't read your mind."

Anne proceeded to tell Leslie about the Tower woman and her near abduction by a kidnapping ring. Anne said she cooperated with the police to capture them. She also said she met a cute sergeant in the Paris police force and had to go down to the station a day later to give him her statement.

"You seem more interested in telling me about the sergeant than the near abduction. Is that what this calls is about?" Leslie asked.

"Well, maybe. Guess what? The sergeant asked me out for coffee and I accepted. Can you believe it? I started seeing a policeman."

"So you've met with him."

"I have and I really liked him. He didn't talk about his work and he met me wearing street clothes instead of his uniform. He has an interest in yoga and wanted to find out more."

"Was that a line or is he sincere?" Leslie asked.

"It sounded sincere. He even signed up for some beginning classes and he starts next week. What do you think about that?"

"What are you calling me for, advice on men? Remember, I'm married to William. I just spent the last eighteen months surviving a criminal investigation with him as a key player. You dating a cop has nothing on what I've been through."

"I never did find out how all that turned out. Did the case finally end and the bad guy get put away?"

"The bad guy blew his brains out and William played a big part in the man losing 1.5 billion dollars in the stock market. By the time it was over I was ready for another vacation."

"Are you able to tell me the whole story now? William said he would after everything was over."

"You've just given me a great idea, Anne. How about William and I fly over to Paris and visit you again? That way we can spend more time with you and William can tell you the whole story. Also, we can give our approval of the new man in your life."

"He's not in my life just yet. We're just beginning to see each other. I don't know where it's going but your visit sounds great."

"William made a lot of money on the last venture, so travel expenses are easy to handle. We can stay in a hotel nearby and give you some space in case this new man in your life works out."

"Leslie, just stop. We just met, and I like him but we are a long way from being that involved."

"Anne, you're not that young anymore. Fifty is just around the corner and you don't want to be alone forever do you?"

"Just call me when you're coming for a visit. He's new and who knows where it will go."

"I'll talk to William. We can bring mom and you two can spend some time together. You don't get back to the States much so we'll bring her to you."

"That is a great idea, Leslie. I know she can't travel all over Europe, due to her legs tiring easily, but having her in Paris will be a good chance for us to visit."

"Have you talked to Heather in a while?" Leslie

asked.

"No, and let's leave it at that. You know we don't see eye to eye on almost everything. I'll visit with mom, but please don't bring the whole family. I can't handle everyone at once."

"Talk to you in a few days after I speak to William. I'm looking forward to visiting again. Maybe William and I can take off for a few days and leave mom with you. I want to visit Amsterdam. William lived there in 1984 and he's never taken me there."

"Bye, Leslie, and thanks for bringing mom. I'm looking forward to it."

"Love you, Anne."

Just as Leslie hung up, William walked into the room. "Who was that?" he asked.

"Anne. Says she met someone in Paris and there was an attempted kidnapping in front of her studio last week. She wants all of us to come and visit. How about next month?"

"Why wait a whole month? If we bring your mom, we can go anytime. What's this about a kidnapping?"

"You'll have to ask her yourself. She didn't talk about it."

"Right now the weather is the best time of year for

Europe. September has cooler nights but the days are still warm. We don't have to make a lot of plans. Tell her we can be there in a few weeks," William said.

"I'm fine with that. Do we have to tell anyone we're going?" Leslie asked.

"Not really. We were going to visit Robert and Julia but I'll call and let them know we can do that when we get back."

"Fine, just don't sign up for any more cases with that madman. I love Robert, but his lifestyle is way over the top for me. He must get a rush going after bad guys and Julia is a lot like him. The best thing about her is that she believes in nonviolence and follows the teachings of the Dali Lama."

"I don't think there'll be anything he needs from me. I did hear they captured both men who kidnapped Cathy. Alan told me Robert and Julia went to Paris to get the second guy. They're now involved in some kind of international case with the Paris police. Robert should write a newsletter and keep us up on his case load."

"You said he went to Paris to capture the second kidnapper. When did this happen?" Leslie asked.

"About three weeks ago. They caught him living in an apartment and flew him back to Albuquerque to stand trial."

"So he's not in Paris now? If he's not there, then it should be safe for us to go. If he were there I'd stay home. Somehow you two attract each other like polar opposites."

"Taking down Ian was an exciting time in my life. It filled several chapters in my memoirs. Now all I do is play cards, practice yoga, and go shopping."

"Yes, and all I do is volunteer at the animal shelter, practice yoga, and shop. What's wrong with that?"

"I guess our ideas for retirement are not completely the same. A little adventure doesn't hurt once in a while."

"Taking down a corrupt CEO of a company is more than a little adventure. Let's keep our traveling to tourist sites and nothing more, okay?" Leslie was serious.

"Fine with me. We'll have mom with us so no clandestine adventures are on my agenda," William said.

"Well, that's good, Mr. Bond."

Leslie used 007 references when she was angry with William during his previous involvements with Robert.

"I'm off to volunteer at the animal shelter and will be home by six. Put the potatoes in the oven at five and we'll eat when I get back."

Leslie left and as soon as she did, William called Robert.

"Hi, Julia, is Robert there? This is William."

"William. How have you been? We haven't seen you and Leslie in a while."

"I know. After your wedding and Cathy's kidnapping ended, we've kept to ourselves. Leslie and I are heading back to Paris to visit her sister, Anne. She's the one with excitement in her life."

"What do you mean?" Julia asked.

"She met a police sergeant after he and his team set up a sting operation at her yoga studio and captured three people in a kidnapping ring."

"Wait. What did you say?" Julia asked. "You said kidnappers at a yoga studio? That was Leslie's sister? Are you kidding me? You need to talk to Robert. We had something to do with that."

"No way," William said. "You were involved in that case all the way from Albuquerque. How's that possible?"

"I'm going to let you talk to Robert. Here he is." Julia passed the phone over to Robert who seated himself next to her on the couch.

"Hi, William. I heard Julia say 'Leslie's sister' and 'yoga studio'. Is she referring to the sting operation in Paris?"

"I was calling to tell you that we are planning to visit Anne in Paris. She told tell us she met a policeman after an attempted kidnapping happened in front of her yoga studio. Now Julia tells me you two were involved in that?"

"Yes, but in an indirect way. We helped a French police Captain capture a mole in their police force and broke up a kidnapping ring in Paris. It's a long story with Jeff and Laura involved. Laura wanted no part of it but Jeff was interested and tried to help."

"Tried to help?" William asked.

"He answered the door of his house, pretending to be me, and got zapped with a stun gun. He survived and the police captured the criminal. I don't think Jeff will join in with police work for a while."

"This is too friggin wild. All I wanted to call you about was to say we have to visit later. We're going to Paris to visit Anne and now there's a connection to you. Whatever happens, you can't tell Leslie about any of this. She can't handle my involvements with you and now her sister is in the mix."

"The yoga studio was an isolated incident. It just happened to belong to your sister-in-law and nothing more. Why the kidnappers choose that location, I'll never know. We're now trying to capture the mastermind behind the team that was busted. It turns out he's a gun runner as well."

"He what? Runs guns? How is that connected with kidnapping?" William asked.

"The police think he used the income from the kidnappings to purchase the guns, which he sells to revolutionary groups. We're trying to set him up and expose the main man working for the gun manufacturer. We know who the middle man is but not the main seller."

"How in the hell are you going to do that, Robert? Kidnappers, gunrunners and yoga studios. Wow, I'm pumped."

"I can't tell you anything right now. I know Leslie wouldn't approve if she found out you had anything to do with this case. I'll tell you about it after we capture the guy."

"Wait, Robert. You have my cell number. We'll be in Paris for a few weeks. If you need any help, you call me, and only me. I'll do what I can but Leslie is out of the picture."

"Are you sure, William? I don't want to break up your marriage because you helped me on a case."

"She won't leave me but I may have to sleep on the couch for a few months if she finds out. This stuff gets my blood pumping. Give me a call if you need me over there. Let's leave it at that."

"Okay, William. You know what you're doing in regards to Leslie. Have a good trip and if anything comes up I'll call."

"You've made my day for sure," William said. He then hung up.

*****

Two weeks later, the Rays and Leslie's mom landed in Paris. The plan was for the couple to check into Pension Luca about a block from Anne's apartment, and for Lois to spend time at her daughter's apartment. William and Leslie even signed up for several classes at the yoga studio in between touring the city and a side trip to Amsterdam.

"Mom," Anne yelled after they came through customs. "I'm so happy you made it over here. You finally get to see my studio and apartment."

"And even spend some time with you," Lois said. "Let's get to your place so I can lay down for a while. The flight really took it out of me."

Lois was now eighty years old and this was her last trip abroad. Travel was not easy for her anymore.

"Are you hungry?" Anne asked. "There is a café near my apartment and the Pension where you're staying."

"We could all eat," Leslie said. "After that, we better

get mom into bed for a while. She's on pain medication, but it'll wear off and bed-rest is what she needs," Leslie added.

William kept quiet during most of the interactions between the sisters and their mother. He was happy they were able to see each other.

"We can catch a taxi in front of the terminal, and be at the restaurant in twenty minutes," Anne said as the family walked out the sliding doors of the airport lobby.

After hiring a cab, the party of four drove through the streets of Paris and got out in front of Café du Ponte. The pleasant weather allowed them to sit outside under the green umbrellas with the petite patio furniture.

"Do you work today?" Leslie asked after everyone was seated.

"My assistant can handle almost everything I do except the payroll. She wants the extra hours and I'll cover for her when she goes on vacation next month."

"Leslie mentioned you've fallen for a police officer," Lois said. "Does your mother get to meet him or is he under wraps?"

"Leslie tends to be overdramatic, mother. I've met a policeman but fallen for him is a bit of a stretch. We've gone out five or six times and he takes classes in the studio twice a week before going into work. Nothing too serious yet."

"But do we get to meet him?" Lois persisted.

Anne rolled her eyes and stared at Leslie. "You came to visit me, not the men I date. Anyway, he's working on a big case right now and might not have a lot of free time."

Lois would not let it go. "Anne, I'm getting old. I don't have time for your avoidance games. If this is someone you're interested in, then this could be the last time I have a chance to meet him. Have him make time."

"Okay, I give up. I'll produce him when I find out his schedule. Remember, he's a policeman and could get called away at any time."

"Good, now that we settled that, let's eat," Lois said.

During the meal, the conversation centered on events in the family past and how they missed being together.

After the meal, the family headed back to the Pension to drop off William and Leslie's luggage. Lois planned to spend as many nights as possible with Anne. An elevator had been added to the apartment building since the last time the Rays visited. That was the only way Lois could get to the third floor. The stairway was no longer an option for her.

"We're heading back to our room," Leslie said after

securing her mother in Anne's apartment. "We need to lay down for a while as well. What shall we do for dinner?"

"I'm cooking tonight," Anne said. "Be back around six and we can have a glass of wine before we eat. I made a casserole this morning. All I have to do is put it in the oven. If you could pick up some bread at the *boulangerie* on the way here, it would be great. There is one not far from your Pension."

"Six o'clock is fine," William said. "I'll get the bread and look forward to a home-cooked meal."

The family planned to be in the city for two or three weeks.

*****

Poppy finally got a message to Paula in prison. He wanted to know what went wrong at the yoga studio. He couldn't call her himself so he relied on an employee to get him the information.

"Poppy, I think I have what you want," Pierre said over the phone. He visited Paula posing as her brother. "She still does not know exactly what happened. Everything played out so fast and the next thing she knew the police were there."

"What exactly did she say?" Poppy asked.

"She said as soon as she grabbed the Tower woman, and put a rag in her mouth, two policemen appeared out of nowhere. They were in uniform and came at them from behind. The bodyguard for the woman grabbed his own gun away from Dante and kneed him in the groin. Also, two plain-clothes police arrived a minute later and arrested your driver trying to get away."

"All that and the police just happened to be in the neighborhood. That's hard to believe," Poppy said.

"Paula also wondered why there were so many cops on the scene so quickly. They were taken away before the reporters arrived which seemed strange. Most cops like to get their pictures taken putting cuffs on the culprits."

"It sounds like the police were waiting for them," Poppy said a bit agitated. "The only other person who knew about the grab is out of the country and I can't reach him."

"Do you want me to visit Paula again? She was expecting to see you but I explained to her how you need to stay under cover."

"I'll pay for a good legal advisor for her as well as the other two. We'll pretend you're the one giving them help. I'll call you when I have one lined up. Just tell her I'm doing my best."

"I don't think they're going anywhere, Poppy. Paula

and the driver understand the need to keep quiet but I'm not so sure about Mr. Bodybuilder. He's new at this and I suspect prison life is not something he may do well with. He'll be a constant target, and the next biggest prisoner may try to beat him up. Keeping him quiet may take more effort on our part."

"I can shut people up when I have to," Poppy said. "After my legal advisor visits him I'll know more about Dante and see if he's able to do time. If he's going to flip, then another plan has to be activated."

"I understand, Poppy. Do this right away. We don't want any names going to the police."

*****

"Christophe has been transferred to another station, sir. That's all I know. I was told he went on vacation and requested a transfer when he returned."

Poppy got through to someone who had some information on Christophe but not a way to reach him. Christophe's personal phone was no longer in use and a man hired by Poppy went by the policeman's apartment complex. He reported a rent sign outside the building and the vacated apartment was the one Christophe used to live in.

Poppy thought Christophe was no longer a part of his team. He had to be in custody and the police held him somewhere. He was the only other person who knew about the attempted grab of the Tower woman in front of the yoga studio.

If the police were on to Poppy, he might have to move to a new residence. He didn't want to leave Paris. His weapons business was located here. None of his employees knew where he lived.

Poppy needed to make another weapons deal soon. The sale of guns was less complicated than kidnapping rich Americans.

The website Poppy used was accessed through a private password. It was a secret site because it involved groups looking for guns used for their various causes. Poppy scrolled past the middle-east countries wanting guns. Most of those weapons were coming from Russia anyway and Poppy didn't like the Muslim fanatics.

Not much was happening in Africa. He just sent a shipment there and the Americas were the only region wanting any firepower. A militant group in Idaho caught his eye. They wanted fifty crates of automatic rifles and would pay top dollar. That worked out to be around $300,000 in profit to Poppy after expenses. It was not as much income as other orders because the quantity was large so the price went down. He needed the cash flow. An encrypted message was sent to the site with the price and make of rifle Poppy sold.

He then left the site to look for a new apartment on the web. The militant groups that used this site were careful and would make sure Poppy's web address was legit before they answered. They didn't want any Federal investigators finding out who they were or where they were located. He would check them out as well if they responded.

Poppy called a real estate agent after he found an ideal apartment in the St Maurice district of Paris. He knew about a high-end gay bar within walking distance from the location and the apartment was large enough for his needs.

"Is this the Blurr Agency?"

"Yes, it is. How can I help you?" the agent asked.

"My name is *Monsieur* Bolivar and I'm interested in the C 14 apartment on your site. Is it still available?"

"Give me a second and I'll look it up." Thirty seconds later, the agent answered. "*Qui, monsieur*, it just went on the market. It's in an exclusive district in St Maurice and not far from public transportation. Would you like to see it?"

"Yes, I would. Do you have time right now to show me the place?"

"Of course," the agent answered. "I can meet you there or pick you up. Whatever is convenient?"

"I'll meet your there," Poppy said. No one was going to see where he lived. Using a false name and paying six months in advance in cash also made sure he would remain hidden. "I can be there in an hour. Just give me directions."

The agent told Poppy where to meet him. A new home and a new start in the city he loved was his focus for now.

Chapter 26

"*Salute*, Julia," *Capitaine* Le Cure said after the call went through. "We have a hit on the website."

"That was fast. Here, I'll let you talk to Robert." Julia handed the phone to her husband.

"*Capitaine*. Did I hear right? You think Poppy responded to the site?"

"We think so. The weapons he had to sell are the same ones sold to those African groups. The fact that he responded so quickly tells us he may be in need of some quick cash because he lost out on the Towers' kidnapping. We've also been monitoring people visiting the three prisoners in jail."

"Really? Poppy didn't show up did he?"

"No, he's too smart for that," Le Cure said. "A visitor said he was the brother of the woman. We taped the conversation, which dealt mainly with the attempted kidnapping. I don't believe we can pretend the bust was by chance. She told the fake brother everything."

"What about the mole at the police station. How did you keep him hidden from Poppy?" Robert asked.

"Anyone asking for Christophe was told that he'd been transferred after he returned from vacation. We had several people inquiring about him so we think Poppy put the information together and realized his mole is no longer available. Christophe's apartment is up for rent and his cell phone account is closed."

"That might shut down his kidnapping line of work for a while but not the weapons," Robert said. "Is he doing that business with a different crew?"

"We believe so. There was a different driver for the truck that picked up the guns."

"Are we any closer to finding out who's the seller at the factory?" Robert asked.

"All we have is a few taped conversations. No names mentioned and we couldn't trace the calls. Our best bet is to arrest Poppy and make him talk," Le Cure said. "We have our ways when it comes to National Security."

"That sounds like Guantanamo in our country," said Robert.

The *Capitaine* continued. "We're going to respond to Poppy and try to locate him. Our computer person is working on that right now. Poppy will have to make contact with the seller at the factory in France because the order is rather large. Fifty cases are a lot more than the last shipment Poppy sold to Africa."

"Isn't Poppy going to meet the buyer before he sends guns to the States? He has to make sure they're legit and can be trusted, right?"

"Who in this business can be trusted?" Le Cure asked. "It's not like getting an order ready for a French winery. These fanatical groups are usually the bottom of societies pile no matter what country they come from. They see normal people living normal lives and they have no clue how to do it themselves. Many times there is a leader who has a high IQ and is leading his disciples in the name of God, country or some other bullshit reason. We have a few Nazi groups like that in France and Germany, but the States has a lot of them."

"I realize that," Robert said. "Keeping weapons out of their hands is not a priority in this country. Gun people scream it is their right to own a gun and people continue to get killed. Nothing changes. It's almost like the country goes to sleep and wants to have it all sorted out when they wake up."

"All we can do on our end is to bring these groups down and the people who are supplying them with the guns. If we can do that, then we've done our job," Le Cure said.

"What's the plan now?" Robert asked.

"I'll call you when we know more. I suspect Poppy is checking you out and making sure you're a legit group. He'll want to make contact at some point in time and meet a representative."

Robert's thoughts went to his only American contact

in Europe, William.

"I have a possibility in Paris right now. His name is William Ray and he helped me with my biggest case I've ever closed. He's visiting his sister-in-law in Paris with his family right now. You won't believe this but guess who the relative is?"

"*Monsieur* Robert, I may be a good detective, but not a mind reader. Can I have a hint?"

"Okay, here goes. She owns a yoga studio," Robert answered.

"She owns a……. wait a minute. You're telling me she owns the studio where the kidnapping attempt happened with Poppy's crew?"

"Not only that, William offered his services while he's there. His biggest problem is his wife. She's not happy when he helps me. He loves the excitement and I believe he could pass as a representative for the radical group in Idaho."

"Get in contact with him right away, Robert. If Poppy wants to meet him, then we have to set it up and brief him on what to say."

"I'll call him right now and get back to you."

"I'll wait for your call," Le Cure said.

*****

"Our possible witness is dead," Lieutenant Alain's *Sergent* said after he received a call from the prison.

"Who's dead?" Alain asked.

"The muscle man from that kidnapping case. He ended up dead in the shower room with several stab wounds in his chest and a broomstick up his butt and into his stomach. The warden thinks it was a planned killing. Rumors circulated he was going to turn evidence and try and get a lesser sentence."

"How did this happen? Don't the guards watch these men 24/7?"

"Not in the shower area. That's where most sexual contacts take place. The guards believe a couple of large prisoners held him while someone stuck him with a sharpened spoon. They left the murder weapon in him and added the broom to let the rest of the population know he was gay. Queers are not popular in prisons. Especially muscular ones and this guy was big."

"Someone on the outside must have paid for the hit. I'll call Le Cure and inform him we lost the one person who might have turned on Poppy."

Lieutenant Alain made the call and passed on the information to *Capitaine* Le Cure. The police report stated that Dante told several guards that he was willing to make a deal. Dante was new to the prison system and didn't know he shouldn't talk to guards. Any one of them could sell the information to the right person rather quickly. This is probably what happened to Dante. Now he's dead.

"Everything's not lost," Le Cure said after receiving the news. "We're working on a new angle to take down Poppy. We think he knows Christoph is gone. There's evidence he's working on his other business to raise money. He's probably staying away from kidnapping for a while, now that his team is behind bars. He is setting up a sale in the United States."

"Is there anything you want me to do from my office?" Lieutenant Alain asked.

"Not at the moment. We may have an American who'll step in and have a meeting with Poppy. I'll let you know if we need backup."

"*Au revoir, Capitaine.* Good luck with catching Poppy."

Le Cure put down his phone and called in his *Sergent*. He needed to talk to him and see if there was any more activity on the website.

*****

"William, hi. It's Robert. Can we talk?" Robert knew he couldn't ask William anything if Leslie was around.

"We just got back from two days in Amsterdam. Leslie's napping so I can talk in private. Let me step out on the balcony and close the door."

Robert could hear the door shut over his phone.

"Are you calling me because you need me?" William asked. "Let me guess. You need a 'cat burglar', right?"

"Funny, William. I always knew you would come up with a joke about any case we're working on. Can you act at all? I need someone to take a meeting with an arms dealer and pretend to be the financial accountant for a paramilitary group from Idaho. They're interested in buying weapons. If the meeting happens, then we need someone in Paris to represent the group. You might even get to handle a lot of money if the deal goes through."

"You want me to do what?" William asked. "Act like I'm in a radical group from the States buying weapons. Don't I have to be covered with tattoos and talk like a hillbilly?"

"No, you're the educated person in the group, handling the money and finances. Poppy might not want to deal with a hick and you'd be perfect. All you have to do is act like a retired teacher who is disgruntled with the American system and wants to tear it down."

"This has to happen in the next two weeks," William said. "We are only here for that long. Any dates yet?"

"You'll need to sneak away. No dates so far and Poppy hasn't taken the bait. If you're in, I'll do my best to work with your schedule."

"What are the odds I'll come out of this alive, Robert?"

"Stop being so dramatic, William. You're just taking a meeting and sealing the deal. If it's a go, and Poppy thinks you're legit, then we have a chance."

"Will I be in any danger, because danger's my middle name," William said with a smile.

"I thought it was Neal. At least that's what you told me." Robert played along with William's sense of humor as best he could.

"Okay, you got me there. I'll get away from the family. I want to see Versailles and Leslie and her mother have already done that tour. I can use that as an excuse to take the meeting as long as it's not at midnight."

"We'll set it up for an afternoon. I'm waiting for the French Captain to get back to me. They're the ones setting up the meeting with Poppy. He'll also want to talk to you before this happens."

"Okay then. You've got my blood pumping again," William said.

*****

Poppy had one more job to do before he completed the weapon sale. He needed to meet with a representative of 'The Brotherhood' and screen him with some questions. Shipping guns to someone he'd never met was not good business. All the African groups used a go-between in Europe to set up the deals. Poppy sent a message to the website asking for a meeting.

Poppy was moving items around in his new apartment when the computer alerted him he had a response. There was an actual number to call so Poppy dialed it from a burner phone.

"Is this account number P94735?" Poppy asked. No names appeared on the weapons website.

"Yes, it is," answered the French policeman who spoke English with an American accent. "Can I verify your name, please?"

"RT8852," Poppy said. "I'm answering the message you sent me."

"Yes, we are interested in your product and want to set up a transfer as soon as possible. What do you need from us?"

"I have never done business with you so I need to meet with one of your people. Do you have someone in Europe to represent you?" Poppy asked.

"It just so happens we do," the officer answered.

"Can you get that person to Paris in twenty-four hours? I need to talk to them before we proceed any further."

"It can be arranged. When and where would you like to meet?" the officer asked.

"Get your person to Paris and I'll call back in twelve hours. I'll give the place and time then."

"We'll wait for your call, RT8852. Goodbye."

The conversation was short and to the point.

"Do you think he'll call back?" Le Cure asked his assistant.

"I got the sense Poppy's being cautious. I'll bet we'll get a call back so we should get our American agent in place."

"If Poppy calls in twelve hours, it'll be midnight. The meeting has to be tomorrow. That's the best time for our agent."

"We'll try and set it up in the afternoon," the officer answered.

"I'll call my contact and get our person prepared. This has to work."

Le Cure called Robert. It was early morning in

Albuquerque. Le Cure didn't know who the American in Paris was but he needed to get him ready as soon as possible.

Robert's phone rang five times before he answered. "This better be good," he said. "It's five a.m."

"Robert, it's *Capitaine* Le Cure and I'm sorry for calling so early. We need your contact now."

"Give me a second. I'll go in the living room and let Julia sleep." Robert slipped on a robe, walked to the kitchen and hit the coffee machine switch. He had to have something to wake up. "Okay, *Capitaine*, I'm ready to talk. Is there a meeting with Poppy set up?"

"Yes and no. He'll call back in twelve hours. The person taking the meeting needs to be in Paris tomorrow so your man needs to be ready. Maybe you could give me your agent my number so I won't have to bother you like this."

"That's a good idea, *Capitaine*. I'll give William your name and number and let you handle it from there. Do you want Julia and me there as well?"

"If you have your agent here, then we need a contact in the States in case Poppy calls."

"There's another person I can use here," Robert said. "I'll make some calls and prepare him. Julia and I should fly to Paris today and be there when William goes to the meeting. We could follow Poppy back to his apartment. We look like tourists so we could pull that off."

"That might work but get here right away. We have to have everyone in place or we might lose an opportunity to catch this guy."

"I'll call William and tell him he can expect a call from you soon. If his wife answers the phone, ask for William. She does not know about this investigation at all and it needs to stay that way."

"Don't you Americans talk to your wives? Our French partners know everything about their husbands. That's why we have a lower divorce rate than you do."

"You're probably right, *Capitaine*. It's easy when your wife works with you but in the case of William, his wife is afraid most of the time. William has to work in secret."

Robert gave William's phone number to Le Cure. "I'll call him now."

Le Cure thanked Robert and apologized again for calling so early.

By now the coffee was ready and Robert drank his first cup black. He needed a quick 'wake up fix'.

*****

The phone rang several times before William answered. He could see the call was from Robert so he excused himself from the café where the family was sitting and eating lunch. "I have to take this," he told Leslie. "I'll be just a minute."

The look on Leslie's face told William he needed to make up a good story regarding the call.

"Robert, make it quick," William said. "I'm with Leslie and her mother."

"Okay. You'll be getting a call from a *Capitaine* Le Cure. They expect the meeting with Poppy tomorrow. He'll be your contact in Paris. Julia and I are flying there today and will be your back up. I'll call when we get there. Goodbye."

Wow, thought William. That was quick. He walked back to the table and sat down.

"Who was that," asked Leslie.

"Confirmation regarding the tour at Versailles," William said. "I'm scheduled for tomorrow so I'll be gone most of the day."

"You're going tomorrow?" Anne asked. "I was planning on showing you a winery in the countryside."

"Take Mom and Leslie. They've been to Versailles and I may not get another chance. I can do a winery another time with you."

William could tell Leslie was suspicious. "Be sure to

take a lot of pictures, William. I want to see what you did on the tour."

Shit, thought William. "I thought you should take the camera with you tomorrow. I can buy some postcards of Versailles because they'll be much better images than anything I'd take."

"That's right, we only have one camera and you don't have that feature on your phone. Oh well, buy a lot of cards. I want to see them when you get back."

Dodged a bullet on that one, thought William. I can buy postcards of Versailles from anywhere in Paris.

"I want to take you to a special place for dinner tomorrow night," Anne said. "It's not far from my apartment so let's meet there around seven. Will you be back by then, William?"

"I hope so. I'm taking one of those tour buses to the palace. If I'm late, I'll call."

"Don't be late," Leslie said in a stern voice.

"It's a special dinner, dear," William said. "I'll do my best to be on time."

The four family members finished lunch and took a taxi to Anne's yoga studio. She wanted her mother to see what she put together on her own.

While on the tour of the studio, William got a call

from *Capitaine* Le Cure. His phone was on vibration, and when it rang. William excused himself and asked where the bathroom was. When he was seated in the WC he dialed back the number that had gone to voicemail.

"Hello, this is William Ray. Is this *Capitaine* Le Cure?"

"Yes, it is. Did Robert tell you I'd call?"

"He did. We have to make this quick. I'm in the WC at a yoga studio. I can't talk long. My family is here."

"We expect Poppy to call us tonight to set up the interview meeting. He wants to be sure you're who you say you are."

"I know how to balance a checkbook. I can do this," William said. He always made a joke when he could.

"Good. I'll call you as soon as we know the time and location. Robert and Julia should be here by then. We plan on having them follow Poppy to where he lives. We'll have some officers nearby as well. Talk to you soon."

Le Cure hung up and William flushed the toilet before entering the hallway. He was excited, especially when he found out Robert and Julia would be in Paris. His 007 persona was taking over and he loved it.

"We're in here," Anne said as she spotted William

walking down the narrow hallway. "This is the belt wall room."

"We have one of those at the studio in Tucson," Leslie said. "They usually conduct the class on weekends. I don't hang upside down like some of the women but I can get into some unusual positions."

"I'd like you three to meet my boyfriend. The class he's taking is about to get out."

"You set this up, didn't you," Lois said. "You're finally letting us meet someone special in your life."

"It's still a new relationship, Mom. Don't get too involved with questions or you'll scare him away."

Five minutes later *Sergent* Paul came out of the Yoga class with his rubber yoga mat rolled up under his arm. He was wearing green shorts and a tee shirt that advertised the studio. His muscular legs, dark black hair, and Roman nose fit perfectly onto his six-foot frame and handsome features.

"Mom, Leslie, William, this is *Sergent* Paul Trudeau."

"So happy to meet you," Paul said. "Just call me Paul. I'm not a *Sergent* when I'm off duty."

He shook hands with William and kissed the hands of Lois and Leslie.

This guy is suave, thought William. Maybe he's a

keeper.

"I'm glad to finally meet someone Anne is interested in," Lois said. This is a rare moment for all of us."

"I've haven't had that many boyfriends, Mom," Anne said, "and you haven't visited in a long time."

"Leave Anne alone," Leslie said, coming to her defense. "Be glad you get to meet someone in her life right now."

"You're right, Leslie. That was rude of me," Lois said.

"Anyway, Paul has the evening off and we thought a ride to Sacre Coeur would be in order. How does that sound? We could get a bite to eat there after touring the area and be home by ten."

"Perfect," said William. "I have a palace to visit tomorrow, and I need to get to sleep early."

"All right then. I'll get changed and we can go in my car," Paul said. "I'll be five minutes."

The family all fit into Paul's Renault Captur. It was a trendy looking SUV that sat everybody comfortably. They spent the rest of the day touring Paris with dinner around eight. William thought that Paul held up well with all the questions Lois asked him.

Chapter 27

At 12:10 a.m., the call came through to the phone number from the website. Poppy was ready to meet at two p.m. at a café near the Eiffel Tower. He chose a public place with plenty of tourists around in case something went wrong.

The police officer, acting as a go-between, told Poppy the representative would be at the café. He gave William's description to him based on the photo he was sent by Robert. William would pose as a disgruntled retired teacher who disliked his government and everything the education system taught kids today.

Le Cure made calls to William and Robert the next morning to discuss last minute details. The Forrester team was in their Paris hotel. William was now the fly positioned to lure the gun running Poppy into the web.

At 1:30 p.m., Julia and Robert arrived at the café. A plainclothes policeman and policewoman posed as another couple enjoying the afternoon together. They had a voice-monitoring device they could aim at any table and record the conversation. The couples sat at opposite sides of the outdoor patio and ordered lunch. They planned to be at their tables during the entire meeting.

William drove up in a taxi and walked across the plaza to the café. He was fifteen minutes early. Robert and Julia sat at a table but William avoided eye contact when he walked by. Countless spy movies on TV told him what not to do.

The patio area was almost full when Poppy arrived at 2:05. He was late. Poppy wore a red flower in his lapel so William knew who he was.

William rose from his table when he saw Poppy walking towards him. Poppy was short and had a feminine look about him. Truman Capote came to mind. His slight build, balding head, and clear tight facial skin told William that Poppy was older than he looked and had gone 'under the knife'.

"My name is Bill Geist," William said.

"Yes, I recognize you from the picture your contact sent me. My name is Walter Crow. Please sit. I have a few questions as you must for me."

"Shall we order something before we start talking?" William asked.

"That's a good idea," Poppy answered. "I'm only having coffee. If you want to eat something then please order lunch."

The waiter approached the table and took the order. William decided on a sandwich and mineral water while Poppy ordered an espresso. Poppy began with the first question.

"How long has your organization been operating?" Poppy asked. "I've read a little about you from the website but it doesn't have a date when you first started."

"We organized in Mississippi in 1964 soon after the Civil Rights Act. Everything was working fine in the South until President Johnson ruined our control down there. My parents were Democrats before and elected Johnson but for him to turn on his roots and give power back to the niggers was more than we could stand."

"What did you do before you joined the group?" Poppy asked. "You seem to be an educated man."

"I was a teacher for twenty-five years in Dallas, Texas. I stopped teaching when I couldn't stand what the new textbooks were saying about the south. Texas is now making attempts to change all that and rewrite some of the propaganda in our history. As soon as we drop this idea of separation of church and state and get some real Christian values back in the White House, the country will be much better off."

By now, Poppy knew he had a racial nut case sitting in front of him. All Poppy tried to do was establish if this idiot was for real. He was here to sell him weapons, not try to change his world views.

"Do you have any questions for me, Mr. Geist?"

"Yes. How long have you been doing this? We've

never purchased French-made rifles, but the reports on your assault rifle have been good."

"Ten years. I usually sell to African groups. You're the first American faction that has shown interest in our rifle. The quantity is rather large and I'm still communicating with my seller to provide that amount. Please bear with me if it takes a few days." Poppy studied the face of William, looking for any indication he was not who he said he was.

"I don't care who else you sell to. If the 'niggers' are buying guns in Africa and killing each other, then so be it. We have our hands full in America. We need to get a stockpile and show our members we're in this fight to the end. The 'niggers' and the Mexicans have gained too much power in the South and the white Texan could be a minority in a few more years. Can you imagine a Mexican as governor of Texas?"

"I don't get mixed up in American politics. I just sell weapons. What you do with them is your business."

"Then do we have a deal, Mr. Crow? I have to get back to the States and the sooner I know this is happening, the better."

"Do you have a cell phone with you, Mr. Gueist? When the shipment is ready, I'll give you a call. I can deliver them to any port in Europe but if you pick them up yourself at our warehouse, I can give you a 5%

discount on the price."

"We'll stick to the original deal and have you deliver them to Le Havre. We already have a cargo ship ready. I know nothing about moving guns through France. If this works out, the brotherhood can get you in touch with other groups like ours. The fight for the white man is not over."

"Don't you have a black president, Mr. Geist? I thought your country elected him twice?"

"Propaganda and brainwashing got him elected. We now have our own news channel educating the American people so they won't make that mistake again."

"Whatever you do with the weapons is your business. You'll receive a call in a couple of days for a delivery date. A ten percent down payment is required from you first. I discussed that with your European contact. Also, you cell phone number."

William reached into his coat pocket and handed Poppy the envelope containing the money.

Everything was taped by the video camera on the roof of an adjacent building as well as the conversation from the table nearby.

"Here is the agreed amount. My number is on the envelope. Thank you for your time. If we do this again I'd like to come myself. I like this country but I have one question. How do you control the niggers here?"

"Like I said, I don't get involved in politics, Mr. Gueist. I just sell guns." William finished his sandwich and water while Poppy reached into the envelope and pulled out a hundred Euro bill to pay for the meal. Poppy stood up and shook William's hand.

"Expect my call in the next day or two. The crates will arrive at Le Havre and I'll have a man there to pick up the final payment after the weapons are accounted for. The ammunition is available in the States or it can be ordered and shipped to you."

"We have a powerful lobby in American government. The NRA has a lot of wealthy people who share my views making sure everyone can get a gun."

"Enjoy your meal. I have to go," Poppy said as he turned and walked away.

*****

William watched Poppy make his exit. He had an earpiece and knew he was being taped and sound monitored. He whispered in a low voice, "Did you get all of that?"

The French officer, who spoke English, was the person with the sound equipment. "Yes, we got it all. You were so convincing you even scared me. Are you sure you don't share the same views as the man you were trying to portray?"

"Hell no. Those idiots live in isolated parts of the country like Idaho and feed on each other's misery. Now they're arming themselves and telling their followers the federal government is coming after them for their beliefs."

"I lived in the States for a while when I was younger," the French officer said. "That's how I speak English with an American accent. I went to school in San Francisco so I never met any racists. If I went to some place like Texas, it might have been a different story."

"That's true. Are Robert and Julia following Poppy? I saw them leave soon after Poppy did."

"They have contact with *Capitaine* Le Cure. Hopefully, they can find out where Poppy lives and we can tap his phone."

"What do you want me to do now," William asked.

"Your work is done. We expect you'll get a call from Poppy in a day or two unless he is arrested, so be prepared. Go home and I'll have Robert fill you in when he returns to his hotel."

William prepared to take an elevator ride up the tower. He had time and not expected back at the Pension until six. He also needed to buy some postcards of Versailles. If he could keep his mission secret until the case was over, he stood a chance of escaping Leslie's wrath with only minor scratches.

*****

"Make sure we don't lose contact with that taxi," Robert told the driver. "A double tip is waiting for you if we find out where he lives."

"Qui monsieur," the driver answered.

"I don't think Poppy knows he's being followed," Julia said. "The traffic is so bad in Paris there is no way one could escape in a car."

"What area are we heading to?" Robert asked the driver.

"St. Maurice. This section of Paris has nice homes and apartments. I think the taxi is going to pull over, *monsieur.*"

Poppy's cab pulled up in front of a beautiful apartment complex overlooking the city. After Robert and Julia's taxi drove by, Poppy got out. The tinted car windows kept their faces hidden.

"Pull over and park," Robert told the driver. "We need to see which apartment he goes into." Both Robert and Julia stayed in their taxi and watched through the back window as Poppy crossed the street and walked up the stone stairs to apartment 317. They waited until he opened the front door and walked in.

"Capitaine, this is Robert. We followed Poppy to his apartment in the St. Maurice district. The address is 317 Vision. Poppy must be doing quite well to live up here."

"That is a nice area of Paris," Le Cure commented. "I'll get a court order to tap into any land lines in the apartment. When he leaves, we'll point a sound receiver at the front window and bug the inside as well. National Security laws permit us a lot of room to operate so we should hear everything he says while he's home."

"See if you can find out who owns this place. There's another apartment next door for rent so his is probably a rental," Robert said. "We're leaving. You now have his residence so all that is needed is the seller."

"I'll do my best," Le Cure said.

On the way back to their hotel, Robert called William. "Well 008, how did the meeting go? Did you get your detective fix with Poppy?"

"That was awesome," William answered. "I just got back to the room and the family is still gone so I can talk. I want a copy of my conversation with Poppy. The guy I pretended to be was such an asshole I wanted to strangle him after the meeting, except that would be suicide. Poppy had to believe me. I was the perfect racist."

"Don't get too carried away, 008. We don't have him

or his seller yet."

"He's going to do this deal, Robert. I had to give him 10% as a down payment. The guns will be delivered to Le Havre and he expects the rest of the money then. The call from Poppy is in the next two days after he makes sure his seller gets the order ready."

"That means he'll be talking to the mystery man soon. We need to get ears on that apartment as fast as possible. Let me know when he calls, William. Does Leslie know anything about this?"

"You know she doesn't. I don't want to lose my buzz just yet. This is better than going after Ian. Also, I believe Poppy is gay. He has too many of the stereotype characteristics to be straight."

"And what would that be, William. Well dressed and checking out the single men walking by?"

"Well-dressed, yes. He did watch a few men walk by. It's more in his mannerisms and hand movements. I'm 95% sure he's gay, but I don't know how that'll help us."

"I'll say something to Le Cure and see what he thinks," Robert said. "The *Capitaine* knows the neighborhoods in Paris so maybe he can use the information. I'll call him now."

"Agent 008, signing off." William hung up.

Robert turned off his cell phone and turned to Julia. "William's lost it. He's having too much fun with this spy business. I hope he doesn't kid around too much, and lose his focus. Poppy and his seller are not people I'd mess with."

"Didn't Poppy have that bodybuilder killed in jail?" Julia asked. "He was going to flip, and ended up dead in the shower, right?"

"Yes, Le Cure believes so. I'm calling him now and pass on the new development William discovered."

"And what's that?"

"William is sure Poppy is gay."

Robert speed dialed the Le Cure's number and waited for him to answer. "Hello, *Capitaine*, it's me, Robert. I may have something for you."

"Did you talk to William?" Le Cure asked.

"Yes. William thinks Poppy is gay. We don't know if this information will help, but at least you have it."

"It may," Le Cure said. "I do know there is a famous gay bar in the area where Poppy lives. He may go there at night. We have his picture so I'll get a plainclothes cop to hang out and see if he shows up. We have his apartment under surveillance. As soon as he leaves we're bugging the place."

"Call us back if something comes up. Julia and I are staying around our hotel. We're ready to back up William if he needs it. He's carried away with his detective role and thinks he's agent 008. His humor is more like Peter Sellers."

"Isn't Peter Sellers the actor who played a French detective in The Pink Panther? I love that movie. Made the French police look like crap, but it was funny."

"That's the same guy," Robert said.

"I'll get someone on this and check out the bar. It's called Le Beefcake. Only the gay population with money can afford to drink there."

"Okay, talk to you later," Robert said.

*****

Poppy arrived at Le Beefcake around eight. He wasn't looking for any companionship but wanted to have a few drinks around other men like him. He'd been harassed too many times in straight bars when he was younger.

"You were here last night," the bartender said to Poppy. "Are you new in the area?"

"I moved here last week. I'm not looking for anyone to connect with. Just give me a whiskey sour and a plate of fries, please. I'll be over in that booth."

"Yes, sir. I'll get it right to you." The bartender sent

the food order back to the kitchen and prepared the drink.

Poppy sat in the soft cushioned, red velvet seat. He needed a few drinks to unwind as he called his contact, Oscar Norman, regarding the shipment on Wednesday. Poppy now had a driver to take the rifles to Le Havre.

*****

The plainclothes officer spotted Poppy as soon as he walked in the door. Pierre had done undercover work with the gay community before, and he looked the part. His handsome, boyish looks, and applied makeup to his eyes allowed him to fit in. The listening device was in his hand and he needed to place it near Poppy as soon as he could.

"Hello," Pierre said to Poppy as he approached his table. "Are you looking for company?"

"No, not really," Poppy said. "Maybe another night. I have business to conduct and I can't be interrupted."

Pierre leaned forward and placed his left hand on the tabletop to distract Poppy and slipped his right hand under the wood surface and pressed the listening device, with the adhesive, into the table bottom. "I'll look forward to talking to you another time," Pierre said.

He turned to leave just as the fries and drink arrived.

He's pretty damn cute, thought Poppy. Too bad I have

business or I'd look into that one. After a few sips of his drink, he was ready to make the call.

"Hello, Oscar, Poppy here. Sorry to call you at home but I've been busy with that American representative."

"I hope you're in a safe place because you used my name. Where are you?"

"Le Beefcake. It's a bar and one of the reasons I moved to this area. I have to be around my people and I live only a few blocks from here."

"Oh, that's right. You moved recently. I can hear a lot of talking in the background. Are you alone?"

"Yes. I came here to be sure the call was safe. The police have devices that pick up signals from anywhere so inside a bar seemed to be a good place."

"My wife is taking a bath so I'll make this conversation quick. The shipment will be at the warehouse tomorrow night. Midnight seems to be the best. The night guard is on my payroll and has no problem signing for anything."

"My driver is the same," Poppy said. "This is a big shipment, so I had to hire a larger truck. Should I wire the money to the same account?"

"Nothing has changed," Oscar said. "I have the guns marked as going to Australia. The police in Sydney are on the invoice. As long as law enforcements are building up their arms cache, we'll stay in business for a long time, Poppy. We just make sure the people on the other side can get them as well to keep the playing field level."

Poppy had no problem with who bought weapons. The police beat him when he was a young gay man taking part in protest marches for gay rights. This was payback for the treatment he received from those who were suppose to protect its citizens. Screw them. Screw them all, he thought. He had the power now.

"I have to go," Poppy said. "I'm new here, and the regulars are dropping by to see if I'm available."

"Stay out of trouble, Poppy. Maybe the Americans will become better clients than the Africans."

Poppy paused for a moment before speaking. He hoped he didn't have to deal with another insane group like 'The Brotherhood' again.

"Maybe, but they're crazy. I may hire someone to take a meeting if I need to sell to them again. If they find out I'm gay, they might use me as target practice."

"They're that bad? Anyway, stay safe. We'll both make money on this deal and we could use the expanded market."

"*Au revoir.*" Poppy put his phone in his pocket and ordered another drink. The fries were gone. He didn't want to stay much longer or he might be tempted to take one of these men home with him. He had work to do.

*****

"We got it all on tape, *Capitaine*. We have the seller's first name. Pierre got there just in time and placed the bug under Poppy's table. Poppy called a minute later. After another drink, he left the bar and is probably heading home."

"Did Pierre retrieve the device from the table?" Le Cure asked.

"Yes, he grabbed it as soon as Poppy left. Do we have Poppy's apartment bugged yet?"

"That team finished twenty minutes ago. They got in and got out. Now we have to find out who this mystery seller is," Le Cure said. "We'll grab the driver and night watchman at the warehouse instead of following the guns to Le Havre. What was the name of the seller?" Le Cure asked.

"Oscar," the sergeant said. "We could only hear Poppy talking but we are sure the same warehouse is the location. It's owned by the gun factory named ATP."

Le Cure gave a sigh of relief. "Good work, *Sergent*. I'll get my computer hacker to access the employee files of ATP and see how many Oscars there are. He has to be a person in a high position to be able to pull this off so that should narrow down the search a bit."

"Correct, *Capitaine*. If you find the name Oscar in the business office and you have your man."

"I'm starting the search right now. Maybe we can make an arrest tomorrow and wrap up this case."

"Let's hope so, *Capitaine*. A French automatic rifle in the hands of radical extremists does not make us look good. This is a National Security problem and we have the government backing us on this."

"I have to go. Thank you, *Sergent*."

Chapter 28

"How did you like the palace, William?" Anne asked. "Versailles is as popular to visit as the Eiffel Tower."

"Really. There were a lot of tour busses, but the palace is so big and spread out I never felt crowded. The tour guide said there are over seven hundred rooms." William Googled the palace online to get a few facts he could throw out in case Leslie quizzed him.

"How about the garden? Did you get to walk around on your tour?" Leslie asked.

William purchased several postcards of the well-groomed back yard and gave his comment. "That was amazing. There must be hundreds of people keeping that place in shape. I was really impressed. I bought a few cards so I could remember what it looked like. How was your wine tour?" William did his best to divert the conversation away from himself.

"We bought several bottles of the local brand at the winery and had them sent home. What was the type of wine we bought, Anne?" Leslie asked.

"The local grapes are Cabernet and every year the wine tastes a little different depending up what happens during the growing season. I don't remember the years we bought, but we filled a case box and the wine should be in Arizona when you get home."

"Speaking of wine, are we going out to that special restaurant you were thinking about, Anne?" William asked.

"We have reservations. I eat there on special occasions and Paul will meet us. We'll take a taxi and he'll drive us home. He's coming from work and only has time to change his clothes."

"What time do you want us ready?" Lois asked. "I need about an hour to get ready."

"Start getting ready now. I'll help you," said Anne. "The taxi will come by here first and then pick you two up." Anne nodded towards William and Leslie.

"We better head back to the Pension then," Leslie said. "We'll be ready when the taxi arrives. See you in an hour."

*****

Capitaine Le Cure's team was sure they had their man. Of all the office staff in the company ATP, only one had the first name of Oscar. Oscar Norman.

"There is one obstacle we could encounter, *Capitaine*. Oscar is married to the daughter of one of the three founders of the company. The owners are third generation and *Monsieur* Norman is the head of the export department. I doubt he worked his way up through the company. He probably married into that job."

"So you're telling me we have to embarrass one of the three owners if we bust this guy. We need foolproof evidence before we go crashing into their factory to make an arrest," the Sergent said. "These powerful businessmen won't let us in without a warrant."

"Let's pick up Poppy the same time we raid the warehouse. When we have all three in separate rooms, we make a deal with whoever breaks first. One of them should. If not then we threaten each one with the maximum sentence. Selling illegal arms internationally has to be twenty years or more."

The team laid out their plan and made a few bets as to who would flip first.

"Poppy and the driver know each other, but probably not the company boss. Oscar and the midnight warehouse worker will know each other. I'm not too concerned with either of these men. Poppy and Monsieur Norman are the real players," Le Cure said.

Sergent Bruno continued. "We need to grill them tonight and get one of them to talk."

"You set up a team for the warehouse bust, Sergent and I'll take two men with me to pick up Poppy. We'll meet back here at the station and prepare the rooms. First one who gets their man to talk gets dinner at Le Bistro on me."

"Our best bet is either the driver or the warehouse worker. Poppy has too much to lose by giving up *Monsieur* Norman. Gays in prison don't have it so good so he probably won't tell us much."

"Let's get this done, *Capitaine*. We have a long night ahead of us."

*****

Robert and Julia were asleep when they got the call from Le Cure. It was eleven p.m. Both were invited to come down to the station and witness the interrogations or be a part of the team that went to the gun factory to make the bust. Being up all night did not seem exciting for either him or Julia.

"How about we accompany you to the factory for the final take down," Robert said. "Do you think you'll get one of the men to break? I don't think Poppy will."

"We don't either," Le Cure said. "We'll give the other two a chance to redeem ten years of their life. The driver should give up Poppy and we believe the warehouse worker will turn on his boss. After that, we'll make the arrest at the factory and wrap up this case."

"We can get a taxi to the factory when you make the bust. I want to see the face of *Monsieur* Norman when this happens," Robert said.

"The wife's father may cooperate if we promise to

keep this bust out of the news. Something like this will damage the name of their company," Le Cure said. "I'll send a police car to pick you up. You'll never get past the main gate in a taxi."

"Good idea. We'll be ready tomorrow morning, *Capitaine*. Thank you for including us."

"You're a good ally, Robert. Even William is a huge asset. When this is over we have an award for him."

"An award? What kind of award?" Robert asked.

"I'm going to make one up. How about the 'Pink Panther' metal of honor, exclusively for Americans who help the French Police solve cases. Anyway, it's late. I'll call in the morning after we get one of the men to sign a confession. If we get two confessions, we'll have both Poppy and Oscar over a barrel."

"We'll expect your call, *Capitaine*."

Robert turned to face Julia. She handed him a glass of wine to help him relax and go back to sleep.

"We're invited to attend the arrest of the man selling guns to Poppy. They're arresting Poppy tonight at the same time they bust the warehouse."

"So we can go back to sleep now," Julia said. "I'm a little wound up and might need help sleeping."

"What kind of help?"

"What do you think?" Julia asked in her most seductive voice.

Robert didn't need any more hints. He set his wine on the table next to the bed, ducked under the covers and hit her special spot on the first attempt. Julia's face registered a smile when he made contacted. She then let out a moan.

*****

By 11:45 p.m. the trap at the warehouse was set. The police parked several blocks away while several officers positioned themselves on the rooftop across the street. The plan was to arrest the driver and warehouse worker when the exchange was made, take them to the police station and bring the shipment of rifles as evidence.

While the factory bust took place, Le Cure and his two officers waited outside Poppy's apartment. The lights were off and Le Cure waited for a call from his *Sergent* at the warehouse.

12:15 the call came. "*Capitaine*, we have them," *Sergent* Bruno said. "They didn't put up a fight at all. The weapons are on the way back to the station and we have each man in a separate car. I believe each man will tell us what we want."

"Good work, *Sergent*. We're about to arrest Poppy. We'll meet you back at the station. Three separate interrogation rooms are set up. Let's complete this before sunrise."

"Will do. See you in an hour," *Sergent* Bruno said.

*****

Capitaine Le Cure and two of his men approached the front door of Poppy's apartment. One officer held a door slammer while the other two stood behind him. The handle was crushed with one swing and all three officers entered the apartment with guns drawn. They didn't know if Poppy carried a weapon.

The apartment bedroom door was open and Poppy sat up in bed wearing pajamas. He reached for the phone as the police entered. He had the bedroom light on, waiting for a call from his driver.

"This is the police, Poppy," Le Cure announced. "You're under arrest for selling weapons to foreign organizations and violating French law."

Poppy had a surprised look on his face that told *Capitaine* Le Cure he had no idea what was happening.

"*Merde*," Poppy said loud enough that the arresting officers could hear him. "You have no right to break into my apartment without a warrant."

"The arrest warrant is in my hand," *Capitaine* Le Cure answered. "Assholes like you give France a bad name and this time you and your partner, Oscar Norman, will pay."

"Norman, who's that," Poppy said with a straight face. "I've never heard of anyone named Norman."

"We'll give you time to remember down at the station," Le Cure said. "Grab his computer and cell phone. I can see several phones on the dresser so take them as well. Officer Crusio, I want you to go through the apartment and take anything you think we can use as evidence. Office Barley and I will take Poppy to the station and send a car back for you."

"Sir. It looks like a lot of his belongings are still in boxes. It shouldn't take long."

Le Cure and officer Barley each took a hold of Poppy's arms and lifted him up. He was still in his pajamas so Le Cure grabbed the street clothes he found neatly folded on the chair next to the bed as well as a pair of shoes under the chair.

"Do you need any underwear and socks?" Le Cure asked.

"You can't get away with this," Poppy answered.

"I'll take that as a no," Le Cure said. "Get him in the car and let's get him to talk back at the station. This could be a long night."

*****

The drive to the station was uneventful. Only Le Cure and officer Barley spoke while Poppy sat in silence in the back seat. Shock and disbelief muddled his thinking process. He had to get a message to Oscar. Hopefully, he could warn him what was happening.

The squad car with Poppy pulled up to the station around two a.m. The other suspects were already in their separate interrogation rooms, waiting for someone to come in and start the questioning process. Poppy remained in his own enclosure.

"Don't I get a phone call? I do have a lawyer," Poppy said.

"You can have your call when we feel you've had time to think about what you're faced with. Give us your connection with *Monsieur* Norman at ATP, and we can reduce your sentence. You're looking at 30 years. Your driver has already given us your name and he'll be out in a couple of years. Same thing goes with the warehouse employee. After he confirms *Monsieur* Norman at the factory, then he gets the break and not you. I'll be back to get your answer."

"My lawyer. I need to call him," Poppy screamed as the door slammed shut.

By four a.m., the driver and the warehouseman signed

confessions. Poppy only had his lawyer to save him now. Le Cure came into the room and placed a phone on the table. Poppy made a call.

"Francois, it's me, Poppy. I've been arrested for selling weapons. I'm at the 3rd precinct. You know what to do." He then hung up.

Le Cure walked into the room where Poppy was and unplugged the phone and removed it.

"You've had your call. Now we have a signed confession by the factory worker so you are too late to save yourself."

"Put me in a cell with a bed. I'm done talking to you. I need some sleep," Poppy said.

Le Cure was confused. This was not the response he expected. He then led Poppy to a proper cell and within minutes the prisoner was asleep.

*****

Poppy's lawyer, Francois knew what he had to do. He couldn't make a call directly to Norman because he only had his work number at the factory. Norman kept his personal phone and address unlisted. He made a call to the office number message box, telling Norman about Poppy's arrest and the police coming for him. Francois planned to visit Poppy in the morning, and he went back to sleep. He couldn't do much more until he visited his client and found out all the facts.

*****

The next morning Oscar Norman arrived at his office and listened to his message. There was only one. "Poppy is arrested for selling guns and the police are on their way to you. Good Luck."

After calling the night watchman on his cell phone and not getting an answer, Oscar made a call to the warehouse where the guns were located. The person on duty told Oscar when he arrived all the doors were locked and no one was around. The night watchman had not clocked out and the thirty crates of rifles going to Le Havre were missing.

Something went wrong, thought Oscar. If the night watchman was arrested, his name could be involved. Why else would the police be coming to the factory? His mind was spinning. This could be the end. All the extra money he made from the gun sales was for naught. Someone would do a follow-up and see that the weapons he sold did not go where they were supposed to go. He couldn't keep his wife in the lifestyle she was accustomed to. He had to prepare for the end because he wasn't going down quietly.

It was not yet nine o'clock. From his office window, Oscar had a view of the parking lot and entrance into the gated factory door. In the distance, he could see two blue police cars approaching with the lights flashing on the hoods of the vehicles. There were no sirens, only lights.

Norman calmly walked down to the factory floor and grabbed one of the newest automatic rifles from the display case. The workers were starting to assemble the weapons and a few of them stared at Norman as he passed them. He had a crazed look on his face.

His next move was to get ammunition and bullet magazines. He punched in the code to the cabinet and opened the door. Once inside he grabbed a case of ammo and put on a bulletproof vest that the testers used.

Oscar needed a secure position to make his last stand. He wasn't going to jail, and what he did next would damage the company when it hit the nightly news.

The workers in the factory knew something was not right but no one made an attempt to interfere with one of their bosses. They gave him room to walk to the back of the factory with the weapon and ammunition.

*****

By now, the police cars were in the parking lot. They had no idea that their suspect knew they had arrived as they made their way to the business offices. *Capitaine* Le Curc led the way. Robert and Julia were in the second car. When they got out they followed the *Capitaine* to the elevator.

The factory floor was in a panic. The workers shut down any machines that were used to assemble the weapons and headed towards the exits. They wanted no part in what might come next.

"We're here to talk to *Monsieur* Norman," *Capitaine* Le Cure told the secretary outside the main office. We have an arrest warrant and we need to do this without incident."

The president on duty came out of his office. All the machinery was off and the workers had exited from the building to the parking lot.

"What's the meaning of this?" he asked. "Why are you here?"

"We have an arrest warrant for *Monsieur* Oscar Norman. We also would like to do this quietly and keep it out of the press. Something like this is not good publicity for your company. That's possible if you cooperate with us," *Captaine* Le Cure said.

The secretary's phone rang and she answered. After listening for a minute, she spoke. "*Monsieur* Canne. That was the factory foreman. He reported the workers left the building and *Monsieur* Norman is in the corner of the factory wearing a protection vest and has fortified an area with metal crates. He has our best automatic rifle and ammunition. The foreman thinks *Monsieur* Norman snapped. All the workers are now out of harm's way."

"Where is he now?" Canne asked. "Can we see him from the windows overlooking the factory?"

Le Cure knew they had walked into a dangerous situation. Someone must have tipped Norman off, he thought.

"We were trying to avoid a situation like this," Le Cure said.

"What did he do?" Canne asked. "He's married to the daughter of one of the other owners and has a good position with the company."

"He sells your rifles to gun dealers, who in turn sells them to illegal organizations throughout the world. We have one of his buyers in custody right now along with your night watchman at the warehouse. The driver of a truck is also behind bars. The last client was an extremist group from America."

"America?" Canne said. "We don't sell weapons to America. They have their own factories. Why would they buy from us?"

"I don't think we have time to discuss this right now, *Monsieur* Canne. We seem to be in a crisis situation. Is there any way we can see where *Monsieur* Norman is in the factory. Maybe I can get one of my snipers in position and neutralize him before someone gets hurt."

Suddenly, the sound of automatic gunfire came from

the factory below. Oscar assembled a cave with heavy metal crates and laid out all the magazines for the automatic rifle in order to quickly reload. He was tired of waiting and wanted the police to know he was ready for them.

"You have to kill me because I'm not going to jail," he yelled. "Let's see what you've got."

Monsieur Canne and the police heard the challenge through the glass windows overlooking the factory below.

"I have a monitor in my office. We can see him from there," Canne said.

Le Cure and Robert entered the office and assessed the situation after seeing the screen.

"It looks like Norman is not going to give up," Robert said.

"I think we have a madman on our hands," Le Cure said. "This is exactly what I wanted to avoid. Poppy's lawyer might have sent a message warning him. That bastard will pay if any of my men get hurt."

Monsieur Canne made a call to the other two owners of the factory to tell them the situation. Both men were on their way and would be there in thirty minutes.

"I never did like Norman," Canne said. "Giving

executive jobs to in-laws doesn't work. This is a perfect example. I have two sons and they worked their way up in this company."

"This is not the time to voice grievances about your staff. This man is dangerous and will kill someone if we don't do something," Le Cure said.

Another round of automatic fire came from the fortified cave. "Is anyone out there? I'm waiting," Norman yelled.

"Can we get a negotiator here in the next twenty minutes?" Robert asked.

"No, not that soon." Le Cure said. "If Norman gets tired of waiting and starts firing out the factory door, someone could get killed. We've got to get one of my snipers in position and fill that cave with bullets. We can try to talk to him first but I doubt it'll work. He sounds like he's too far gone."

"One of us has to try and talk to him before we go to plan B," *Sergent* Bruno said.

"I don't want anyone killed," Le Cure said. "I think we have to get everyone away from the exit doors and seal this place off. He can't get out and so maybe we can wait him out."

The order went down to the foreman to seal off the factory and get everyone away from any doors. Two of

Le Cure's marksmen took positions upstairs on opposite sides of the factory. Each had a clear shot at the fortified cave.

By now, *Captaine* Le Cure retrieved his megaphone from the police car and stood to the side of the fort where Norman was located. If Oscar continued to fire the weapon, the orders were to shoot.

"Oscar Norman , I'm *Capitaine* Le Cure of the Paris police." His voice on the bullhorn rang out loud and clear. "You have nowhere to go. We came here to arrest you, not harm you. You have put us in a difficult position. If you don't surrender then we have no alternative but to stop you from hurting anyone else. Is this what you want?"

"Stop the bullshit," Oscar yelled. He then fired ten rounds in the direction of Le Cure's voice. One of the snipers had a shot at Norman's arm for a split second but the rifle retreated into the metal cave before he could get a shot off.

Le Cure was faced with a dilemma. He returned to the safety of the second floor. "What do you want us to do?" he asked Canne. "If we neutralize him, we can be gone before the press arrives. If Oscar doesn't give up and the news gets wind of this incident, there is no preventing this from this making the headlines."

"I'll get back to you," Canne said. He speed dialed the

other two owners to get their input. Five minutes later he returned with the answer.

"We all want to keep this from the news. Finish it. I can control my workers but those two Americans with you are different. Can you keep them quiet?'

"When they leave France we have no control over what they do. Maybe you could offer them a reward for helping solve this case. Other than that, they're free to do what they want."

"Take him out and we will clean up the mess," Canne said. "I'll offer them two million Euros and take care of everything else."

Julia and Robert were in the room when the conversation between Le Cure and Canne took place.

"You're going to kill him to keep this out of the press?" Julia asked. She was clearly upset.

"You speak French?" Canne asked, looking at Julia. "This is really French business. We are paying to stop any bad publicity."

Julia was in shock. She turned to Robert. "*Monsieur* Canne wants to offer two million Euros for them to keep quiet about the incident. The police will kill Norman and leave before the press arrived."

"This is their business, Julia. We're not in the States.

We have no control over what they do."

"I know, Robert, but that is still a life down there. If we're going to turn our backs on him, then we should make them really pay. These men make these weapons and are rich from this business."

"What can we do, Julia? I see your point but we are out of our element. Do you have a plan?"

Julia turned to *Capitaine* Le Cure and said in English. "Tell Monsieur Canne that we want a trust fund set up for five million Euros. The money should be in the name of the French police and used for the families of the victims who die in street killings. These are our terms. We want it in writing before we leave the country."

Capitaine Le Cure had a whole new level of respect for Julia. He didn't like street weapons either because they made his job more difficult. He turned to Canne but was cut short before he spoke.

"I speak English, *Capitaine*." He then turned to Julia. "It's a deal. I'll get the papers signed, and have the police set up the trust. We have your word nothing gets to the press, correct?"

"You have our word," Julia said. "Let's get out of here, Robert. This situation distresses me and I don't want to see the how this ends."

*****

Robert and Julia left the office and headed back to the waiting police car. The factory employees were still milling around in the parking lot. A multitude of gunshots rang out followed by silence. Both Robert and Julia knew it was over. Killing Norman was like shooting fish in a barrel.

"This has been the worst ending of a case I've ever been a part of, Robert. I never want to be in a situation like this again. That man's life was bought and paid for just to keep the incident from leaking out. That was the only solution I could think of to make this right. I think I'm going to be sick," she said as she held a handkerchief to her mouth.

Robert shook his head. "I'm sorry, Julia, I really am. We solved the case, but this is not our country. Money seems to be the deciding factor in most nations. This could have happen in the States as well. You did what you could to make it right. Let's get back to the hotel and pack. I ready to go home."

*****

Robert and Julia spent the next two days tying up loose ends. Le Cure contacted them and the trust fund was established in the name of the Paris police. Not a word of the incident made it into the newspapers or on the evening news. The only mention of anything was a fire drill at the factory conducted by the police to account for the employees seen standing in the parking lot. The gunfire noise was explained to the press as testing.

The only thing related to the factory in the news was a report of an executive named Oscar Norman, who died in a drowning accident. His body was never recovered. The article mentioned he liked to swim in the English Channel by himself. The police found his car parked on an isolated beach near the water.

He was survived only by his wife of five years. They had no children.

*****

Poppy received the news of Oscar's death from his lawyer. When he told Poppy to plead out and hope to reduce his sentence five years, Poppy refused. He knew he wouldn't last five years, let alone fifteen. Being gay in prison was a nightmare. The gay population either 'put out' and adjusted to being abused daily or ended their lives.

Chapter 29

A month later Julia and Robert hosted a party at their home in Albuquerque. Laura and Jeff, married two weeks before, arrived with wine left over from their wedding. Cathy and Alan made the mile drive down the same road to the Forrester home. William and Leslie came from Tucson. Detective Louis and his soon to be wife, June, were also invited. Neither of them knew that Robert Woods was still alive. That information would be shared privately.

Julia met the two police officers at the door and took them to a side room. Robert and Julia discussed this delicate situation earlier. They had to share their secret with these two guardians of the law because they were now entrenched in solving cases together. So far, the Ian McClure investigation, the kidnapping of Cathy and the capture of Marcos was a successful joint effort. These two officers were an important part of the network Robert and Julia established and they wanted to secure their partnership with them.

"The reason I wanted to talk to you two has to do with our continued ability to work with each other. What you're about to find out in the next minute is going to either bond us, or make life difficult. My hope is that you two can be a part of our team and remain police officers protecting our city from crime."

"This is starting to freak me out, Julia," Louis said. "What is so important that we have to keep it to ourselves?"

Julia raised her voice and said, "Time to come in."

The side door opened and Robert entered. His face was changed so he looked different than the photos Louis had of him on file. Nothing was said. Suddenly, June made a gasping sound. "You're Robert Woods, aren't you?"

Louis's jaw dropped when he finally made the connection. "Damn, you're right June, it's him."

Robert came in and sat down. He looked at Louis but still didn't say anything. He hoped his secret was safe with these two police officers. Finally, he said, "My name is Robert Forrester now because Robert Woods is dead. Our wish is you can live with that, and be a part of what we're trying to do."

"What are you trying to do, Robert?" June asked.

"You've been involved in three cases. In all of them, the police received the credit and we worked with you to make this happen. Our plan is to keep this relationship going and you become our contact with the department in solving more cases. Robert Woods needs to remain dead, and my looks are altered enough to make this possible. As far as anyone knows, he died in that house explosion last year."

Louis was still in shock. He had no idea he'd been working with a 'dead man'. All this time he thought he was solving cases with Julia and her assistant.

"How do we do this?" Louis finally asked. "Do we continue as though you're dead, and do everything through Julia?"

"For now, that's the best solution. That way you don't have to lie about me, and Julia is your only contact."

"Our boss knows nothing about any of this. If we work together on anything in the future, do you think we can continue this hidden identity game? June asked.

"I don't see why not," Robert said. "We also have an ally in France. *Capitaine* Le Cure knows me, but nothing about my past. He only knows us as Julia and Robert Forrester. The only difference is that you know who I was before."

Silence filled the room. Finally, June spoke. "Louis, we can do this. Martin only sees headlines and so far our department has solved three cases with the help of Robert and Julia. They haven't broken any laws, and it's been a big plus for us. You're in line for a promotion, and in a few years, Martin will retire. When you're the boss we won't have to answer to anyone."

Louis saw June's practical reasoning. She was smart

and helped balanced out his cop mentality. "I think we can do this," he finally said.

Both Louis and June shook Robert's hand. Nothing more needed to be said. It was their private pact. Who knew what the future would bring between this newly formed alliance? June and Julia smiled at each other. They hoped it would work.

"Let's go back to the party and have a drink," Robert finally said. "We have plenty of food and I want you to formally meet the other members of our team." The two couples entered the living room.

"You mean all these people are a part of your team?" asked Louis.

"Well, let's put it this way. Alan and Cathy have their own business now but he had a lot to do with the Ian case. Cathy was kidnapped and you helped us captured those two idiots. Laura helped with the Ian case and Jeff had a role in capturing Marcos. After being zapped with a stun gun I don't know if he'll volunteer again. William and Leslie are the couple from Tucson. William had a lot to do with shutting down The Company and ruining Ian McClure. Ian did shoot himself, but I gave him a little help in making that decision."

"So that was you in the room with Ian," June said. "We never could figure out who was talking to him at the end."

"Yes, but that's the past. William also played a big part in capturing a gunrunner in Paris. None of you were involved and all that was a favor to *Capitaine* Le Cure. William posed as a buyer for a fake radical group in the States and, because of him, we discovered the name of the seller for the French weapons factory. Now the flow of weapons from that gun company to illegal groups has stopped."

"You've been busy," Louis said. "So June and I are a part of an international investigation team. I'm sure we can keep anything we know secret from Martin. Just keep us informed when we can help. As long as our boss gets some credit, he'll be happy."

"That's it. My computer assistant just arrived with her boyfriend. He knows nothing about us but Peggy is in the loop regarding all our cases. She replaced Alan when he started his Geek Mingle dating service."

"I did notice a few dishes on your roof, Robert. How big of an operation are you?"

"We do okay." Robert was tempted to show Louis his office but decided to wait. Maybe after a few more cases were in the books, he'd show the new partners his computers and other electronic devices.

Robert spent the next ten minutes introducing Detective Louis and Officer June to the rest of the guests. He even presented them to his cook, Carla, who was in the kitchen preparing her favorite Mexican dishes for the group. To Robert, she was a part of the team as well. She kept them going with good nutrition and her personality was always a spark of light in the home.

After the introductions, Alan pulled Robert to the side. "The police know who you are? I thought you were dead to them."

"We're forming a group with only Louis and June from the local police department. With the publicity they're getting, they're happy to continue this relationship."

"I'm sure you know what you're doing, Robert. How about Jeff? Is he still willing to be a part of the team after getting zapped by the Stun Gun Killer? He might think twice before volunteering his services again."

"You could be right, Alan. I'll have to work on him. It's William I worry about. I don't know if Leslie will continue as a roadblock. He's really into this investigation stuff. He calls himself 008 and he's half serious."

"I miss working for you, Robert. That was an exciting part of my life for sure. Cathy and I are getting married January of next year so don't get into any heavy-duty cases around that time. I want you as my best man and Cathy wants Julia as her matron of honor."

"It's about time. Are you two going traditional with a minister and all the trimmings?"

"Cathy's mom is flying out from New York and my parents live in Albuquerque. Weddings are as much for them as they are for us. We're using the minister from the Episcopal Church where my parents attend. They're actually an open-minded group and avoid that fundamentalist crap."

"Amen to that, Alan. That's why we had the type of service for our wedding. Julia is practicing non-violence in the Buddhist tradition and I'm leaning towards a Dr. Martin Luther King approach to life. They both seem compatible."

"Anyway I just wanted to check in and offer our help if you need it," Alan said. "Peggy seems to be doing a great job with you. From what I hear, she thinks it's the most exciting work she's ever done. I don't know if her boyfriend knows everything she does but it's probably best to keep him in the dark."

"I think so too, Alan."

Alan joined Cathy on the sofa while Robert tapped his wine glass with a knife to get everyone's attention.

"Friends and family. We are here to celebrate the end of a series of cases. Cathy is safe after the gallant efforts of the Albuquerque police force including detective

Louis and officer June. The case led Julia and me to Paris, France where we tracked down the second kidnapper and sent him home to stand trial."

So far Robert's story did not include William so Leslie remained in the dark.

"While in France, Julia and I were able to help the Paris Police after they led us to our kidnapper. The man we tracked down lived in Stockholm, Sweden and came to Paris when a kidnapping took place. His boss, who went by the name Poppy, was the ring-leader. Marcos, known as the Stun Gun Killer, was his employee."

The story still did not include William in any way.

"This last case got a little wild and took us to Stockholm where we followed up with some leads. We found where Marcos lived and missed catching him by several hours. He returned to Paris, but was tipped off and fled to London. We then received a letter from Poppy. He said Marcos was on his way to Albuquerque to kill Julia and me."

A gasp came from a few of the guests who hadn't heard about the Paris case.

"We believe Poppy was trying to cover his tracks by having the police in America shoot our man and prevent any connections with him back in France. This is where Jeff comes in."

Everyone in the room looked at Jeff, sitting next to Laura. He had a half smile on his face but he didn't seem as excited as he did when he first volunteered to help Robert capture Marcos.

"Luckily we were able to catch our man with officer June and her police skills. She wounded Marcos and Jeff survived the zapping he received at his doorstep."

"And I still have the burn marks," Jeff said, as he exposed his neck area where he was shocked by Marcos.

"We're thankful for Jeff's volunteer work, and part of the reward goes to him and officer June for helping."

Robert handed both of them an envelope with their share of the reward.

Still, there was no mention of William.

"The last phase of the case led us back to Paris where Poppy had another kidnapping planned. It turns out he was using ransom money to purchase weapons from a French gun manufacturer and selling them to rebel groups in Africa."

"Are you kidding me?" Louis said. "I haven't heard this part of the story at all. This is really wild."

"Not only that, but the kidnapping team under Poppy was about to nab a wealthy wife of a developer who was in Paris at the time. The ring was broken up on the stairs of a yoga studio belonging to the sister of someone right here in this room."

Robert looked over at William who seemed to be anticipating what would come next.

"Wait," protested Leslie. "That was Anne's studio where the arrest happened? She mentioned it but said it was over before the press arrived. Anne was more interested in telling us about the policeman she met and who she is now dating. How in the hell did my family get involved in this case?"

"Oh, there's more, Leslie, so hang on," Robert said. "What I have for your husband is a special award from the French government. They've sent a plaque honoring him for his help in the capture of Poppy and breaking up a gun smuggling ring tied to the weapon company. Captain Le Cure had it made for William. They're calling it the Pink Panther Award, designed for Americans who aid the French government. This, along with 100,000 Euros, is their way of showing their appreciation. The story never appeared in the French papers, which was part of the deal made with the gun company."

"Wait a minute," Leslie called out again. "William was with me the whole time in Paris. When did he…….., oh no! You didn't go to Versailles that day did you, William. I knew something was up when you left the camera. What the hell did you do?"

Robert came to William's defense before the situation got out of hand. Leslie had a temper, and he didn't want her to ruin the awards party.

"William simply posed as a gun buyer and took a meeting with Poppy. He pretended to be the buyer for a fake organization in the States. He did such a good job, that Poppy went through with the sale and the French police were able to capture everyone involved. For his one hour meeting, posing as a disgruntled, racist school teacher from Texas, we were able to take down a gun seller and put Poppy away."

Leslie was at a loss for words. After a minute she finally said, "Part of that reward money has to be mine for being married to you, William. I now can see this investigation stuff is in your blood, and the quiet, retirement years I planned for us is not going to happen, is it?"

"Leslie, I know you're mad at me right now. I can't help that. Robert and I knew we'd have to let you know what happened in Paris, especially after the police sent me this award. I've never acted before, but I have a talent for pretending to be someone else. I fooled Poppy and we broke the case. It was a total rush for me, and the highlight of my Paris experience."

"You're right, William. You do have a knack for pretending to be someone else. You pretending to be my husband for twenty-three years and now I find out you're someone else completely. I give up. If this is how you want to spend your retirement years then so be it. I'm not going to get in your way. All I ask is that you send a postcard occasionally when Robert sends you on assignment."

"You mean if I occasionally work for Robert, you're okay with that?"

"I'm tired of fighting your desire to live on the edge. If you ever do write about your retirement years, I don't want to be seen as the 'stick in the mud' and block you from your true life's calling."

"You're being a little dramatic, Leslie. I just want to help Robert out when I can. It definitely breaks up the routine of staying home and playing cards. Robert doesn't use me that often, and in this case, we happened to be in Paris."

By now several of the guest, including Robert and Julia, were smiling at each other. They knew about the battles these two had over the past few years. The Rays were entertaining, to say the least.

"William, let's put this to rest. If Robert needs you, then go. I'll be home taking care of mom and doing the chores. I'll get by."

"We have a cleaning maid and gardener who come in every week so what else do you want? I'm home all the time. Thank you for understanding my need to help Robert. I'm not moving to Albuquerque."

"He's right, Leslie," Robert said. "William has been a huge piece in solving two big cases. I'd only call him when there is no one else. He's actually good at impersonating people, and he played the racist gun buyer perfectly. Even the French government thought so."

"Enough said. Let's continue the party. I'm done with this. Like I said before, send me a postcard when you're on assignment."

The conversation ended and everyone was ready for some Mexican cuisine.

June turned to Louis and said in a whisper, "That was really funny. I wonder how we'll be after twenty-three years of marriage?"

Louis answered, "I don't know but I think you should get the French maid outfit from the closet. This whole episode has turned me on."

*****

The three separate cases involving yoga, kidnapping and guns were closed. The Robert and Julia's team added two more members including their contacts in Europe. Who knew where their future investigations would take them? Only time would tell.

Poppy was found in his cell a month later, hanging by his neck from strips of bed sheet he'd tied together. It was just a matter of time. Poppy knew he wouldn't last in prison.

Marcos, the Stun Gun Killer, would be an old man when he finally got out. The sentence for the four deaths would be served one after another. There were two murders in Sweden, one in France and one in England.

*****

Sera, the writer from New York who helped take down Ian McClure the previous year, came to Laura's wedding in Albuquerque. She couldn't make it to Robert and Julia's party but she sent her published book, *Woman of Power*, as a gift. The subtitle was, *Sometimes Men Get in the Way*. It was selling well, especially in women's reading groups across the country.

About the author

Jeffrey Crimmel is an author who has seven published books on Amazon ranging from 'Travel, nonfiction' to 'Murder, mystery, fiction' focusing on the investigations of Robert Forrester.

After graduating from UC Santa Barbara in 1969 Jeff decided to move to Europe and see the world. He had a degree in Geography and wanted to visit the planet in person and not observe it from a news reel. He traveled overland three times through Turkey, Iran, Afghanistan, and Pakistan to India. He eventually settled in Australia after continuing through SE Asia and homesteaded in the woods of NSW. He returned to the California in 1979 with his wife and two daughters.

Mr. Crimmel earned a teaching credential and used his degree to teach in California and Arizona. He retired in 2008 and began writing down his adventures while traveling in the 70's. *Living Beneath the Radar*, *A Nine Year Journey Around the World,* is the book documenting that adventure.

A move to San Felipe and Baja California for three years created the time for Mr. Crimmel to write three more books. He eventually began the *Brain Bleed* murder mystery series based on his own visit to Sharp Memorial in San Diego and events that followed after he developed a blood clot in his leg.

He is currently living in Ramona, CA with his wife, Suzanne, and two cats. Plans are to settle in Oregon in the near future and be near his daughter in Portland.

The current book, *Nab Yoga* is the third in this series. *The Hemp Papers,* scheduled for release in early 2017, is the fourth.

Made in the USA
San Bernardino, CA
05 February 2018